CHILDREN'S OMNIBUS VOLUME ②

RUSKIN BOND

CHILDREN'S OMNIBUS

VOLUME ②

RUPA

Published by
Rupa Publications India Pvt. Ltd 2013
7/16, Ansari Road, Daryaganj
New Delhi 110002

Sales centres:
Allahabad Bengaluru Chennai
Hyderabad Jaipur Kathmandu
Kolkata Mumbai

ISBN: 978-81-291-2974-1

First impression 2013

10 9 8 7 6 5 4 3 2 1

The moral right of the author has been asserted.

Printed at Parksons Graphics, Mumbai

Contents

Introduction

'The writer on the hill…'

That line probably sums me up perfectly. I have never had pretensions to being anything but a writer, having grown up in an era when writers—even successful ones—did not become TV celebrities or Booker Prize winners or media personalities. It wasn't fashionable to be a writer. Only a few became famous; even fewer made money out of writing.

When I came home after finishing my last year at school, my mother asked me what I wanted to do with myself.

'I'm going to be a writer,' I said

'Don't be silly,' she said. 'Go and join the army!'

Well, if I'd joined the army, there would have been one more Beetle Bailey in the ranks.

Not that the army would have taken me. Certainly not the Indian army. I couldn't do the rope-trick—that is, climb a rope or disappear up a cliff-face!

And so, a writer I became…

For over sixty years I have made a living with my pen, bringing out stories, essays, poems, memoirs and novels, so that I now have well over a hundred books in print.

About fifteen years ago, my publishers at Rupa put some of my best children's stories into an omnibus volume. *Children's Omnibus* has probably been my most popular book, now about to go into its 40th impression.

Since then, I have written at least one hundred new stories and personal essays, and the best of these appear in this new collection.

The selection was made with the help of Sudeshna Shome Ghosh and her team of editors at Rupa and I hope this second omnibus will find favour with young readers and have as long a life as the first.

We are planning a Jungle Omnibus and a Spooky Omnibus as well. And if you have any other suggestions, please write to me, care of Rupa Publications.

Ruskin Bond
October, 2013

The Writer on the Hill

IT'S HARD to realize that I've been here all these years—forty summers and monsoons and winters and Himalayan springs—because, when I look back to the time of my first coming here, it really does seem like yesterday.

That probably sums it all up. Time passes, and yet it doesn't pass (it is only you and I who are passing). People come and go, the mountains remain. Mountains are permanent things. They are stubborn, they refuse to move. You can blast holes out of them for their mineral wealth; or strip them of their trees and foliage; or dam their streams and divert their torrents; or make tunnels and roads and bridges; but no matter how hard they try, humans cannot actually get rid of these mountains. That's what I like about them—they are here to stay.

I like to think that I have become a part of this mountain, this particular range, and that by living here for so long, I am able to claim a relationship with the trees, wild flowers, even the rocks that are an integral part of it. Yesterday, at twilight, when I passed beneath the canopy of oak leaves, I felt that I was a part of the forest. I put out my hand and touched the bark of an old tree and as I turned away, its leaves brushed against my face as if to acknowledge me.

One day I thought, if we trouble these great creatures too much, and hack away at them and destroy their young, they will simply uproot themselves and march away—whole forests on the move—over the next range and the next, far from the haunts of man. Over the years, I have seen many forests and green places dwindle and disappear.

Now there is an outcry. It is suddenly fashionable to be an environmentalist. That's all right. Perhaps it isn't too late to save the little that's left. They could start by curbing the property developers, who have been spreading their tentacles far and wide.

The sea has been celebrated by many great writers—Conrad, Melville, Stevenson, Masefield—but I cannot think of anyone comparable for whom the mountains have been a recurring theme. I must turn to the Taoist poets from old China to find a true feeling for mountains. Kipling does occasionally look to the hills, but the Himalayas do not appear to have given rise to any memorable Indian literature, at least not in modern times.

By and large, I suppose, writers have to stay in the plains to make a living. Hill people have their work cut out just trying to wrest a livelihood from their thin, calcinated soil.

And as for mountaineers, they climb their peaks and move on, in search of other peaks; they do not take up residence in the mountains.

But to me, as a writer, the mountains have been kind. They were kind from the beginning, when I threw up a job in Delhi and rented a small cottage on the outskirts of the hill station. Today, most hill stations are rich men's playgrounds, but twenty-five years ago, they were places where people of modest means could live quite cheaply. There were very few cars and everyone walked about.

The cottage was situated on the edge of an oak and maple forest and I spent eight or nine years in it, most of them happy years, writing stories, essays, poems, books for children. It was only after I came to live in the hills that I began writing for children.

I think this had something to do with Prem's children. Prem

Singh came to work for me as a boy, fresh from his village near Rudraprayag, in Pauri Garhwal. He was taller and darker than most of the young men from his area. Although in those days the village school did not go beyond the primary stage, he had an aptitude for reading and a good head for figures.

After he had been with me for a couple of years, he went home to get married, and then he and his wife Chandra took on the job of looking after the house and all practical matters; I remain helpless with electric fuses, clogged cisterns, leaking gas cylinders, ruptured water pipes, tin roofs that blow away whenever there's a storm, and the do-it-yourself world of hill station India. In other words, they made it possible for a writer to write.

They also nursed me when I was ill, and gave me a feeling of belonging to a family, something which I hadn't known since childhood.

Their sons Rakesh and Mukesh, and daughter Savitri, grew up in Maplewood Cottage and then in other houses and cottages when we moved. I became, for them, an adopted grandfather. For Rakesh I wrote a story about a cherry tree that had difficulty in growing up (he was rather frail as a child). For Mukesh, who liked upheavals, I wrote a story about an earthquake and put him in it; and for Savitri I wrote a whole bunch of rhymes and poems.

One seldom ran short of material. There was a stream at the bottom of the hill and this gave me many subjects in the way of small (occasionally large) animals, wild flowers, birds, trees, insects, ferns. The nearby villages were of absorbing interest. So were the old houses and old families of the Landour and Mussoorie hill stations.

There were walks into the mountains and along the pilgrim trails, and sometimes I slept at a roadside tea shop or at a village school. Sadly, many of these villages are still without basic medical and educational facilities taken for granted elsewhere.

'Who goes to the hills, goes to his mother.' So wrote Kipling in *Kim* and he seldom wrote truer words, for living in the hills was like living in the bosom of a strong, sometimes proud, but always comforting, mother. And every time I went away, the homecoming would be more tender and precious. It became increasingly difficult for me to go away. Once the mountains are in your blood, there is no escape.

It has not always been happiness and light. Two-year-old Suresh (who came between Rakesh and Mukesh) died of tetanus. I had bouts of ill health, and there were times when money ran out. Freelancing can be daunting at times, and I never could make enough to buy a house like almost everyone else I know.

Editorial doors close; but when one door closes, another has, for me, almost immediately, miraculously opened. I could perhaps have done a little better living in London or Hong Kong, or even Bombay. But given the choice, I would not have done differently. When you have received love from people and the freedom that only the mountains can give, you have come very near the borders of heaven.

And now, Rakesh and Beena have three lovely children, and Mukesh and Vinita have two little scamps.

Growing Up with Trees

DEHRADUN WAS a good place for trees, and Grandfather's house was surrounded by several kinds—peepul, neem, mango, jackfruit and papaya. There was also an ancient banyan tree. I grew up amongst these trees, and some of them planted by Grandfather grew with me.

There were two types of trees that were of special interest to a boy—trees that were good for climbing, and trees that provided fruit.

The jackfruit tree was both these things. The fruit itself—the largest in the world—grew only on the trunk and main branches. I did not care much for the fruit, although cooked as a vegetable it made a good curry. But the tree was large and leafy and easy to climb. It was a very dark tree and if I hid in it, I could not be easily seen from below. In a hole in the tree trunk I kept various banned items—a catapult, some lurid comics, and a large stock of chewing-gum. Perhaps they are still there, because I forgot to collect them when we finally went away.

The banyan tree grew behind the house. Its spreading branches, which hung to the ground and took root again, formed a number of twisting passageways and gave me endless pleasure. The tree was older than the house, older than my grandparents, as old as Dehra. I could hide myself in its branches, behind thick green leaves, and spy on the world below. I could read in it, too, propped up against the bole of the tree, with *Treasure Island* or the *Jungle Books* or comics like *Wizard* or *Hotspur* which, unlike the forbidden Superman and others like him, were full of clean-cut schoolboy heroes.

The banyan tree was a world in itself, populated with small beasts and large insects. While the leaves were still pink and tender, they would be visited by the delicate map butterfly, who committed her eggs to their care. The 'honey' on the leaves—an edible smear— also attracted the little striped squirrels, who soon grew used to my presence and became quite bold. Red-headed parakeets swarmed about the tree early in the morning.

But the banyan really came to life during the monsoon, when the branches were thick with scarlet figs. These berries were not fit for human consumption, but the many birds that gathered in the tree—gossipy rosy pastors, quarrelsome mynas, cheerful bulbuls and coppersmiths, and sometimes a raucous bullying crow—feasted on them. And when night fell, and the birds were resting, the dark flying foxes flapped heavily about the tree, chewing and munching as they clambered over the branches.

Among nocturnal visitors to the jackfruit and banyan trees was the Brainfever bird, whose real name is theHawk-Cuckoo. 'Brainfever, brainfever!' it seems to call, and this shrill, nagging cry will keep the soundest of sleepers awake on a hot summer night.

The British called it the Brainfever bird, but there are other names for it. The Mahrattas called it 'Paos-ala' which means 'Rain is coming!' Perhaps Grandfather's interpretation of its call was the best. According to him, when the bird was tuning up for its main concert, it seemed to say: 'Oh dear, oh dear! How very hot it's getting! we feel it...WE FEEL IT...WE FEEL IT!'

Yes, the banyan tree was a noisy place during the rains. If the Brainfever bird made music by night, the crickets and cicadas orchestrated during the day. As musicians, the cicadas were in a class by themselves. All through the hot weather their chorus rang through the garden, while a shower of rain, far from damping their spirits, only roused them to a greater vocal effort.

The tree crickets were a band of willing artistes who commenced their performance at almost any time of the day, but preferably in the evenings. Delicate pale green creatures with transparent green wings, they were hard to find amongst the lush monsoon foliage; but once located, a tap on the leaf or bush on which they sat would put an immediate end to the performance.

At the height of the monsoon, the banyan tree was like an orchestra pit with the musicians constantly turning up. Birds, insects and squirrels expressed their joy at the end of the hot weather and the cool quenching relief of the rains.

A flute in my hands, I would try adding my shrill piping to theirs. But they thought poorly of my musical ability, for whenever I played on the flute, the birds and insects would subside into a pained and puzzled silence.

Birdsong in the Hills

BIRD-WATCHING IS more difficult in the hills than on the plains. Many birds are difficult to spot against the dark green of the trees or the varying shades of the hillsides. Large gardens and open fields make bird-watching much easier on the plains; but up here in the mountains one has to be quick of eye to spot a flycatcher flitting from tree to tree, or a mottled brown treecreeper ascending the trunk of oak or spruce. But few birds remain silent, and one learns of their presence from their calls or songs. Birdsong is with you wherever you go in the hills, from the foothills to the tree line; and it is often easier to recognize a bird from its voice than from its colourful but brief appearance.

The barbet is one of those birds which are heard more than they are seen. Summer visitors to our hill stations must have heard their monotonous, far-reaching call, *pee-oh, pee-oh,* or *un-nee-ow, un-nee-ow.* They would probably not have seen the birds, as they keep to the tops of high trees where they are not easily distinguished from the foliage. Apart from that, the sound carries for about half a mile, and as the bird has the habit of turning its head from side to side while calling, it is very difficult to know in which direction to look for it.

Barbets love listening to their own voices and often two or three birds answer each other from different trees, each trying to outdo the other in a shrill shouting match. Most birds are noisy during the mating season. Barbets are noisy all the year round!

Some people like the barbet's call and consider it both striking and pleasant. Some don't like it and simply consider it striking!

In parts of the Garhwal Himalayas, there is a legend that the bird is the reincarnation of a moneylender who died of grief at the unjust termination of a law suit. Eternally his plaint rises to heaven, *un-nee-ow, un-nee-ow!* which means, 'injustice, injustice'.

Barbets are found throughout the tropical world, but probably the finest of these birds is the Great Himalayan Barbet. Just over a foot in length, it has a massive yellow bill, almost as large as that of a toucan. The head and neck are a rich violet; the upper back is olive brown with pale green streaks. The wings are green, washed with blue, brown and yellow. In spite of all these brilliant colours, the barbet is not easily distinguished from its leafy surroundings. It goes for the highest treetops and seldom comes down to earth.

Hodgson's Grey-Headed Flycatcher-Warbler is the long name that ornithologists, in their infinite wisdom, have given to a very small bird. This tiny bird is heard, if not seen, more often than any other bird throughout the Western Himalayas. It is almost impossible to visit any hill station between Naini Tal and Dalhousie without noticing this warbler; its voice is heard in every second tree; and yet there are few who can say what it looks like.

Its song (if you can call it that) is not very musical, and Douglas Dewar in writing about it was reminded of a notice that once appeared in a third-rate music hall: The audience is respectfully requested not to throw things at the pianist. He is doing his best.

Our little warbler does his best, incessantly emitting four or five unmusical but joyful and penetrating notes.

He is much smaller than a sparrow, being only some four inches in length, of which one-third consists of tail. His lower plumage is bright yellow, his upper parts olive green; the head and neck are grey, the head being set off by cream-coloured eyebrows. He is an active little bird always on the move, and both he and his mate, and sometimes a few friends, hop about from leaf to leaf, looking for insects both large and small. And the way he puts away an inch long caterpillar would please the most accomplished spaghetti eater!

Another tiny bird more often than it is seen is the Green-Backed Tit, a smart little bird about the size of a sparrow. It constantly utters a sharp, rather metallic but not unpleasant, call which sounds like 'kiss me, kiss me, kiss me...'

Another fine singer is the sunbird, which is found in Kumaon and Garhwal. But perhaps the finest songster is the Grey-Winged Ouzel. Throughout the early summer he makes the wooded hillsides ring with his blackbird-like melody. The hill people call this bird the Kastura or Kasturi, a name also applied to the Himalayan Whistling Thrush. But the whistling thrush has a yellow bill, whereas the ouzel is red-billed and is much the sweeter singer.

Nightjars (or goatsuckers, to give them their ancient name) are birds that lie concealed during the day in shady woods, coming out at dusk on silent wings to hunt for insects. The nightjar has a huge frog-like mouth, but is best recognized by its long tail and wings and its curiously silent flight. After dusk and just before dawn, you can hear its curious call, *tonk-tonk, tonk-tonk*—a note like that produced by striking a plank with a hammer.

As we pass from the plains to the hills, the traveller is transported from one bird realm to another.

Rajpur is separated from Mussoorie by a five-mile footpath, and within that brief distance we find the caw of the house crow replaced by the deeper note of the corby. Instead of the crescendo shriek of the koel, the double note of the cuckoo meets the ear. For the eternal cooing of the little brown dove, the melodious kokla green pigeon is substituted. The harsh cries of the rose-ringed parakeets give place to the softer call of the slate-headed species. The dissonant voices of the seven sisters no longer issue from the bushes; their place is taken by the weird but more pleasing calls of the Himalayan streaked laughing thrushes.

When I first came to live in the hills, it was the song of the Himalayan Whistling Thrush that caught my attention. I did not see the bird that day. It kept to the deep shadows of the ravine below the old stone cottage.

The following day I was sitting at my window, gazing out at the new leaves on the walnut and wild pear trees. All was still, the wind was at peace with itself, the mountains brooded massively under the darkening sky. And then, emerging from the depths of that sunless chasm like a dark sweet secret, came the indescribably beautiful call of the whistling thrush.

It is a song that never fails to thrill and enchant me. The bird starts with a hesitant schoolboy whistle, as though trying out the tune; then, confident of the melody, it bursts into full song, a crescendo of sweet notes and variations that ring clearly across the hillside. Suddenly the song breaks off right in the middle of a cadenza, and I am left wondering what happened to make the bird stop so suddenly.

At first the bird was heard but never seen. Then one day I found the whistling thrush perched on the broken garden fence. He was deep glistening purple, his shoulders flecked with white; he has sturdy black legs and a strong yellow beak. A dapper fellow who would have looked just right in a top hat! When he saw me coming down the path, he uttered a sharp *kree-ee*—unexpectedly harsh when compared to his singing—and flew off into the shadowed ravine.

As the months passed, he grew used to my presence and became less shy. Once the rain water pipes were blocked, and this resulted in an overflow of water and a small permanent puddle under the steps. This became the whistling thrush's favourite bathing place. On sultry summer afternoons, while I was taking a siesta upstairs, I would hear the bird flapping about in the rainwater pool. A little later, refreshed and sunning himself on the roof, he would treat me to a little concert—performed, I could not help feeling, especially for my benefit.

It was Govind, the milkman, who told me the legend of the whistling thrush, locally called Kastura by the hill people, but also going by the name of Krishan-patti.

According to the story, Lord Krishna fell asleep near a mountain stream and while he slept, a small boy made off with the god's famous flute. Upon waking and finding his flute gone, Krishna was so angry that he changed the culprit into a bird. But having once played on the flute, the bird had learnt bits and pieces of Krishna's wonderful music. And so he continued, in his disrespectful way, to play the music of the gods, only stopping now and then (as the whistling thrush does) when he couldn't remember the tune.

It wasn't long before my whistling thrush was joined by a female, who looked exactly like him. (I am sure there are subtle points of difference, but not to my myopic eyes!) Sometimes they gave solo performances, sometimes they sang duets; and these, no doubt, were love calls, because it wasn't long before the pair were making forays into the rocky ledges of the ravine, looking for a suitable maternity home. But a few breeding seasons were to pass before I saw any of their young.

After almost three years in the hills, I came to the conclusion that these were 'birds for all seasons'. They were liveliest in midsummer; but even in the depths of winter, with snow lying on the ground, they would suddenly start singing, as they flitted from pine to oak to naked chestnut.

As I write, there is a strong wind rushing through the trees and bustling about in the chimney, while distant thunder threatens a storm. Undismayed, the whistling thrushes are calling to each other as they roam the wind-threshed forest.

Whistling thrushes usually nest on rocky ledges near water; but my overtures of friendship may have given my visitors other ideas. Recently I was away from Mussoorie for about a fortnight. When I returned, I was about to open the window when I noticed a large bundle of ferns, lichen, grass, mud and moss balanced outside on the window ledge. Peering through the glass, I was able to recognize this untidy bundle as a nest.

It meant, of course, that I couldn't open the window, as this would have resulted in the nest toppling over the edge. Fortunately the room had another window and I kept this one open to let in sunshine, fresh air, the music of birds, and, always welcome, the call of the postman! The postman's call may not be as musical as birdsong, but this writer never tires of it, for it heralds the arrival of the occasional cheque that makes it possible for him to live close to nature.

And now, this very day, three pink freckled eggs lie in the cup of moss that forms the nursery in this jumble of a nest. The parent birds, both male and female, come and go, bustling about very efficiently, fully prepared for a great day that's coming soon.

The wild cherry trees, which I grew especially for birds, attract a great many small birds, both when it is in flower and when it is in fruit.

When it is covered with pale pink blossoms, the most common visitor is a little yellow-backed sunbird, who emits a squeaky little song as he flits from branch to branch. He extracts the nectar from the blossoms with his tubular tongue, sometimes while hovering on the wing but usually while clinging to the slender twigs.

Just as some vegetarians will occasionally condescend to eat meat, the sunbird (like the barbet) will vary his diet with insects. Small spiders, caterpillars, beetles, bugs and flies (probably in most cases themselves visitors to these flowers), fall prey to these birds. I have also seen a sunbird flying up and catching insects on the wing.

The flycatchers are gorgeous birds, especially the Paradise

Flycatcher with its long white tail and ghost-like flight; and although they are largely insectivorous, like some meat-eaters they will also take a little fruit! And so they will occasionally visit the cherry tree when its sour little cherries are ripening. While travelling over the boughs, they utter twittering notes with occasional louder calls, and now and then the male bird breaks out into a sweet little song, thus justifying the name of Shah Bulbul by which he is known in northern India.

A Special Tree

ONE DAY, when Rakesh was six, he walked home from the Mussoorie bazaar eating cherries. They were a little sweet, a little sour; small, bright red cherries, which had come all the way from the Kashmir Valley.

Here in the Himalayan foothills where Rakesh lived, there were not many fruit trees. The soil was stony, and the dry cold winds stunted the growth of most plants. But on the more sheltered slopes there were forests of oak and deodar.

Rakesh lived with his grandfather on the outskirts of Mussoorie, just where the forest began. His father and mother lived in a small village fifty miles away, where they grew maize and rice and barley in narrow terraced fields on the lower slopes of the mountain. But there were no schools in the village, and Rakesh's parents were keen that he should go to school. As soon as he was of school-going age, they sent him to stay with his grandfather in Mussoorie. He had a little cottage outside the town.

Rakesh was on his way home from school when he bought the cherries. He paid fifty paise for the bunch. It took him about half an hour to walk home, and by the time he reached the cottage there were only three cherries left.

'Have a cherry, Grandfather,' he said, as soon as he saw his grandfather in the garden.

Grandfather took one cherry and Rakesh promptly ate the other two. He kept the last seed in his mouth for some time, rolling it round and round on his tongue until all the tang had gone. Then he placed the seed on the palm of his hand and studied it.

'Are cherry seeds lucky?' asked Rakesh.

'Of course.'

'Then I'll keep it.'

'Nothing is lucky if you put it away. If you want luck, you must put it to some use.'

'What can I do with a seed?'

'Plant it.'

So Rakesh found a small space and began to dig up a flowerbed.

'Hey, not there,' said Grandfather, 'I've sown mustard in that bed. Plant it in that shady corner, where it won't be disturbed.'

Rakesh went to a corner of the garden where the earth was soft and yielding. He did not have to dig. He pressed the seed into the soil with his thumb and it went right in.

Then he had his lunch, and ran off to play cricket with his friends, and forgot all about the cherry seed.

When it was winter in the hills, a cold wind blew down from the snows and went *whoo-whoo-whoo* in the deodar trees, and the garden was dry and bare. In the evenings Grandfather and Rakesh sat over a charcoal fire, and Grandfather told Rakesh stories—stories about people who turned into animals, and ghosts who lived in trees, and beans that jumped and stones that wept—and in turn Rakesh would read to him from the newspaper, Grandfather's eyesight being rather weak. Rakesh found the newspaper very dull—especially after the stories—but Grandfather wanted all the news...

They knew it was spring when the wild duck flew north again, to Siberia. Early in the morning, when he got up to chop wood and light a fire, Rakesh saw the V-shaped formation streaming northward, the calls of the birds carrying clearly through the thin mountain air.

One morning in the garden he bent to pick up what he thought was a small twig and found to his surprise that it was well rooted. He stared at it for a moment, then ran to fetch Grandfather, calling, 'Dada, come and look, the cherry tree has come up!'

'What cherry tree?' asked Grandfather, who had forgotten about it.

'The seed we planted last year—look, it's come up!'

Rakesh went down on his haunches, while Grandfather bent almost double and peered down at the tiny tree. It was about four inches high.

'Yes, it's a cherry tree,' said Grandfather. 'You should water it now and then.'

Rakesh ran indoors and came back with a bucket of water.

'Don't drown it!' said Grandfather.

Rakesh gave it a sprinkling and circled it with pebbles.

'What are the pebbles for?' asked Grandfather.

'For privacy,' said Rakesh.

He looked at the tree every morning but it did not seem to be growing very fast, so he stopped looking at it except quickly, out of the corner of his eye. And, after a week or two, when he allowed himself to look at it properly, he found that it had grown—at least an inch!

That year the monsoon rains came early and Rakesh plodded to and from school in raincoat and chappals. Ferns sprang from the trunks of trees, strange-looking lilies came up in the long grass, and even when it wasn't raining the trees dripped and mist came curling up the valley. The cherry tree grew quickly in this season.

It was about two feet high when a goat entered the garden and ate all the leaves. Only the main stem and two thin branches remained.

'Never mind,' said Grandfather, seeing that Rakesh was upset. 'It will grow again, cherry trees are tough.'

Towards the end of the rainy season new leaves appeared on

the tree. Then a woman cutting grass scrambled down the hillside, her scythe swishing through the heavy monsoon foliage. She did not try to avoid the tree: one sweep, and the cherry tree was cut in two.

When Grandfather saw what had happened, he went after the woman and scolded her; but the damage could not be repaired.

'Maybe it will die now,' said Rakesh.

'Maybe,' said Grandfather.

But the cherry tree had no intention of dying.

By the time summer came round again, it had sent out several new shoots with tender green leaves. Rakesh had grown taller too. He was eight now, a sturdy boy with curly black hair and deep black eyes. 'Blackberry eyes,' Grandfather called them.

That monsoon Rakesh went home to his village, to help his father and mother with the planting and ploughing and sowing. He was thinner but stronger when he came back to Grandfather's house at the end of the rains to find that the cherry tree had grown another foot. It was now up to his chest.

Even when there was rain, Rakesh would sometimes water the tree. He wanted it to know that he was there.

One day he found a bright green praying-mantis perched on a branch, peering at him with bulging eyes. Rakesh let it remain there; it was the cherry tree's first visitor.

The next visitor was a hairy caterpillar, who started making a meal of the leaves. Rakesh removed it quickly and dropped it on a heap of dry leaves.

'Come back when you're a butterfly,' he said.

Winter came early. The cherry tree bent low with the weight of snow. Field mice sought shelter in the roof of the cottage. The road from the valley was blocked, and for several days there was no newspaper, and this made Grandfather quite grumpy. His stories began to have unhappy endings.

In February it was Rakesh's birthday. He was nine—and the tree was four, but almost as tall as Rakesh.

One morning, when the sun came out, Grandfather came into the garden to 'let some warmth get into my bones,' as he put it. He stopped in front of the cherry tree, stared at it for a few moments, and then called out, 'Rakesh! Come and look! Come quickly before it falls!'

Rakesh and Grandfather gazed at the tree as though it had performed a miracle. There was a pale pink blossom at the end of a branch.

The following year there were more blossoms. And suddenly the tree was taller than Rakesh, even though it was less than half his age. And then it was taller than Grandfather, who was older than some of the oak trees.

But Rakesh had grown too. He could run and jump and climb trees as well as most boys, and he read a lot of books, although he still liked listening to Grandfather's tales.

In the cherry tree, bees came to feed on the nectar in the blossoms, and tiny birds pecked at the blossoms and broke them off. But the tree kept blossoming right through the spring, and there were always more blossoms than birds.

That summer there were small cherries on the tree. Rakesh tasted one and spat it out.

'It's too sour,' he said.

'They'll be better next year,' said Grandfather.

But the birds liked them—especially the bigger birds, such as the bulbuls and scarlet minivets—and they flitted in and out of the foliage, feasting on the cherries.

On a warm sunny afternoon, when even the bees looked sleepy, Rakesh was looking for Grandfather without finding him in any of his favourite places around the house. Then he looked out of the bedroom window and saw Grandfather reclining on a cane chair under the cherry tree.

'There's just the right amount of shade here,' said Grandfather. 'And I like looking at the leaves.'

'They're pretty leaves,' said Rakesh. 'And they are always ready to dance if there's a breeze.'

After Grandfather had come indoors, Rakesh went into the garden and lay down on the grass beneath the tree. He gazed up through the leaves at the great blue sky; and turning on his side, he could see the mountains striding away into the clouds. He was still lying beneath the tree when the evening shadows crept across the garden. Grandfather came back and sat down beside Rakesh, and they waited in silence until the stars came out and the nightjar began to call. In the forest below, the crickets and cicadas began tuning up; and suddenly the trees were full of the sound of insects.

'There are so many trees in the forest,' said Rakesh. 'What's so special about this tree? Why do we like it so much?'

'We planted it ourselves,' said Grandfather. 'That's why it's special.'

'Just one small seed,' said Rakesh, and he touched the smooth bark of the tree that he had grown. He ran his hand along the trunk of the tree and put his finger to the tip of a leaf. 'I wonder,' he whispered. 'Is this what it feels to be God?'

The School among the Pines

1

A LEOPARD, LITHE and sinewy, drank at the mountain stream, and then lay down on the grass to bask in the late February sunshine. Its tail twitched occasionally and the animal appeared to be sleeping. At the sound of distant voices it raised its head to listen, then stood up and leapt lightly over the boulders in the stream, disappearing among the trees on the opposite bank.

A minute or two later, three children came walking down the forest path. They were a girl and two boys, and they were singing in their local dialect an old song they had learnt from their grandparents.

> *Five more miles to go!*
> *We climb through rain and snow.*
> *A river to cross...*
> *A mountain to pass...*
> *Now we've four more miles to go!*

Their school satchels looked new, their clothes had been washed and pressed. Their loud and cheerful singing startled a Spotted Forktail. The bird left its favourite rock in the stream and flew down the dark ravine.

'Well, we have only three more miles to go,' said the bigger boy, Prakash, who had been this way hundreds of times. 'But first we have to cross the stream.'

He was a sturdy twelve-year-old with eyes like raspberries and a mop of bushy hair that refused to settle down on his head. The girl and her small brother were taking this path for the first time.

'I'm feeling tired, Bina,' said the little boy.

Bina smiled at him, and Prakash said, 'Don't worry, Sonu, you'll get used to the walk. There's plenty of time.' He glanced at the old watch he'd been given by his grandfather. It needed constant winding. 'We can rest here for five or six minutes.'

They sat down on a smooth boulder and watched the clear water of the shallow stream tumbling downhill. Bina examined the old watch on Prakash's wrist. The glass was badly scratched and she could barely make out the figures on the dial. 'Are you sure it still gives the right time?' she asked.

'Well, it loses five minutes every day, so I put it ten minutes forward at night. That means by morning it's quite accurate! Even our teacher, Mr Mani, asks me for the time. If he doesn't ask, I tell him! The clock in our classroom keeps stopping.'

They removed their shoes and let the cold mountain water run over their feet. Bina was the same age as Prakash. She had pink cheeks, soft brown eyes, and hair that was just beginning to lose its natural curls. Hers was a gentle face, but a determined little chin showed that she could be a strong person. Sonu, her younger brother, was ten. He was a thin boy who had been sickly as a child but was now beginning to fill out. Although he did not look very athletic, he could run like the wind.

Bina had been going to school in her own village of Koli, on the other side of the mountain. But it had been a primary school, finishing at Class Five. Now, in order to study in the Sixth, she would have to walk several miles every day to Nauti, where there was a high school going up to the Eighth. It had been decided that Sonu would also shift to the new school, to give Bina company. Prakash, their neighbour in Koli, was already a pupil at the Nauti school. His mischievous nature, which sometimes got him into trouble, had resulted in his having to repeat a year.

But this didn't seem to bother him. 'What's the hurry?' he had told his indignant parents. 'You're not sending me to a foreign land when I finish school. And our cows aren't running away, are they?'

'You would prefer to look after the cows, wouldn't you?' asked Bina, as they got up to continue their walk.

'Oh, school's all right. Wait till you see old Mr Mani. He always gets our names mixed up, as well as the subjects he's supposed to be teaching. At out last lesson, instead of maths, he gave us a geography lesson!'

'More fun than maths,' said Bina.

'Yes, but there's a new teacher this year. She's very young, they say, just out of college. I wonder what she'll be like.'

Bina walked faster and Sonu had some trouble keeping up with them. She was excited about the new school and the prospect of different surroundings. She had seldom been outside her own village, with its small school and single ration shop. The day's routine never varied—helping her mother in the fields or with household tasks like fetching water from the spring or cutting grass and fodder for the cattle. Her father, who was a soldier, was away for nine months in the year and Sonu was still too small for the heavier tasks.

As they neared Nauti village, they were joined by other children coming from different directions. Even where there were no major roads, the mountains were full of little lanes and short cuts. Like a game of snakes and ladders, these narrow paths zigzagged around the hills and villages, cutting through fields and crossing narrow ravines until they came together to form a fairly busy road along which mules, cattle and goats joined the throng.

Nauti was a fairly large village, and from here a broader but dustier road started for Tehri. There was a small bus, several trucks and (for part of the way) a road-roller. The road hadn't been completed because the heavy diesel roller couldn't take the steep climb to Nauti. It stood on the roadside half way up the road from Tehri.

Prakash knew almost everyone in the area, and exchanged greetings and gossip with other children as well as with muleteers, bus drivers, milkmen and labourers working on the road. He loved telling everyone the time, even if they weren't interested.

'It's nine o'clock,' he would announce, glancing at his wrist. 'Isn't your bus leaving today?'

'Off with you!' the bus driver would respond, 'I'll leave when I'm ready.'

As the children approached Nauti, the small flat school buildings came into view on the outskirts of the village, fringed with a line of long-leaved pines. A small crowd had assembled on the playing field. Something unusual seemed to have happened. Prakash ran forward to see what it was all about. Bina and Sonu stood aside, waiting in a patch of sunlight near the boundary wall.

Prakash soon came running back to them. He was bubbling over with excitement.

'It's Mr Mani!' he gasped. 'He's disappeared! People are saying a leopard must have carried him off!'

2

Mr Mani wasn't really old. He was about fifty-five and was expected to retire soon. But for the children, adults over forty seemed ancient! And Mr Mani had always been a bit absent-minded, even as a young man.

He had gone out for his early morning walk, saying he'd be back by eight o'clock, in time to have his breakfast and be ready for class.

He wasn't married, but his sister and her husband stayed with him. When it was past nine o'clock his sister presumed he'd stopped at a neighbour's house for breakfast (he loved tucking into other people's breakfast) and that he had gone on to school from there. But when the school bell rang at ten o'clock, and everyone but Mr Mani was present, questions were asked and guesses were made.

No one had seen him return from his walk and enquiries made in the village showed that he had not stopped at anyone's house. For Mr Mani to disappear was puzzling; for him to disappear without his breakfast was extraordinary.

Then a milkman returning from the next village said he had seen a leopard sitting on a rock on the outskirts of the pine forest. There had been talk of a cattle-killer in the valley, of leopards and other animals being displaced by the construction of a dam. But as yet no one had heard of a leopard attacking a man. Could Mr Mani have been its first victim? Someone found a strip of red cloth entangled in a blackberry bush and went running through the village showing it to everyone. Mr Mani had been known to wear red pyjamas. Surely, he had been seized and eaten! But where were his remains? And why had he been in his pyjamas?

Meanwhile, Bina and Sonu and the rest of the children had followed their teachers into the school playground. Feeling a little lost, Bina looked around for Prakash. She found herself facing a dark slender young woman wearing spectacles, who must have been in her early twenties—just a little too old to be another student. She had a kind expressive face and she seemed a little concerned by all that had been happening.

Bina noticed that she had lovely hands; it was obvious that the new teacher hadn't milked cows or worked in the fields!

'You must be new here,' said the teacher, smiling at Bina. 'And is this your little brother?'

'Yes, we've come from Koli village. We were at school there.'

'It's a long walk from Koli. You didn't see any leopards, did you? Well, I'm new too. Are you in the Sixth class?'

'Sonu is in the Third. I'm in the Sixth.'

'Then I'm your new teacher. My name is Tania Ramola. Come along, let's see if we can settle down in our classroom.'

Mr Mani turned up at twelve o'clock, wondering what all the fuss was about. No, he snapped, he had not been attacked by a leopard; and yes, he had lost his pyjamas and would someone kindly return them to him?

'How did you lose your pyjamas, sir?' asked Prakash.

'They were blown off the washing line!' snapped Mr Mani.

After much questioning, Mr Mani admitted that he had gone further than he had intended, and that he had lost his way coming back. He had been a bit upset because the new teacher, a slip of a girl, had been given charge of the Sixth, while he was still with the Fifth, along with that troublesome boy Prakash, who kept on reminding him of the time! The headmaster had explained that as Mr Mani was due to retire at the end of the year, the school did not wish to burden him with a senior class. But Mr Mani looked upon the whole thing as a plot to get rid of him. He glowered at Miss Ramola whenever he passed her. And when she smiled back at him, he looked the other way!

Mr Mani had been getting even more absent-minded of late—putting on his shoes without his socks, wearing his homespun waistcoat inside out, mixing up people's names and, of course, eating other people's lunches and dinners. His sister had made a special mutton broth (*pai*) for the postmaster, who was down with flu and had asked Mr Mani to take it over in a thermos. When the postmaster opened the thermos, he found only a few drops of broth at the bottom—Mr Mani had drunk the rest somewhere along the way.

When sometimes Mr Mani spoke of his coming retirement, it

was to describe his plans for the small field he owned just behind the house. Right now, it was full of potatoes, which did not require much looking after; but he had plans for growing dahlias, roses, French beans, and other fruits and flowers.

The next time he visited Tehri, he promised himself, he would buy some dahlia bulbs and rose cuttings. The monsoon season would be a good time to put them down. And meanwhile, his potatoes were still flourishing.

3

Bina enjoyed her first day at the new school. She felt at ease with Miss Ramola, as did most of the boys and girls in her class. Tania Ramola had been to distant towns such as Delhi and Lucknow—places they had only read about—and it was said that she had a brother who was a pilot and flew planes all over the world. Perhaps he'd fly over Nauti some day!

Most of the children had, of course, seen planes flying overhead, but none of them had seen a ship, and only a few had been in a train. Tehri mountain was far from the railway and hundreds of miles from the sea. But they all knew about the big dam that was being built at Tehri, just forty miles away.

Bina, Sonu and Prakash had company for part of the way home, but gradually the other children went off in different directions. Once they had crossed the stream, they were on their own again.

It was a steep climb all the way back to their village. Prakash had a supply of peanuts which he shared with Bina and Sonu, and at a small spring they quenched their thirst.

When they were less than a mile from home, they met a postman who had finished his round of the villages in the area and was now returning to Nauti.

'Don't waste time along the way,' he told them. 'Try to get home before dark.'

'What's the hurry?' asked Prakash, glancing at his watch. 'It's only five o'clock.'

'There's a leopard around. I saw it this morning, not far from the stream. No one is sure how it got here. So don't take any chances. Get home early.'

'So there really is a leopard,' said Sonu.

They took his advice and walked faster, and Sonu forgot to complain about his aching feet.

They were home well before sunset.

There was a smell of cooking in the air and they were hungry.

'Cabbage and roti,' said Prakash gloomily. 'But I could eat anything today.' He stopped outside his small slate-roofed house, and Bina and Sonu waved him goodbye, then carried on across a couple of ploughed fields until they reached their small stone house.

'Stuffed tomatoes,' said Sonu, sniffing just outside the front door.

'And lemon pickle,' said Bina, who had helped cut, sun and salt the lemons a month previously.

Their mother was lighting the kitchen stove. They greeted her with great hugs and demands for an immediate dinner. She was a good cook who could make even the simplest of dishes taste delicious. Her favourite saying was, 'Homemade *pai* is better than chicken soup in Delhi,' and Bina and Sonu had to agree.

Electricity had yet to reach their village, and they took their meal by the light of a kerosene lamp. After the meal, Sonu settled down to do a little homework, while Bina stepped outside to look at the stars.

Across the fields, someone was playing a flute. 'It must be Prakash,' thought Bina. 'He always breaks off on the high notes.' But the flute music was simple and appealing, and she began singing softly to herself in the dark.

4

Mr Mani was having trouble with the porcupines. They had been getting into his garden at night and digging up and eating his potatoes.

From his bedroom window—left open, now that the mild-April weather had arrived—he could listen to them enjoying the vegetables he had worked hard to grow. Scrunch, scrunch! *Katar, katar,* as their sharp teeth sliced through the largest and juiciest of potatoes. For Mr Mani it was as though they were biting through his own flesh. And the sound of them digging industriously as they rooted up those healthy, leafy plants, made him tremble with rage and indignation. The unfairness of it all!

Yes, Mr Mani hated porcupines. He prayed for their destruction, their removal from the face of the earth. But, as his friends were quick to point out, 'Bhagwan protected porcupines too,' and in any case you could never see the creatures or catch them, they were completely nocturnal.

Mr Mani got out of bed every night, torch in one hand, a stout stick in the other, but as soon as he stepped into the garden the crunching and digging stopped and he was greeted by the most infuriating of silences. He would grope around in the dark, swinging wildly with the stick, but not a single porcupine was to be seen or heard. As soon as he was back in bed—the sounds would start all over again. Scrunch, scrunch, *katar, katar*…

Mr Mani came to his class tired and dishevelled, with rings beneath his eyes and a permanent frown on his face. It took some time for his pupils to discover the reason for his misery, but when they did, they felt sorry for their teacher and took to discussing ways and means of saving his potatoes from the porcupines.

It was Prakash who came up with the idea of a moat or waterditch. 'Porcupines don't like water,' he said knowledgeably.

'How do you know?' asked one of his friends.

'Throw water on one and see how it runs! They don't like getting their quills wet.'

There was no one who could disprove Prakash's theory, and the class fell in with the idea of building a moat, especially as it meant getting most of the day off.

'Anything to make Mr Mani happy,' said the headmaster, and the rest of the school watched with envy as the pupils of Class Five, armed with spades and shovels collected from all parts of the village, took up their positions around Mr Mani's potato field and began digging a ditch.

By evening the moat was ready, but it was still dry and the porcupines got in again that night and had a great feast.

'At this rate,' said Mr Mani gloomily 'there won't be any potatoes left to save.'

But next day Prakash and the other boys and girls managed to divert the water from a stream that flowed past the village. They had the satisfaction of watching it flow gently into the ditch. Everyone went home in a good mood. By nightfall, the ditch had overflowed, the potato field was flooded, and Mr Mani found himself trapped inside his house. But Prakash and his friends had won the day. The porcupines stayed away that night!

A month had passed, and wild violets, daisies and buttercups now sprinkled the hill slopes, and on her way to school Bina gathered enough to make a little posy. The bunch of flowers fitted easily into an old ink well. Miss Ramola was delighted to find this little display in the middle of her desk.

'Who put these here?' she asked in surprise.

Bina kept quiet, and the rest of the class smiled secretively. After that, they took turns bringing flowers for the classroom.

On her long walks to school and home again, Bina became aware that April was the month of new leaves. The oak leaves were bright green above and silver beneath, and when they rippled in the breeze they were like clouds of silvery green. The path was strewn with old leaves, dry and crackly. Sonu loved kicking them around.

Clouds of white butterflies floated across the stream. Sonu was chasing a butterfly when he stumbled over something dark and repulsive. He went sprawling on the grass. When he got to his feet, he looked down at the remains of a small animal.

'Bina! Prakash! Come quickly!' he shouted.

It was part of a sheep, killed some days earlier by a much larger animal.

'Only a leopard could have done this,' said Prakash.

'Let's get away, then,' said Sonu. 'It might still be around!'

'No, there's nothing left to eat. The leopard will be hunting elsewhere by now. Perhaps it's moved on to the next valley.'

'Still, I'm frightened,' said Sonu. 'There may be more leopards!'

Bina took him by the hand. 'Leopards don't attack humans!' she said.

'They will, if they get a taste for people!' insisted Prakash.

'Well, this one hasn't attacked any people as yet,' said Bina, although she couldn't be sure. Hadn't there been rumours of a leopard attacking some workers near the dam? But she did not want Sonu to feel afraid, so she did not mention the story. All she said was, 'It has probably come here because of all the activity near the dam.'

All the same, they hurried home. And for a few days, whenever they reached the stream, they crossed over very quickly, unwilling to linger too long at that lovely spot.

5

A few days later, a school party was on its way to Tehri to see the new dam that was being built.

Miss Ramola had arranged to take her class, and Mr Mani, not wishing to be left out, insisted on taking his class as well. That meant there were about fifty boys and girls taking part in the outing. The little bus could only take thirty. A friendly truck driver agreed to take some children if they were prepared to sit on sacks of potatoes. And

Prakash persuaded the owner of the diesel roller to turn it round and head it back to Tehri—with him and a couple of friends up on the driving seat.

Prakash's small group set off at sunrise, as they had to walk some distance in order to reach the stranded road roller. The bus left at 9 a.m. with Miss Ramola and her class, and Mr Mani and some of his pupils. The truck was to follow later.

It was Bina's first visit to a large town and her first bus ride.

The sharp curves along the winding, downhill road made several children feel sick. The bus driver seemed to be in a tearing hurry. He took them along at rolling, rollicking speed, which made Bina feel quite giddy. She rested her head on her arms and refused to look out of the window. Hairpin bends and cliff edges, pine forests and snowcapped peaks, all swept past her, but she felt too ill to want to look at anything. It was just as well—those sudden drops, hundreds of feet to the valley below, were quite frightening. Bina began to wish that she hadn't come—or that she had joined Prakash on the road roller instead!

Miss Ramola and Mr Mani didn't seem to notice the lurching and groaning of the old bus. They had made this journey many times. They were busy arguing about the advantages and disadvantages of large dams—an argument that was to continue on and off for much of the day; sometimes in Hindi, sometimes in English, sometimes in the local dialect!

Meanwhile, Prakash and his friends had reached the roller. The driver hadn't turned up, but they managed to reverse it and get it going in the direction of Tehri. They were soon overtaken by both the bus and the truck but kept moving along at a steady chug. Prakash spotted Bina at the window of the bus and waved cheerfully. She responded feebly.

Bina felt better when the road levelled out near Tehri. As they crossed an old bridge over the wide river, they were startled by a loud bang which made the bus shudder. A cloud of dust rose above the town.

'They're blasting the mountain,' said Miss Ramola.

'End of a mountain,' said Mr Mani mournfully.

While they were drinking cups of tea at the bus stop, waiting for the potato truck and the road roller, Miss Ramola and Mr Mani continued their argument about the dam. Miss Ramola maintained that it would bring electric power and water for irrigation to large areas of the country, including the surrounding area. Mr Mani declared that it was a menace, as it was situated in an earthquake zone. There would be a terrible disaster if the dam burst! Bina found it all very confusing. And what about the animals in the area, she wondered, what would happen to them?

The argument was becoming quite heated when the potato truck arrived. There was no sign of the road roller, so it was decided that Mr Mani should wait for Prakash and his friends while Miss Ramola's group went ahead.

Some eight or nine miles before Tehri the road roller had broken down, and Prakash and his friends were forced to walk. They had not gone far, however, when a mule train came along—five or six mules that had been delivering sacks of grain in Nauti. A boy rode on the first mule, but the others had no loads.

'Can you give us a ride to Tehri?' called Prakash.

'Make yourselves comfortable,' said the boy.

There were no saddles, only gunny sacks strapped on to the mules with rope. They had a rough but jolly ride down to the Tehri bus stop. None of them had ever ridden mules; but they had saved at least an hour on the road.

Looking around the bus stop for the rest of the party, they could find no one from their school. And Mr Mani, who should have been waiting for them, had vanished.

6

Tania Ramola and her group had taken the steep road to the hill above Tehri. Half an hour's climbing brought them to a little plateau which overlooked the town, the river and the dam site.

The earthworks for the dam were only just coming up, but a wide tunnel had been bored through the mountain to divert the river into another channel. Down below, the old town was still spread out across the valley and from a distance it looked quite charming and picturesque.

'Will the whole town be swallowed up by the waters of the dam?' asked Bina.

'Yes, all of it,' said Miss Ramola. 'The clock tower and the old palace. The long bazaar, and the temples, the schools and the jail, and hundreds of houses, for many miles up the valley. All those people will have to go—thousands of them! Of course, they'll be resettled elsewhere.'

'But the town's been here for hundreds of years,' said Bina. 'They were quite happy without the dam, weren't they?'

'I suppose they were. But the dam isn't just for them—it's for the millions who live further downstream, across the plains.'

'And it doesn't matter what happens to this place?'

'The local people will be given new homes, somewhere else.' Miss Ramola found herself on the defensive and decided to change the subject. 'Everyone must be hungry. It's time we had our lunch.'

Bina kept quiet. She didn't think the local people would want to go away. And it was a good thing, she mused, that there was only a small stream and not a big river running past her village. To be uprooted like this—a town and hundreds of villages—and put down somewhere on the hot, dusty plains—seemed to her unbearable.

'Well, I'm glad I don't live in Tehri,' she said.

She did not know it, but all the animals and most of the birds had already left the area. The leopard had been among them.

They walked through the colourful, crowded bazaar, where fruit sellers did business beside silversmiths, and pavement vendors sold everything from umbrellas to glass bangles. Sparrows attacked sacks of grain, monkeys made off with bananas, and stray cows and dogs rummaged in refuse bins, but nobody took any notice. Music blared from radios. Buses blew their horns. Sonu bought a whistle to add to the general din, but Miss Ramola told him to put it away. Bina had kept ten rupees aside, and now she used it to buy a cotton head scarf for her mother.

As they were about to enter a small restaurant for a meal, they were joined by Prakash and his companions; but of Mr Mani there was still no sign.

'He must have met one of his relatives,' said Prakash. 'He has relatives everywhere.'

After a simple meal of rice and lentils, they walked the length of the bazaar without seeing Mr Mani. At last, when they were about to give up the search, they saw him emerge from a bylane, a large sack slung over his shoulder.

'Sir, where have you been?' asked Prakash. 'We have been looking for you everywhere.'

On Mr Mani's face was a look of triumph.

'Help me with this bag,' he said breathlessly.

'You've bought more potatoes, sir,' said Prakash.

'Not potatoes, boy. Dahlia bulbs!'

7

It was dark by the time they were all back in Nauti. Mr Mani had refused to be separated from his sack of dahlia bulbs, and had been forced to sit in the back of the truck with Prakash and most of the boys.

Bina did not feel so ill on the return journey. Going uphill was definitely better than going downhill! But by the time the bus reached Nauti it was too late for most of the children to walk back to the more distant villages. The boys were put up in different homes, while the girls were given beds in the school verandah.

The night was warm and still. Large moths fluttered around the single bulb that lit the verandah. Counting moths, Sonu soon fell asleep. But Bina stayed awake for some time, listening to the sounds of the night. A nightjar went *tonk-tonk* in the bushes, and somewhere in the forest an owl hooted softly. The sharp call of a barking deer travelled up the valley, from the direction of the stream. Jackals kept howling. It seemed that there were more of them than ever before.

Bina was not the only one to hear the barking deer. The leopard, stretched full length on a rocky ledge, heard it too. The leopard raised its head and then got up slowly. The deer was its natural prey. But there weren't many left, and that was why the leopard, robbed of its forest by the dam, had taken to attacking dogs and cattle near the villages.

As the cry of the barking deer sounded nearer, the leopard left its lookout point and moved swiftly through the shadows towards the stream.

8

In early June the hills were dry and dusty, and forest fires broke out, destroying shrubs and trees, killing birds and small animals. The resin in the pines made these trees burn more fiercely, and the wind would take sparks from the trees and carry them into the dry grass and leaves, so that new fires would spring up before the old ones had died out. Fortunately, Bina's village was not in the pine belt; the fires did not reach it. But Nauti was surrounded by a fire that raged for three days, and the children had to stay away from school.

And then, towards the end of June, the monsoon rains arrived and there was an end to forest fires. The monsoon lasts three months and the lower Himalayas would be drenched in rain, mist and cloud for the next three months.

The first rain arrived while Bina, Prakash and Sonu were

returning home from school. Those first few drops on the dusty path made them cry out with excitement. Then the rain grew heavier and a wonderful aroma rose from the earth.

'The best smell in the world!' exclaimed Bina.

Everything suddenly came to life. The grass, the crops, the trees, the birds. Even the leaves of the trees glistened and looked new.

That first wet weekend, Bina and Sonu helped their mother plant beans, maize and cucumbers. Sometimes, when the rain was very heavy, they had to run indoors. Otherwise they worked in the rain, the soft mud clinging to their bare legs.

Prakash now owned a black dog with one ear up and one ear down. The dog ran around getting in everyone's way, barking at cows, goats, hens and humans, without frightening any of them. Prakash said it was a very clever dog, but no one else seemed to think so. Prakash also said it would protect the village from the leopard, but others said the dog would be the first to be taken—he'd run straight into the jaws of Mr Spots!

In Nauti, Tania Ramola was trying to find a dry spot in the quarters she'd been given. It was an old building and the roof was leaking in several places. Mugs and buckets were scattered about the floor in order to catch the drip.

Mr Mani had dug up all his potatoes and presented them to the friends and neighbours who had given him lunches and dinners. He was having the time of his life, planting dahlia bulbs all over his garden.

'I'll have a field of many-coloured dahlias!' he announced. 'Just wait till the end of August!'

'Watch out for those porcupines,' warned his sister. 'They eat dahlia bulbs too!'

Mr Mani made an inspection tour of his moat, no longer in flood, and found everything in good order. Prakash had done his job well.

Now, when the children crossed the stream, they found that the water level had risen by about a foot. Small cascades had turned into waterfalls. Ferns had sprung up on the banks. Frogs chanted.

Prakash and his dog dashed across the stream. Bina and Sonu followed more cautiously. The current was much stronger now and the water was almost up to their knees. Once they had crossed the stream, they hurried along the path, anxious not to be caught in a sudden downpour.

By the time they reached school, each of them had two or three leeches clinging to their legs. They had to use salt to remove them. The leeches were the most troublesome part of the rainy season. Even the leopard did not like them. It could not lie in the long grass without getting leeches on its paws and face.

One day, when Bina, Prakash and Sonu were about to cross the stream they heard a low rumble, which grew louder every second. Looking up at the opposite hill, they saw several trees shudder, tilt outwards and begin to fall. Earth and rocks bulged out from the mountain, then came crashing down into the ravine.

'Landslide!' shouted Sonu.

'It's carried away the path,' said Bina. 'Don't go any further.'

There was a tremendous roar as more rocks, trees and bushes fell away and crashed down the hillside.

Prakash's dog, who had gone ahead, came running back, tail between his legs.

They remained rooted to the spot until the rocks had stopped falling and the dust had settled. Birds circled the area, calling wildly. A frightened barking deer ran past them.

'We can't go to school now,' said Prakash. 'There's no way around.'

They turned and trudged home through the gathering mist.

In Koli, Prakash's parents had heard the roar of the landslide. They were setting out in search of the children when they saw them emerge from the mist, waving cheerfully.

9

They had to miss school for another three days, and Bina was afraid they might not be able to take their final exams. Although Prakash was not really troubled at the thought of missing exams, he did not like feeling helpless just because their path had been swept away. So he explored the hillside until he found a goat track going around the mountain. It joined up with another path near Nauti. This made their walk longer by a mile, but Bina did not mind. It was much cooler now that the rains were in full swing.

The only trouble with the new route was that it passed close to the leopard's lair. The animal had made this area its own since being forced to leave the dam area.

One day Prakash's dog ran ahead of them, barking furiously. Then he ran back, whimpering.

'He's always running away from something,' observed Sonu. But a minute later he understood the reason for the dog's fear.

They rounded a bend and Sonu saw the leopard standing in their way. They were struck dumb—too terrified to run. It was a strong, sinewy creature. A low growl rose from its throat. It seemed ready to spring.

They stood perfectly still, afraid to move or say a word. And the leopard must have been equally surprised. It stared at them for a few seconds, then bounded across the path and into the oak forest.

Sonu was shaking. Bina could hear her heart hammering. Prakash could only stammer: 'Did you see the way he sprang? Wasn't he beautiful?'

He forgot to look at his watch for the rest of the day.

A few days later Sonu stopped and pointed to a large outcrop of rock on the next hill.

The leopard stood far above them, outlined against the sky. It looked strong, majestic. Standing beside it were two young cubs.

'Look at those little ones!' exclaimed Sonu.

'So it's a female, not a male,' said Prakash.

'That's why she was killing so often,' said Bina. 'She had to feed her cubs too.'

They remained still for several minutes, gazing up at the leopard and her cubs. The leopard family took no notice of them.

'She knows we are here,' said Prakash, 'but she doesn't care. She knows we won't harm them.'

'We are cubs too!' said Sonu.

'Yes,' said Bina. 'And there's still plenty of space for all of us. Even when the dam is ready there will still be room for leopards and humans.'

10

The school exams were over. The rains were nearly over too. The landslide had been cleared, and Bina, Prakash and Sonu were once again crossing the stream.

There was a chill in the air, for it was the end of September.

Prakash had learnt to play the flute quite well, and he played on the way to school and then again on the way home. As a result he did not look at his watch so often.

One morning they found a small crowd in front of Mr Mani's house.

'What could have happened?' wondered Bina. 'I hope he hasn't got lost again.'

'Maybe he's sick,' said Sonu.

'Maybe it's the porcupines,' said Prakash.

But it was none of these things.

Mr Mani's first dahlia was in bloom, and half the village had turned out to look at it! It was a huge red double dahlia, so heavy that it had to be supported with sticks. No one had ever seen such a magnificent flower!

Mr Mani was a happy man. And his mood only improved over the coming week, as more and more dahlias flowered—crimson, yellow, purple, mauve, white—button dahlias, pompom dahlias, spotted dahlias, striped dahlias... Mr Mani had them all! A dahlia even turned up on Tania Romola's desk—he got on quite well with her now—and another brightened up the headmaster's study.

A week later, on their way home—it was almost the last day of the school term—Bina, Prakash and Sonu talked about what they might do when they grew up.

'I think I'll become a teacher,' said Bina. 'I'll teach children about animals and birds, and trees and flowers.'

'Better than maths!' said Prakash.

'I'll be a pilot,' said Sonu. 'I want to fly a plane like Miss Ramola's brother.'

'And what about you, Prakash?' asked Bina.

Prakash just smiled and said, 'Maybe I'll be a flute player,' and he put the flute to he lips and played a sweet melody.

'Well, the world needs flute players too,' said Bina, as they fell into step beside him.

The leopard had been stalking a barking deer. She paused when she heard the flute and the voices of the children. Her own young ones were growing quickly, but the girl and the two boys did not look much older.

They had started singing their favourite song again.

> *Five more miles to go!*
> *We climb through rain and snow.*
> *A river to cross...*
> *A mountain to pass...*
> *Now we've four more miles to go!*

The leopard waited until they had passed, before returning to the trail of the barking deer.

The Wind on Haunted Hill

WHOO, WHOO, *whoo*, cried the wind as it swept down from the Himalayan snows. It hurried over the hills and passed and hummed and moaned through the tall pines and deodars. There was little on Haunted Hill to stop the wind—only a few stunted trees and bushes and the ruins of a small settlement.

On the slopes of the next hill was a village. People kept large stones on their tin roofs to prevent them from being blown off. There was nearly always a strong wind in these parts. Three children were spreading clothes out to dry on a low stone wall, putting a stone on each piece.

Eleven-year-old Usha, dark-haired and rose-cheeked, struggled with her grandfather's long, loose shirt. Her younger brother, Suresh, was doing his best to hold down a bedsheet, while Usha's friend, Binya, a slightly older girl, helped.

Once everything was firmly held down by stones, they climbed up on the flat rocks and sat there sunbathing and staring across the fields at the ruins on Haunted Hill.

'I must go to the bazaar today,' said Usha.

'I wish I could come too,' said Binya. 'But I have to help with the cows.'

'I can come!' said eight-year-old Suresh. He was always ready to visit the bazaar, which was three miles away, on the other side of the hill.

'No, you can't,' said Usha. 'You must help Grandfather chop wood.'

'Won't you feel scared returning alone?' he asked. 'There are ghosts on Haunted Hill!'

'I'll be back before dark. Ghosts don't appear during the day.'

'Are there lots of ghosts in the ruins?' asked Binya.

'Grandfather says so. He says that over a hundred years ago, some Britishers lived on the hill. But the settlement was always being struck by lightning, so they moved away.'

'But if they left, why is the place visited by ghosts?'

'Because, Grandfather says, during a terrible storm, one of the houses was hit by lightning, and everyone in it was killed. Even the children.'

'How many children?'

'Two. A boy and his sister. Grandfather saw them playing there in the moonlight.'

'Wasn't he frightened?'

'No. Old people don't mind ghosts.'

Usha set out for the bazaar at two in the afternoon. It was about an hour's walk. The path went through yellow fields of flowering mustard, then along the saddle of the hill, and up, straight through the ruins. Usha had often gone that way to shop at the bazaar or to see her aunt, who lived in the town nearby.

Wild flowers bloomed on the crumbling walls of the ruins, and a wild plum tree grew straight out of the floor of what had once been a hall. It was covered with soft, white blossoms. Lizards scuttled over the stones, while a whistling thrush, its deep purple plumage glistening in the sunshine, sat on a windowsill and sang its heart out.

Usha sang, too, as she skipped lightly along the path, which dipped steeply down to the valley and led to the little town with its quaint bazaar.

Moving leisurely, Usha bought spices, sugar and matches. With the two rupees she had saved from her pocket money, she chose a necklace of amber-coloured beads for herself and some marbles for Suresh. Then she had her mother's slippers repaired at a cobbler's shop.

Finally, Usha went to visit Aunt Lakshmi at her flat above the shops. They were talking and drinking cups of hot, sweet tea when Usha realized that dark clouds had gathered over the mountains. She quickly picked up her things, said goodbye to her aunt, and set out for the village.

Strangely, the wind had dropped. The trees were still, the crickets silent. The crows flew round in circles, then settled on an oak tree.

'I must get home before dark,' thought Usha, hurrying along the path.

But the sky had darkened and a deep rumble echoed over the hills. Usha felt the first heavy drop of rain hit her cheek. Holding the shopping bag close to her body, she quickened her pace until she was almost running. The raindrops were coming down faster now—cold, stinging pellets of rain. A flash of lightning sharply outlined the ruins on the hill, and then all was dark again. Night had fallen.

'I'll have to find shelter in the ruins,' Usha thought and began to run. Suddenly the wind sprang up again, but she did not have to fight it. It was behind her now, helping her along, up the steep path and on to the brow of the hill. There was another flash of lightning, followed by a peal of thunder. The ruins loomed before her, grim and forbidding.

Usha remembered part of an old roof that would give some shelter. It would be better than trying to go on. In the dark, with the howling wind, she might stray off the path and fall over the edge of the cliff.

Whoo, whoo, whoo, howled the wind. Usha saw the wild plum tree swaying, its foliage thrashing against the ground. She found her way into the ruins, helped by the constant flicker of lightning. Usha placed her hands flat against a stone wall and moved sideways, hoping to reach the sheltered corner. Suddenly, her hand touched something soft and furry, and she gave a startled cry. Her cry was answered by another—half snarl, half screech—as something leapt away in the darkness.

With a sigh of relief Usha realized that it was the cat that lived in the ruins. For a moment she had been frightened, but now she moved quickly along the wall until she heard the rain drumming on a remnant of a tin roof. Crouched in a corner, she found some shelter. But the tin sheet groaned and clattered as if it would sail away any moment.

Usha remembered that across this empty room stood an old fireplace. Perhaps it would be drier there under the blocked chimney. But she would not attempt to find it just now—she might lose her way altogether.

Her clothes were soaked and water streamed down from her hair, forming a puddle at her feet. She thought she heard a faint cry—the cat again, or an owl? Then the storm blotted out all other sounds.

There had been no time to think of ghosts, but now that she was settled in one place, Usha remembered Grandfather's story about the lightning-blasted ruins. She hoped and prayed that lightning would not strike her.

Thunder boomed over the hills, and the lightning came quicker now. Then there was a bigger flash, and for a moment the entire ruin was lit up. A streak of blue sizzled along the floor of the building. Usha was staring straight ahead, and, as the opposite wall lit up, she saw, crouching in front of the unused fireplace, two small figures—children!

The ghostly figures seemed to look up and stare back at Usha. And then everything was dark again.

Usha's heart was in her mouth. She had seen without doubt, two ghosts on the other side of the room. She wasn't going to remain in the ruins one minute longer.

She ran towards the big gap in the wall through which she had entered. She was halfway across the open space when something—someone—fell against her. Usha stumbled, got up, and again bumped into something. She gave a frightened scream. Someone else screamed. And then there was a shout, a boy's shout, and Usha instantly recognized the voice.

'Suresh!'

'Usha!'

'Binya!'

They fell into each other's arms, so surprised and relieved that all they could do was laugh and giggle and repeat each other's names.

Then Usha said, 'I thought you were ghosts.'

'We thought you were a ghost,' said Suresh.

'Come back under the roof,' said Usha.

They huddled together in the corner, chattering with excitement and relief.

'When it grew dark, we came looking for you,' said Binya. 'And then the storm broke.'

'Shall we run back together?' asked Usha. 'I don't want to stay here any longer.'

'We'll have to wait,' said Binya. 'The path has fallen away at one place. It won't be safe in the dark, in all this rain.'

'We'll have to wait till morning,' said Suresh, 'and I'm so hungry!'

The storm continued, but they were not afraid now. They gave each other warmth and confidence. Even the ruins did not seem so forbidding.

After an hour the rain stopped, and the thunder grew more distant.

Towards dawn the whistling thrush began to sing. Its sweet, broken notes flooded the ruins with music. As the sky grew lighter, they saw that the plum tree stood upright again, though it had lost all its blossoms.

'Let's go,' said Usha.

Outside the ruins, walking along the brow of the hill, they watched the sky grow pink. When they were some distance away, Usha looked back and said, 'Can you see something behind the wall? It's like a hand waving.'

'It's just the top of the plum tree,' said Binya.

'Goodbye, goodbye...' They heard voices.

'Who said "goodbye"?' asked Usha.

'Not I,' said Suresh.

'Nor I,' said Binya.

'I heard someone calling,' said Usha.

'It's only the wind,' assured Binya.

Usha looked back at the ruins. The sun had come up and was touching the top of the wall.

'Come on,' said Suresh. 'I'm *hungry*.'

They hurried along the path to the village.

'Goodbye, goodbye...' Usha heard them calling. Or was it just the wind?

A Face in the Dark

IT MAY give you some idea of rural humour if I begin this tale with an anecdote that concerns me. I was walking alone through a village at night when I met an old man carrying a lantern. I found, to my surprise, that the man was blind. 'Old man,' I asked, 'if you cannot see, why do you carry a lamp?'

'I carry this,' he replied, 'so that fools do not stumble against me in the dark.'

This incident has only a slight connection with the story that follows, but I think it provides the right sort of tone and setting. Mr Oliver, an Anglo-Indian teacher, was returning to his school late one night, on the outskirts of the hill station of Shimla. The school was conducted on English public school lines and the boys, most of them from well-to-do Indian families, wore blazers, caps and ties. *Life* magazine, in a feature on India, had once called this school the 'Eton of the East'.

Individuality was not encouraged; they were all destined to become 'leaders of men'.

Mr Oliver had been teaching in the school for several years. Sometimes it seemed like an eternity, for one day followed another with the same monotonous routine. The Shimla bazaar, with its cinemas and restaurants, was about two miles from the school; and

Mr Oliver, a bachelor, usually strolled into the town in the evening, returning after dark, when he would take a short cut through a pine forest.

When there was a strong wind, the pine trees made sad, eerie sounds that kept most people to the main road. But Mr Oliver was not a nervous or imaginative man. He carried a torch and, on the night I write of, its pale gleam—the batteries were running down—moved fitfully over the narrow forest path. When its flickering light fell on the figure of a boy, who was sitting alone on a rock, Mr Oliver stopped. Boys were not supposed to be out of school after 7 p.m., and it was now well past nine.

'What are you doing out here, boy?' asked Mr Oliver sharply, moving closer so that he could recognize the miscreant. But even as he approached the boy, Mr Oliver sensed that something was wrong. The boy appeared to be crying. His head hung down, he held his face in his hands, and his body shook convulsively. It was a strange, soundless weeping, and Mr Oliver felt distinctly uneasy.

'Well, what's the matter?' he asked, his anger giving way to concern. 'What are you crying for?' The boy would not answer or look up. His body continued to be racked with silent sobbing.

'Come on, boy, you shouldn't be out here at this hour. Tell me the trouble. Look up!'

The boy looked up. He took his hands from his face and looked up at his teacher. The light from Mr Oliver's torch fell on the boy's face—if you could call it a face.

He had no eyes, ears, nose or mouth. It was just a round smooth head—with a school cap on top of it. And that's where the story should end—as indeed it has for several people who have had similar experiences and dropped dead of inexplicable heart attacks. But for Mr Oliver it did not end there.

The torch fell from his trembling hand. He turned and scrambled down the path, running blindly through the trees and calling for help. He was still running towards the school buildings when he saw a lantern swinging in the middle of the path. Mr Oliver had never before been so pleased to see the night watchman. He stumbled up to the watchman, gasping for breath and speaking incoherently.

'What is it, sir?' asked the watchman. 'Has there been an accident? Why are you running?'

'I saw something—something horrible—a boy weeping in the forest—and he had no face!'

'No face, sir?'

'No eyes, nose, mouth—nothing.'

'Do you mean it was like this, sir?' asked the watchman, and raised the lamp to his own face. The watchman had no eyes, no ears, no features at all—not even an eyebrow!

The wind blew the lamp out, and Mr Oliver had his heart attack.

If Mice could Roar

If mice could roar,
And elephants soar,
And trees grow up in the sky;
If tigers could dine,
On biscuits and wine,
And the fattest of men could fly!
If pebbles could sing,
And bells never ring,
And teachers get lost in the post;
If a tortoise could run,
And losses be won,
And bullies be buttered on toast;
If a song brought a shower,
And a gun grew a flower,
This world would be nicer than most!

Monkey Trouble

GRANDFATHER BOUGHT Tutu from a street entertainer for the sum of ten rupees. The man had three monkeys. Tutu was the smallest, but the most mischievous. She was tied up most of the time. The little monkey looked so miserable with a collar and chain that Grandfather decided it would be much happier in our home. Grandfather had a weakness for keeping unusual pets. It was a habit that I, at the age of eight or nine, used to encourage.

Grandmother at first objected to having a monkey in the house. 'You have enough pets as it is,' she said, referring to Grandfather's goat, several white mice, and a small tortoise.

'But I don't have any,' I said.

'You're wicked enough for two monkeys. One boy in the house is all I can take.'

'Ah, but Tutu isn't a boy,' said Grandfather triumphantly. 'This is a little girl monkey!'

Grandmother gave in. She had always wanted a little girl in the house. She believed girls were less troublesome than boys. Tutu was to prove her wrong.

She was a pretty little monkey. Her bright eyes sparkled with mischief beneath deep-set eyebrows. And her teeth, which were a pearly white, were often revealed in a grin that frightened the wits out of Aunt Ruby, whose nerves had already suffered from the presence of Grandfather's pet python. But this was my grandparents' house, and aunts and uncles had to put up with our pets.

Tutu's hands had a dried-up look, as though they had been pickled in the sun for many years. One of the first things I taught her was to shake hands, and this she insisted on doing with all who visited the house. Peppery Major Malik would have to stoop and shake hands with Tutu before he could enter the drawing room, otherwise Tutu would climb onto his shoulder and stay there, roughing up his hair and playing with his moustache.

Uncle Benji couldn't stand any of our pets and took a particular dislike to Tutu, who was always making faces at him. But as Uncle Benji was never in a job for long, and depended on Grandfather's good-natured generosity, he had to shake hands with Tutu, like everyone else.

Tutu's fingers were quick and wicked. And her tail, while adding to her good looks (Grandfather believed a tail would add to anyone's good looks!), also served as a third hand. She could use it to hang from a branch, and it was capable of scooping up any delicacy that might be out of reach of her hands.

On one of Aunt Ruby's visits, loud shrieks from her bedroom brought us running to see what was wrong. It was only Tutu trying on Aunt Ruby's petticoats! They were much too large, of course, and when Aunt Ruby entered the room, all she saw was a faceless white blob jumping up and down on the bed.

We disentangled Tutu and soothed Aunt Ruby. I gave Tutu a bunch of sweet peas to make her happy. Granny didn't like anyone plucking her sweet peas, so I took some from Major Malik's garden while he was having his afternoon siesta.

Then Uncle Benji complained that his hairbrush was missing. We found Tutu sunning herself on the back veranda, using the hairbrush to scratch her armpits.

I took it from her and handed it back to Uncle Benji with an apology; but he flung the brush away with an oath.

'Such a fuss about nothing,' I said. 'Tutu doesn't have fleas!'

'No, and she bathes more often than Benji,' said Grandfather, who had borrowed Aunt Ruby's shampoo to give Tutu a bath.

All the same, Grandmother objected to Tutu being given the run of the house. Tutu had to spend her nights in the outhouse, in the company of the goat. They got on quite well, and it was not long before Tutu was seen sitting comfortably on the back of the goat, while the goat roamed the back garden in search of its favourite grass.

The day Grandfather had to visit Meerut to collect his railway pension, he decided to take Tutu and me along to keep us both out of mischief, he said. To prevent Tutu from wandering about on the train, causing inconvenience to passengers, she was provided with a large black travelling bag. This, with some straw at the bottom, became her compartment. Grandfather and I paid for our seats, and we took Tutu along as hand baggage.

There was enough space for Tutu to look out of the bag occasionally, and to be fed with bananas and biscuits, but she could not get her hands through the opening and the canvas was too strong for her to bite her way through.

Tutu's efforts to get out only had the effect of making the bag roll about on the floor or occasionally jump into the air—an exhibition that attracted a curious crowd of onlookers at the Dehra and Meerut railway stations.

Anyway, Tutu remained in the bag as far as Meerut, but while Grandfather was producing our tickets at the turnstile, she suddenly poked her head out of the bag and gave the ticket collector a wide grin.

The poor man was taken aback. But, with great presence of mind and much to Grandfather's annoyance, he said, 'Sir, you have a dog with you. You'll have to buy a ticket for it.'

'It's not a dog!' said Grandfather indignantly. 'This is a baby monkey of the species *macacus mischievous*, closely related to the human species *homus horriblis*! And there is no charge for babies!'

'It's as big as a cat,' said the ticket collector. 'Cats and dogs have to be paid for.'

'But, I tell you, it's only a baby!' protested Grandfather.

'Have you a birth certificate to prove that?' demanded the ticket collector.

'Next, you'll be asking to see her mother,' snapped Grandfather.

In vain did he take Tutu out of the bag. In vain did he try to prove that a young monkey did not qualify as a dog or a cat or even as a quadruped. Tutu was classified as a dog by the ticket collector, and five rupees were handed over as her fare.

Then Grandfather, just to get his own back, took from his pocket the small tortoise that he sometimes carried about, and said: 'And what must I pay for this, since you charge for all creatures great and small?'

The ticket collector looked closely at the tortoise, prodded it with his forefinger, gave Grandfather a triumphant look, and said, 'No charge, sir. It is not a dog!'

Winters in North India can be very cold. A great treat for Tutu on winter evenings was the large bowl of hot water given to her by Grandfather for a bath. Tutu would cunningly test the temperature with her hand, then gradually step into the bath, first one foot, then the other (as she had seen me doing) until she was in the water upto her neck.

Once comfortable, she would take the soap in her hands or feet and rub herself all over. When the water became cold, she would get out and run as quickly as she could to the kitchen fire in order to dry herself. If anyone laughed at her during this performance, Tutu's feelings would be hurt and she would refuse to go on with the bath.

One day Tutu almost succeeded in boiling herself alive.

Grandmother had left a large kettle on the fire for tea. And Tutu, all by herself and with nothing better to do, decided to remove the lid. Finding the water just warm enough for a bath, she got in, with her head sticking out from the open kettle.

This was fine for a while, until the water began to get heated. Tutu raised herself a little. But finding it cold outside, she sat down again. She continued hopping up and down for some time, until Grandmother returned and hauled her, half-boiled, out of the kettle.

'What's for tea today?' asked Uncle Benji gleefully. 'Boiled eggs and a half-boiled monkey?'

But Tutu was none the worse for the adventure and continued to bathe more regularly than Uncle Benji.

Aunt Ruby was a frequent taker of baths. This met with Tutu's approval—so much so that, one day, when Aunt Ruby had finished shampooing her hair, she looked up through a lather of bubbles and soap suds to see Tutu sitting opposite her in the bath, following her example.

One day Aunt Ruby took us all by surprise. She announced that she had become engaged. We had always thought Aunt Ruby would never marry—she had often said so herself—but it appeared that the right man had now come along in the person of Rocky Fernandes, a schoolteacher from Goa.

Rocky was a tall, firm-jawed, good-natured man, a couple of years younger than Aunt Ruby. He had a fine baritone voice and sang in the manner of the great Nelson Eddy. As Grandmother liked baritone singers, Rocky was soon in her good books.

'But what on earth does he see in her?' Uncle Benji wanted to know.

'More than any girl has seen in you!' snapped Grandmother. 'Ruby's a fine girl. And they're both teachers. Maybe they can start a school of their own.'

Rocky visited the house quite often and brought me chocolates and cashew nuts, of which he seemed to have an unlimited supply. He also taught me several marching songs. Naturally, I approved of Rocky. Aunt Ruby won my grudging admiration for having made such a wise choice.

One day I overheard them talking of going to the bazaar to buy an engagement ring. I decided I would go along, too. But as Aunt Ruby had made it clear that she did not want me around, I decided that I had better follow at a discreet distance. Tutu, becoming aware that a mission of some importance was under way, decided to follow me. But as I had not invited her along, she too decided to keep out of sight.

Once in the crowded bazaar, I was able to get quite close to Aunt Ruby and Rocky without being spotted. I waited until they had settled down in a large jewellery shop before sauntering past and spotting them, as though by accident. Aunt Ruby wasn't too pleased at seeing me, but Rocky waved and called out, 'Come and join us! Help your aunt choose a beautiful ring!'

The whole thing seemed to be a waste of good money, but I did not say so—Aunt Ruby was giving me one of her more unloving looks.

'Look, these are pretty!' I said, pointing to some cheap, bright agates set in white metal. But Aunt Ruby wasn't looking. She was immersed in a case of diamonds.

'Why not a ruby for Aunt Ruby?' I suggested, trying to please her.

'That's her lucky stone,' said Rocky. 'Diamonds are the thing for engagements.' And he started singing a song about a diamond being a girl's best friend.

While the jeweller and Aunt Ruby were sifting through the diamond rings, and Rocky was trying out another tune, Tutu had slipped into the shop without being noticed by anyone but me. A little squeal of delight was the first sign she gave of her presence. Everyone looked up to see her trying on a pretty necklace.

'And what are those stones?' I asked.

'They look like pearls,' said Rocky.

'They *are* pearls,' said the shopkeeper, making a grab for them.

'It's that dreadful monkey!' cried Aunt Ruby. 'I knew that boy would bring him here!'

The necklace was already adorning Tutu's neck. I thought she looked rather nice in pearls, but she gave us no time to admire the effect. Springing out of our reach, Tutu dodged around Rocky, slipped between my legs, and made for the crowded road. I ran after her, shouting to her to stop, but she wasn't listening.

There were no branches to assist Tutu in her progress, but she used the heads and shoulders of people as springboards and so made rapid headway through the bazaar.

The jeweller left his shop and ran after us. So did Rocky. So did several bystanders who had seen the incident. And others, who had no idea what it was all about, joined in the chase. As Grandfather used to say, 'In a crowd, everyone plays follow-the-leader, even when they don't know who's leading.' Not everyone knew that the leader was Tutu. Only the front runners could see her.

She tried to make her escape speedier by leaping onto the back of a passing scooterist. The scooter swerved into a fruit stall and came to a standstill under a heap of bananas, while the scooterist found himself in the arms of an indignant fruitseller. Tutu peeled a banana and ate part of it, before deciding to move on.

From an awning, she made an emergency landing on a washerman's donkey. The donkey promptly panicked and rushed down the road, while bundles of washing fell by the wayside. The washerman joined in the chase. Children on their way to school decided that there was something better to do than attend classes. With shouts of glee, they soon overtook their panting elders.

Tutu finally left the bazaar and took a road leading in the direction of our house. But knowing that she would be caught and locked up once she got home, she decided to end the chase by ridding herself of the necklace. Deftly removing it from her neck, she flung it in the small canal that ran down the road.

The jeweller, with a cry of anguish, plunged into the canal. So did Rocky. So did I. So did several other people, both adults and children. It was to be a treasure hunt!

Some twenty minutes later, Rocky shouted, 'I've found it!' Covered in mud, water lilies, ferns and tadpoles, we emerged from the canal, and Rocky presented the necklace to the relieved shopkeeper.

Everyone trudged back to the bazaar to find Aunt Ruby waiting in the shop, still trying to make up her mind about a suitable engagement ring.

Finally the ring was bought, the engagement was announced, and a date was set for the wedding.

'I don't want that monkey anywhere near us on our wedding day,' declared Aunt Ruby.

'We'll lock her up in the outhouse,' promised Grandfather. 'And we'll let her out only after you've left for your honeymoon.'

A few days before the wedding I found Tutu in the kitchen, helping Grandmother prepare the wedding cake. Tutu often helped with the cooking and, when Grandmother wasn't looking, added herbs, spices, and other interesting items to the pots—so that occasionally we found a chilli in the custard or an onion in the jelly or a strawberry floating in the chicken soup.

Sometimes these additions improved a dish, sometimes they did not. Uncle Benji lost a tooth when he bit firmly into a sandwich which contained walnut shells.

I'm not sure exactly what went into that wedding cake when Grandmother wasn't looking—she insisted that Tutu was always very well-behaved in the kitchen—but I did spot Tutu stirring in some red chilli sauce, bitter gourd seeds, and a generous helping of egg shells!

It's true that some of the guests were not seen for several days after the wedding, but no one said anything against the cake. Most people thought it had an interesting flavour.

The great day dawned, and the wedding guests made their way to the little church that stood on the outskirts of Dehra—a town with a church, two mosques, and several temples.

I had offered to dress Tutu up as a bridesmaid and bring her along, but no one except Grandfather thought it was a good idea. So I was an obedient boy and locked Tutu in the outhouse. I did, however, leave the skylight open a little. Grandmother had always said that fresh air was good for growing children, and I thought Tutu should have her share of it.

The wedding ceremony went without a hitch. Aunt Ruby looked a picture, and Rocky looked like a film star.

Grandfather played the organ, and did so with such gusto that the small choir could hardly be heard. Grandmother cried a little. I sat quietly in a corner, with the little tortoise on my lap.

When the service was over, we trooped out into the sunshine and made our way back to the house for the reception.

The feast had been laid out on tables in the garden. As the gardener had been left in charge, everything was in order. Tutu was on her best behaviour. She had, it appeared, used the skylight to avail of more fresh air outside, and now sat beside the three-tier wedding cake, guarding it against crows, squirrels and the goat. She greeted the guests with squeals of delight.

It was too much for Aunt Ruby. She flew at Tutu in a rage. And Tutu, sensing that she was not welcome, leapt away, taking with her the top tier of the wedding cake.

Led by Major Malik, we followed her into the orchard, only to find that she had climbed to the top of the jackfruit tree. From there she proceeded to pelt us with bits of wedding cake. She had also managed to get hold of a bag of confetti, and when she ran out of cake she showered us with confetti.

'That's more like it!' said the good-humoured Rocky. 'Now let's return to the party, folks!'

Uncle Benji remained with Major Malik, determined to chase Tutu away. He kept throwing stones into the tree, until he received a large piece of cake bang on his nose. Muttering threats, he returned to the party, leaving the major to do battle.

When the festivities were finally over, Uncle Benji took the old car out of the garage and drove up the veranda steps. He was going to drive Aunt Ruby and Rocky to the nearby hill resort of Mussoorie, where they would have their honeymoon.

Watched by family and friends, Aunt Ruby climbed into the back seat. She waved regally to everyone. She leant out of the window and offered me her cheek and I had to kiss her farewell. Everyone wished them luck.

As Rocky burst into song, Uncle Benji opened the throttle and stepped on the accelerator. The car shot forward in a cloud of dust.

Rocky and Aunt Ruby continued to wave to us. And so did Tutu, from her perch on the rear bumper! She was clutching a bag in her hands and showering confetti on all who stood in the driveway.

'They don't know Tutu's with them!' I exclaimed. 'She'll go all the way to Mussoorie! Will Aunt Ruby let her stay with them?'

'Tutu might ruin the honeymoon,' said Grandfather. 'But don't worry—our Benji will bring her back!'

Snake Trouble

1

AFTER RETIRING from the Indian Railways and settling in Dehra, Grandfather often made his days (and ours) more exciting by keeping unusual pets. He paid a snake charmer in the bazaar twenty rupees for a young python. Then, to the delight of a curious group of boys and girls, he slung the python over his shoulder and brought it home.

I was with him at the time, and felt very proud walking beside Grandfather. He was popular in Dehra, especially among the poorer people, and everyone greeted him politely without seeming to notice the python. They were, in fact, quite used to seeing him in the company of strange creatures.

The first to see us arrive was Tutu the monkey, who was swinging from a branch of the jackfruit tree. One look at the python, ancient enemy of her race, and she fled into the house squealing with fright. Then our parrot, Popeye, who had his perch on the veranda, set up the most awful shrieking and whistling. His whistle was like that of a steam engine. He had learnt to do this in earlier days, when we had lived near railway stations.

The noise brought Grandmother to the veranda, where she nearly fainted at the sight of the python curled round Grandfather's neck.

Grandmother put up with most of his pets, but she drew the line at reptiles. Even a sweet-tempered lizard made her blood run cold. There was little chance that she would allow a python in the house.

'It will strangle you to death!' she cried.

'Nonsense,' said Grandfather. 'He's only a young fellow.'

'He'll soon get used to us,' I added by way of support.

'He might, indeed,' said Grandmother, 'but I have no intention of getting used to him. And your Aunt Ruby is coming to stay with us tomorrow. She'll leave the minute she knows there's a snake in the house.'

'Well, perhaps we should show it to her first thing,' said Grandfather, who found Aunt Ruby rather tiresome.

'Get rid of it right away,' said Grandmother.

'I can't let it loose in the garden. It might find its way into the chicken shed, and then where will we be?'

'Minus a few chickens,' I said reasonably, but this only made Grandmother more determined to get rid of the python.

'Lock that awful thing in the bathroom,' she said. 'Go and find the man you bought it from, and get him to come here and collect it! He can keep the money you gave him.'

Grandfather and I took the snake into the bathroom and placed it in an empty tub. Looking a bit crestfallen, he said, 'Perhaps your grandmother is right. I'm not worried about Aunt Ruby, but we don't want the python to get hold of Tutu or Popeye.'

We hurried off to the bazaar in search of the snake charmer but hadn't gone far when we found several snake charmers looking for us. They had heard that Grandfather was buying snakes, and they had brought with them snakes of various sizes and descriptions.

'No, no!' protested Grandfather. 'We don't want more snakes. We want to return the one we bought.'

But the man who had sold it to us had, apparently, returned to his village in the jungle, looking for another python for Grandfather;

and the other snake charmers were not interested in buying, only in selling. In order to shake them off, we had to return home by a roundabout route, climbing a wall and cutting through an orchard. We found Grandmother pacing up and down the veranda. One look at our faces and she knew we had failed to get rid of the snake.

'All right,' said Grandmother. 'Just take it away yourselves and see that it doesn't come back.'

'We'll get rid of it, Grandmother,' I said confidently. 'Don't you worry.'

Grandfather opened the bathroom door and stepped into the room. I was close behind him. We couldn't see the python anywhere.

'He's gone,' announced Grandfather.

'We left the window open,' I said.

'Deliberately, no doubt,' said Grandmother. 'But it couldn't have gone far. You'll have to search the grounds.'

A careful search was made of the house, the roof, the kitchen, the garden and the chicken shed, but there was no sign of the python.

'He must have gone over the garden wall,' Grandfather said cheerfully. 'He'll be well away by now!'

The python did not reappear, and when Aunt Ruby arrived with enough luggage to show that she had come for a long visit, there was only the parrot to greet her with a series of long, ear-splitting whistles.

2

For a couple of days Grandfather and I were a little worried that the python might make a sudden reappearance, but when he didn't show up again we felt he had gone for good. Aunt Ruby had to put up with Tutu the monkey making faces at her, something I did only when she wasn't looking; and she complained that Popeye shrieked loudest when she was in the room; but she was used to them, and knew she would have to bear with them if she was going to stay with us.

And then, one evening, we were startled by a scream from the garden.

Seconds later, Aunt Ruby came flying up the veranda steps, gasping, 'In the guava tree! I was reaching for a guava when I saw it staring at me. The look in its eyes! As though it would eat me alive—'

'Calm down, dear,' urged Grandmother, sprinkling rose water over my aunt. 'Tell us, what *did* you see?'

'A snake!' sobbed Aunt Ruby. 'A great boa constrictor in the guava tree. Its eyes were terrible, and it looked at me in such a queer way.'

'Trying to tempt you with a guava, no doubt,' said Grandfather, turning away to hide his smile. He gave me a look full of meaning, and I hurried out into the garden. But when I got to the guava tree, the python (if it had been the python) had gone.

'Aunt Ruby must have frightened it off,' I told Grandfather.

'I'm not surprised,' he said. 'But it will be back, Ranji. I think it has taken a fancy to your aunt.'

Sure enough, the python began to make brief but frequent appearances, usually up in the most unexpected places.

One morning I found him curled up on a dressing table, gazing at his own reflection in the mirror. I went for Grandfather, but by the time we returned the python had moved on.

He was seen again in the garden, and one day I spotted him climbing the iron ladder to the roof. I set off after him, and was soon up the ladder, which I had climbed up many times. I arrived on the flat roof just in time to see the snake disappearing down a drainpipe. The end of his tail was visible for a few moments and then that too disappeared.

'I think he lives in the drainpipe,' I told Grandfather.

'Where does it get its food?' asked Grandmother.

'Probably lives on those field rats that used to be such a nuisance. Remember, they lived in the drainpipes, too.'

'Hmm...' Grandmother looked thoughtful. 'A snake has its uses. Well, as long as it keeps to the roof and prefers rats to chickens...'

But the python did not confine itself to the roof. Piercing shrieks from Aunt Ruby had us all rushing to her room. There was the python on *her* dressing table, apparently admiring himself in the mirror.

'All the attention he's been getting has probably made him conceited,' said Grandfather, picking up the python to the accompaniment of further shrieks from Aunt Ruby. 'Would you like to hold him for a minute, Ruby? He seems to have taken a fancy to you.'

Aunt Ruby ran from the room and onto the veranda, where she was greeted with whistles of derision from Popeye the parrot. Poor Aunt Ruby! She cut short her stay by a week and returned to Lucknow, where she was a schoolteacher. She said she felt safer in her school than she did in our house.

3

Having seen Grandfather handle the python with such ease and confidence, I decided I would do likewise. So the next time I saw the snake climbing the ladder to the roof, I climbed up alongside him. He stopped, and I stopped too. I put out my hand, and he slid over my arm and up to my shoulder. As I did not want him coiling round my neck, I gripped him with both hands and carried him down to the garden. He didn't seem to mind.

The snake felt rather cold and slippery and at first he gave me goose pimples. But I soon got used to him, and he must have liked the way I handled him, because when I set him down he wanted to climb up my leg. As I had other things to do, I dropped him in a large empty basket that had been left out in the garden. He stared out at me with unblinking, expressionless eyes. There was no way of knowing what he was thinking, if indeed he thought at all.

I went off for a bicycle ride, and when I returned, I found Grandmother picking guavas and dropping them into the basket.

The python must have gone elsewhere.

When the basket was full, Grandmother said, 'Will you take these over to Major Malik? It's his birthday and I want to give him a nice surprise.'

I fixed the basket on the carrier of my cycle and pedalled off to Major Malik's house at the end of the road. The major met me on the steps of his house.

'And what has your kind granny sent me today, Ranji?' he asked.

'A surprise for your birthday, sir,' I said, and put the basket down in front of him.

The python, who had been buried beneath all the guavas, chose this moment to wake up and stand straight up to a height of several feet. Guavas tumbled all over the place. The major uttered an oath and dashed indoors.

I pushed the python back into the basket, picked it up, mounted the bicycle, and rode out of the gate in record time. And it was as well that I did so, because Major Malik came charging out of the house armed with a double-barrelled shotgun, which he was waving all over the place.

'Did you deliver the guavas?' asked Grandmother when I got back.

'I delivered them,' I said truthfully.

'And was he pleased?'

'He's going to write and thank you,' I said.

And he did.

'*Thank you for the lovely surprise,*' he wrote. '*Obviously you could not have known that my doctor had advised me against any undue excitement. My blood pressure has been rather high. The sight of your grandson does not improve it. All the same, it's the thought that matters and I take it all in good humour…*'

'What a strange letter,' said Grandmother. 'He must be ill, poor man. Are guavas bad for blood pressure?'

'Not by themselves, they aren't,' said Grandfather, who had an inkling of what had happened. 'But together with other things they can be a bit upsetting.'

4

Just when all of us, including Grandmother, were getting used to having the python about the house and grounds, it was decided that we would be going to Lucknow for a few months.

Lucknow was a large city, about three hundred miles from Dehra. Aunt Ruby lived and worked there. We would be staying with her, and so of course we couldn't take any pythons, monkeys or other unusual pets with us.

'What about Popeye?' I asked.

'Popeye isn't a pet,' said Grandmother. 'He's one of us. He comes too.'

And so the Dehra railway platform was thrown into confusion by the shrieks and whistles of our parrot, who could imitate both the guard's whistle and the whistle of a train. People dashed into their compartments, thinking the train was about to leave, only to realize that the guard hadn't blown his whistle after all. When they got down, Popeye would let out another shrill whistle, which sent everyone rushing for the train again. This happened several times until the guard actually blew his whistle. Then nobody bothered to get on, and several passengers were left behind.

'Can't you gag that parrot?' asked Grandfather, as the train moved out of the station and picked up speed.

'I'll do nothing of the sort,' said Grandmother. 'I've bought a ticket for him, and he's entitled to enjoy the journey as much as anyone.'

Whenever we stopped at a station, Popeye objected to fruit sellers and other people poking their heads in through the windows. Before the journey was over, he had nipped two fingers and a nose, and tweaked a ticket inspector's ear.

It was to be a night journey, and presently Grandmother covered herself with a blanket and stretched out on the berth. 'It's been a tiring day. I think I'll go to sleep,' she said.

'Aren't we going to eat anything?' I asked.

'I'm not hungry—I had something before we left the house. You two help yourselves from the picnic hamper.'

Grandmother dozed off, and even Popeye started nodding, lulled to sleep by the clackety-clack of the wheels and the steady puffing of the steam engine.

'Well, I'm hungry,' I said. 'What did Granny make for us?'

'Stuffed samosas, omelettes, and tandoori chicken. It's all in the hamper under the berth.'

I tugged at the cane box and dragged it into the middle of the compartment. The straps were loosely tied. No sooner had I undone them than the lid flew open, and I let out a gasp of surprise.

In the hamper was a python, curled up contentedly. There was no sign of our dinner.

'It's a python,' I said. 'And it's finished all our dinner.'

'Nonsense,' said Grandfather, joining me near the hamper. 'Pythons won't eat omelette and samosas. They like their food alive! Why, this isn't our hamper. The one with our food in it must have been left behind! Wasn't it Major Malik who helped us with our luggage? I think he's got his own back on us by changing the hamper!'

Grandfather snapped the hamper shut and pushed it back beneath the berth.

'Don't let Grandmother see him,' he said. 'She might think we brought him along on purpose.'

'Well, I'm hungry,' I complained.

'Wait till we get to the next station, then we can buy some pakoras. Meanwhile, try some of Popeye's green chillies.'

'No thanks,' I said. 'You have them, Grandad.'

And Grandfather, who could eat chillies plain, popped a couple into his mouth and munched away contentedly.

A little after midnight there was a great clamour at the end of the corridor. Popeye made complaining squawks, and Grandfather and I got up to see what was wrong.

Suddenly there were cries of 'Snake, snake!'

I looked under the berth. The hamper was open.

'The python's out,' I said, and Grandfather dashed out of the compartment in his pyjamas. I was close behind.

About a dozen passengers were bunched together outside the washroom.

'Anything wrong?' asked Grandfather casually.

'We can't get into the toilet,' said someone. 'There's a huge snake inside.'

'Let me take a look,' said Grandfather. 'I know all about snakes.'

The passengers made way, and Grandfather and I entered the washroom together, but there was no sign of the python.

'He must have got out through the ventilator,' said Grandfather. 'By now he'll be in another compartment!' Emerging from the washroom, he told the assembled passengers, 'It's gone! Nothing to worry about. Just a harmless young python.'

When we got back to our compartment, Grandmother was sitting up on her berth.

'I *knew* you'd do something foolish behind my back,' she scolded. 'You told me you'd left that creature behind, and all the time it was with us on the train.'

Grandfather tried to explain that we had nothing to do with it, that this python had been smuggled onto the train by Major Malik, but Grandmother was unconvinced.

'Anyway, it's gone,' said Grandfather. 'It must have fallen out of the washroom window. We're over a hundred miles from Dehra, so you'll never see it again.'

Even as he spoke, the train slowed down and lurched to a grinding halt.

'No station here,' said Grandfather, putting his head out of the window.

Someone came rushing along the embankment, waving his arms and shouting.

'I do believe it's the stoker,' said Grandfather. 'I'd better go and see what's wrong.'

'I'm coming too,' I said, and together we hurried along the length of the stationary train until we reached the engine.

'What's up?' called Grandfather. 'Anything I can do to help? I know all about engines.'

But the engine driver was speechless. And who could blame him? The python had curled itself about his legs, and the driver was too petrified to move.

'Just leave it to us,' said Grandfather, and, dragging the python off the driver, he dumped the snake in my arms. The engine driver sank down on the floor, pale and trembling.

'I think I'd better drive the engine,' said Grandfather. 'We don't want to be late getting into Lucknow. Your aunt will be expecting us!' And before the astonished driver could protest, Grandfather had released the brakes and set the engine in motion.

'We've left the stoker behind,' I said.

'Never mind. You can shovel the coal.'

Only too glad to help Grandfather drive an engine, I dropped the python in the driver's lap and started shovelling coal. The engine picked up speed and we were soon rushing through the darkness, sparks flying skywards and the steam whistle shrieking almost without pause.

'You're going too fast!' cried the driver.

'Making up for lost time,' said Grandfather. 'Why did the stoker run away?'

'He went for the guard. You've left them both behind!'

5

Early next morning, the train steamed safely into Lucknow. Explanations were in order, but as the Lucknow station master was an old friend of Grandfather's, all was well. We had arrived twenty minutes early, and while Grandfather went off to have a cup of tea with the engine driver and the station master, I returned the python to the hamper and helped Grandmother with the luggage. Popeye stayed perched on Grandmother's shoulder, eyeing the busy platform with deep distrust. He was the first to see Aunt Ruby striding down the platform, and let out a warning whistle.

Aunt Ruby, a lover of good food, immediately spotted the picnic hamper, picked it up and said, 'It's quite heavy. You must have kept something for me! I'll carry it out to the taxi.'

'We hardly ate anything,' I said.

'It seems ages since I tasted something cooked by your granny.' And after that there was no getting the hamper away from Aunt Ruby.

Glancing at it, I thought I saw the lid bulging, but I had tied it down quite firmly this time and there was little likelihood of its suddenly bursting open.

Grandfather joined us outside the station and we were soon settled inside the taxi. Aunt Ruby gave instructions to the driver and we shot off in a cloud of dust.

'I'm dying to see what's in the hamper,' said Aunt Ruby. 'Can't I take just a little peek?'

'Not now,' said Grandfather. 'First let's enjoy the breakfast you've got waiting for us.'

Popeye, perched proudly on Grandmother's shoulder, kept one suspicious eye on the quivering hamper.

When we got to Aunt Ruby's house, we found breakfast laid out on the dining table.

'It isn't much,' said Aunt Ruby. 'But we'll supplement it with what you've brought in the hamper.'

Placing the hamper on the table, she lifted the lid and peered inside. And promptly fainted.

Grandfather picked up the python, took it into the garden, and draped it over a branch of a pomegranate tree.

When Aunt Ruby recovered, she insisted that she had seen a huge snake in the picnic hamper. We showed her the empty basket.

'You're seeing things,' said Grandfather. 'You've been working too hard.'

'Teaching is a very tiring job,' I said solemnly.

Grandmother said nothing. But Popeye broke into loud squawks and whistles, and soon everyone, including a slightly hysterical Aunt Ruby, was doubled up with laughter.

But the snake must have tired of the joke because we never saw it again!

The Trouble with Jinns

MY FRIEND Jimmy has only one arm. He lost the other when he was a young man of twenty-five. The story of how he lost his good right arm is a little difficult to believe, but I swear that it is absolutely true.

To begin with, Jimmy was (and presumably still is) a Jinn. Now a Jinn isn't really a human like us. A Jinn is a spirit creature from another world who has assumed, for a lifetime, the physical aspect of a human being. Jimmy was a true Jinn and he had the Jinn's gift of being able to elongate his arm at will. Most Jinns can stretch their arms to a distance of twenty or thirty feet. Jimmy could attain forty feet. His arm would move through space or up walls or along the ground like a beautiful gliding serpent. I have seen him stretched out beneath a mango tree, helping himself to ripe mangoes from the top of the tree. He loved mangoes. He was a natural glutton and it was probably his gluttony that first led him to misuse his peculiar gifts.

We were at school together at a hill station in northern India. Jimmy was particularly good at basketball. He was clever enough not to lengthen his arm too much because he did not want anyone to know that he was a Jinn. In the boxing ring he generally won his fights. His opponents never seemed to get past his amazing reach. He just kept tapping them on the nose until they retired from the ring bloody and bewildered.

It was during the half-term examinations that I stumbled on Jimmy's secret. We had been set a particularly difficult algebra paper but I had managed to cover a couple of sheets with correct answers and was about to forge ahead on another sheet when I noticed someone's hand on my desk. At first I thought it was the invigilator's. But when I looked up there was no one beside me.

Could it be the boy sitting directly behind? No, he was engrossed in his question paper and had his hands to himself. Meanwhile, the hand on my desk had grasped my answer sheets and was cautiously moving off. Following its descent, I found that it was attached to an arm of amazing length and pliability. This moved stealthily down the desk and slithered across the floor, shrinking all the while, until it was restored to its normal length. Its owner was of course one who had never been any good at algebra.

I had to write out my answers a second time but after the exam I went straight up to Jimmy, told him I didn't like his game and threatened to expose him. He begged me not to let anyone know, assured me that he couldn't really help himself, and offered to be of service to me whenever I wished. It was tempting to have Jimmy as my friend, for with his long reach he would obviously be useful. I agreed to overlook the matter of the pilfered papers and we became the best of pals.

It did not take me long to discover that Jimmy's gift was more of a nuisance than a constructive aid. That was because Jimmy had a second-rate mind and did not know how to make proper use of his powers. He seldom rose above the trivial. He used his long arm in the tuck shop, in the classroom, in the dormitory. And when we were allowed out to the cinema, he used it in the dark of the hall.

Now the trouble with all Jinns is that they have a weakness for women with long black hair. The longer and blacker the hair, the better for Jinns. And should a Jinn manage to take possession of the woman he desires, she goes into a decline and her beauty decays. Everything about her is destroyed except for the beautiful long black hair.

Jimmy was still too young to be able to take possession in this way, but he couldn't resist touching and stroking long black hair. The cinema was the best place for the indulgence of his whims. His arm would start stretching, his fingers would feel their way along the rows of seats, and his lengthening limb would slowly work its way along the aisle until it reached the back of the seat in which sat the object of his admiration. His hand would stroke the long black hair with great tenderness and if the girl felt anything and looked round, Jimmy's hand would disappear behind the seat and lie there poised like the hood of a snake, ready to strike again.

At college two or three years later, Jimmy's first real victim succumbed to his attentions. She was a lecturer in economics, not very good looking, but her hair, black and lustrous, reached almost to her knees. She usually kept it in plaits but Jimmy saw her one morning just after she had taken a head bath, and her hair lay spread out on the cot on which she was reclining. Jimmy could no longer control himself. His spirit, the very essence of his personality, entered the woman's body and the next day she was distraught, feverish and excited. She would not eat, went into a coma, and in a few days dwindled to a mere skeleton. When she died, she was nothing but skin and bone but her hair had lost none of its loveliness.

I took pains to avoid Jimmy after this tragic event. I could not prove that he was the cause of the lady's sad demise but in my own heart I was quite certain of it. For since meeting Jimmy, I had read a good deal about Jinns and knew their ways.

We did not see each other for a few years. And then, holidaying in the hills last year, I found we were staying at the same hotel. I could not very well ignore him and after we had drunk a few beers together I began to feel that I had perhaps misjudged Jimmy and that he was not the irresponsible Jinn I had taken him for. Perhaps the college lecturer had died of some mysterious malady that attacks only college lecturers and Jimmy had nothing at all to do with it.

We had decided to take our lunch and a few bottles of beer to a grassy knoll just below the main motor road. It was late afternoon and I had been sleeping off the effects of the beer when I woke to find Jimmy looking rather agitated.

'What's wrong?' I asked.

'Up there, under the pine trees,' he said. 'Just above the road. Don't you see them?'

'I see two girls,' I said. 'So what?'

'The one on the left. Haven't you noticed her hair?'

'Yes, it is very long and beautiful and—now look, Jimmy, you'd better get a grip on yourself!' But already his hand was out of sight, his arm snaking up the hillside and across the road.

Presently I saw the hand emerge from some bushes near the girls and then cautiously make its way to the girl with the black tresses. So absorbed was Jimmy in the pursuit of his favourite pastime that he failed to hear the blowing of a horn. Around the bend of the road came a speeding Mercedes Benz truck.

Jimmy saw the truck but there wasn't time for him to shrink his arm back to normal. It lay right across the entire width of the road and when the truck had passed over it, it writhed and twisted like a mortally wounded python.

By the time the truck driver and I could fetch a doctor, the arm (or what was left of it) had shrunk to its ordinary size. We took Jimmy to hospital where the doctors found it necessary to amputate. The truck driver, who kept insisting that the arm he ran over was at least thirty feet long, was arrested on a charge of drunken driving.

Some weeks later I asked Jimmy, 'Why are you so depressed? You still have one arm. Isn't it gifted in the same way?'

'I never tried to find out,' he said, 'and I'm not going to try now.'

He is, of course, still a Jinn at heart and whenever he sees a girl with long black hair he must be terribly tempted to try out his one good arm and stroke her beautiful tresses. But he has learnt his lesson. It is better to be a human without any gifts than a Jinn or a genius with one too many.

The Thief's Story

I WAS STILL a thief when I met Romi. And though I was only fifteen years old, I was an experienced and fairly successful hand. Romi was watching a wrestling match when I approached him. He was about twenty-five and he looked easygoing, kind and simple enough for my purpose. I was sure I would be able to win the young man's confidence.

'You look a bit of a wrestler yourself,' I said. There's nothing like flattery to break the ice!

'So do you,' he replied, which put me off for a moment because at that time I was rather thin and bony.

'Well,' I said modestly, 'I do wrestle a bit.'

'What's your name?'

'Hari Singh,' I lied. I took a new name every month, which kept me ahead of the police and former employers.

After these formalities Romi confined himself to commenting on the wrestlers, who were grunting, gasping and heaving each other about. When he walked away, I followed him casually.

'Hello again,' he said.

I gave him my most appealing smile. 'I want to work for you,' I said.

'But I can't pay you anything—not for some time, anyway.'

I thought that over for a minute. Perhaps I had misjudged my man. 'Can you feed me?' I asked.

'Can you cook?'

'I can cook,' I lied again.

'If you can cook, then maybe I can feed you.'

He took me to his room over the Delhi Sweet Shop and told me I could sleep on the balcony. But the meal I cooked that night must have been terrible because Romi gave it to a stray dog and told me to be off.

But I just hung around, smiling in my most appealing way, and he couldn't help laughing.

Later he said, never mind, he'd teach me to cook. He also taught me to write my name and said he would soon teach me to write whole sentences and to add figures. I was grateful. I knew that once I could write like an educated person, there would be no limit to what I could achieve.

It was quite pleasant working for Romi. I made tea in the morning and then took my time buying the day's supplies, usually making a profit of two or three rupees. I think he knew I made a little money this way, but he didn't seem to mind.

Romi made money by fits and starts. He would borrow one week, lend the next. He kept worrying about his next cheque, but as soon as it arrived he would go out and celebrate. He wrote for the *Delhi* and *Bombay* magazines: a strange way to make a living.

One evening he came home with a small bundle of notes, saying he had just sold a book to a publisher. That night I saw him put the money in an envelope and tuck it under the mattress.

I had been working for Romi for almost a month and, apart from cheating on the shopping, had not done anything big in my real line of work. I had every opportunity for doing so. I could come and go as I pleased, and Romi was the most trusting person I had ever met.

That was why it was so difficult to rob him. It was easy for me to rob a greedy man. But robbing a nice man could be a problem.

And if he doesn't notice he's being robbed, then all the spice goes out of the undertaking!

Well, it's time I got down to some real work, I told myself. If I don't take the money, he'll only waste it on his so-called friends. After all, he doesn't even give me a salary.

Romi was sleeping peacefully. A beam of moonlight reached over the balcony and fell on his bed. I sat on the floor, considering the situation. If I took the money, I could catch the 10.30 express to Lucknow. Slipping out of my blanket, I crept over to the bed.

My hand slid under the mattress, searching for the notes. When I found the packet, I drew it out without a sound. Romi sighed in his sleep and turned on his side. Startled, I moved quickly out of the room.

Once on the road, I began to run. I had the money stuffed into a vest pocket under my shirt. When I'd gotten some distance from Romi's place, I slowed to a walk and, taking the envelope from my pocket, counted the money. Seven hundred rupees in fifties. I could live like a prince for a week or two!

When I reached the station, I did not stop at the ticket office (I had never bought a ticket in my life) but dashed straight onto the platform. The Lucknow Express was just moving out. The train had still to pick up speed and I should have been able to jump into one of the compartments, but I hesitated—for some reason I can't explain—and I lost the chance to get away.

When the train had gone, I found myself standing alone on the deserted platform. I had no idea where to spend the night. I had no friends, believing that friends were more trouble than help. And I did not want to arouse curiosity by staying at one of the small hotels nearby. The only person I knew really well was the man I had robbed. Leaving the station, I walked slowly through the bazaar.

In my short career, I had made a study of people's faces after they had discovered the loss of their valuables. The greedy showed panic; the rich showed anger; the poor, resignation. But I knew that Romi's face when he discovered the theft would show only a touch of sadness—not for the loss of money, but for the loss of trust.

The night was chilly—November nights can be cold in northern India—and a shower of rain added to my discomfort. I sat down in the shelter of the clock tower. A few beggars and vagrants lay beside me, rolled up tight in their blankets. The clock showed midnight. I felt for the notes; they were soaked through.

Romi's money. In the morning, he would probably have given me five rupees to go to the movies, but now I had it all: no more cooking meals, running to the bazaar, or learning to write sentences.

Sentences! I had forgotten about them in the excitement of the theft. Writing complete sentences, I knew, could one day bring me more than a few hundred rupees. It was a simple matter to steal. But to be a really big man, a clever and respected man, was something else. I should go back to Romi, I told myself, if only to learn to read and write.

I hurried back to the room feeling very nervous, for it is much easier to steal something than to return it undetected.

I opened the door quietly, then stood in the doorway in clouded moonlight. Romi was still asleep. I crept to the head of the bed, and my hand came up with the packet of notes. I felt his breath on my hand. I remained still for a few moments. Then my fingers found the edge of the mattress, and I slipped the money beneath it.

I awoke late the next morning to find that Romi had already made the tea. He stretched out a hand to me. There was a fifty-rupee note between his fingers. My heart sank.

'I made some money yesterday,' he said. 'Now I'll be able to pay you regularly.'

My spirits rose. But when I took the note, I noticed that it was still wet from the night's rain.

So he knew what I'd done. But neither his lips nor his eyes revealed anything.

'Today we'll start writing sentences,' he said.

I smiled at Romi in my most appealing way. And the smile came by itself, without any effort.

When the Trees Walked

ONE MORNING while I was sitting beside Grandfather on the veranda steps, I noticed the tendril of a creeping vine trailing nearby. As we sat there in the soft sunshine of a North Indian winter, I saw the tendril moving slowly towards Grandfather. Twenty minutes later, it had crossed the step and was touching his feet.

There is probably a scientific explanation for the plant's behaviour—something to do with light and warmth perhaps—but I liked to think it moved across the steps simply because it wanted to be near Grandfather. One always felt like drawing close to him. Sometimes when I sat by myself beneath a tree, I would feel rather lonely but as soon as Grandfather joined me, the garden became a happy place. Grandfather had served many years in the Indian Forest Service and it was natural that he should know trees and like them. On his retirement, he built a bungalow on the outskirts of Dehradun, planting trees all around. Lime, mango, orange and guava, also eucalyptus, jacaranda and Persian lilacs. In the fertile Doon Valley, plants and trees grew tall and strong.

There were other trees in the compound before the house was built, including an old peepul that had forced its way through the walls of an abandoned outhouse, knocking the bricks down with its vigorous growth. Peepul trees are great show-offs. Even when there is no breeze, their broad-chested, slim-waisted leaves will spin like tops, determined to attract your attention and invite you into the shade. Grandmother had wanted the peepul tree cut down but Grandfather had said, 'Let it be, we can always build another outhouse.'

Grandmother didn't mind trees, but she preferred growing flowers and was constantly ordering catalogues and seeds. Grandfather helped her out with the gardening, not because he was crazy about flower gardens but because he liked watching butterflies and 'there's only one way to attract butterflies,' he said, 'and that is to grow flowers for them.'

Grandfather wasn't content with growing trees in our compound. During the rains, he would walk into the jungle beyond the riverbed armed with cuttings and saplings which he would plant in the forest.

'But no one ever comes here!' I had protested the first time we did this. 'Who's going to see them?'

'See, we're not planting them simply to improve the view,' replied Grandfather. 'We're planting them for the forest and for the animals and birds who live here and need more food and shelter.'

'Of course, men need trees, too,' he added. 'To keep the desert away, to attract rain, to prevent the banks of rivers from being washed away, for fruit and flowers, leaf and seed. Yes, for timber, too. But men are cutting down trees without replacing them and if we don't plant a few trees ourselves, a time will come when the world will be one great desert.'

The thought of a world without trees became a sort of nightmare to me and I helped Grandfather in his tree-planting with greater enthusiasm. And while we went about our work, he taught me a poem by George Morris:

> Woodman, spare that tree!
> Touch not a single bough!
> In youth it sheltered me,
> And I'll protect it now.

'One day the trees will move again,' said Grandfather. 'They've been standing still for thousands of years but there was a time when they could walk about like people. Then along came an interfering busybody who cast a spell over them, rooting them to one place. But they're always trying to move. See how they reach out with their arms! And some of them, like the banyan tree with its travelling aerial roots, manage to get quite far.'

We found an island, a small rocky island in a dry riverbed. It was one of those riverbeds so common in the foothills, which are completely dry in summer but flooded during the monsoon rains. A small mango was growing on the island. 'If a small tree can grow here,' said Grandfather, 'so can others.' As soon as the rains set in and while rivers could still be crossed, we set out with a number of tamarind, laburnum and coral tree saplings and cuttings and spent the day planting them on the island.

The monsoon season was the time for rambling about. At every turn, there was something new to see. Out of the earth and rock and leafless boughs, the magic touch of the rains had brought life and greenness. You could see the broad-leaved vines growing. Plants sprang up in the most unlikely of places. A peepul would take root in the ceiling, a mango would sprout on the windowsill. We did not like to remove them but they had to go if the house was to be kept from falling down.

'If you want to live in a tree, that's all right by me,' said Grandmother crossly. 'But I like having a roof over my head and I'm not going to have my roof brought down by the jungle.'

Then came the Second World War and I was sent away to a boarding school. During the holidays, I went to live with my father in Delhi. Meanwhile, my grandparents sold the house and went to England. Two or three years later, I too went to England and was away from India for several years.

Some years later, I returned to Dehradun. After first visiting the old house—it hadn't changed much—I walked out of town towards the riverbed. It was February. As I looked across the dry water course, my eye was immediately caught by the spectacular red blooms of the coral blossom. In contrast with the dry riverbed, the island was a small green paradise. When I went up to the trees, I noticed that some squirrels were living in them and a koel, a crow pheasant, challenged me with a mellow 'who-are-you, who-are-you'.

But the trees seemed to know me; they whispered among themselves and beckoned me nearer. And looking around I noticed that other smaller trees, wild plants and grasses had sprung up under their protection. Yes, the trees we had planted long ago had multiplied. They were walking again. In one small corner of the world, Grandfather's dream had come true.

The Tunnel

It was almost noon, and the jungle was very still, very silent. Heat waves shimmered along the railway embankment where it cut a path through the tall evergreen trees. The railway lines were two straight black serpents disappearing into the tunnel in the hillside.

Suraj stood near the cutting, waiting for the midday train. It wasn't a station, and he wasn't catching a train. He was waiting so that he could watch the steam engine come roaring out of the tunnel.

He had cycled out of the town and taken the jungle path until he had come to a small village. He had left the cycle there, and walked over a low, scrub-covered hill and down to the tunnel exit.

Now he looked up. He had heard, in the distance, the shrill whistle of the engine. He couldn't see anything, because the train was approaching from the other side of the hill; but presently a sound like distant thunder issued from the tunnel, and he knew the train was coming through.

A second or two later, the steam engine shot out of the tunnel, snorting and puffing like some green, black and gold dragon, some beautiful monster out of Suraj's dreams. Showering sparks left and right, it roared a challenge to the jungle.

Instinctively, Suraj stepped back a few paces. And then the train had gone, leaving only a plume of smoke to drift lazily over tall shisham trees.

The jungle was still again. No one moved. Suraj turned from his contemplation of the drifting smoke and began walking along the embankment towards the tunnel.

The tunnel grew darker as he walked further into it. When he had gone about twenty yards, it became pitch black. Suraj had to turn and look back at the opening to reassure himself that there was still daylight outside. Ahead of him, the tunnel's other opening was just a small round circle of light.

The tunnel was still full of smoke from the train, but it would be several hours before another train came through. Till then, it belonged to the jungle again.

Suraj didn't stop, because there was nothing to do in the tunnel and nothing to see. He had simply wanted to walk through, so that he would know what the inside of a tunnel was really like. The walls were damp and sticky. A bat flew past. A lizard scuttled between the lines.

Coming straight from the darkness into the light, Suraj was dazzled by the sudden glare. He put a hand up to shade his eyes and looked up at the tree-covered hillside. He thought he saw something moving between the trees.

It was just a flash of orange and gold, and a long swishing tail. It was there between the trees for a second or two, and then it was gone.

About fifty feet from the entrance to the tunnel stood the watchman's hut. Marigolds grew in front of the hut, and at the back there was a small vegetable patch. It was the watchman's duty to inspect the tunnel and keep it clear of obstacles. Every day, before the train came through, he would walk the length of the tunnel. If all was well, he would return to his hut and take a nap. If something was wrong, he would walk back up the line and wave a red flag and the engine-driver would slow down. At night, the watchman lit an oil lamp and made a similar inspection of the tunnel. Of course, he could not stop the train if there was a porcupine on the line. But if there was any danger to the train, he'd go back up the line and wave his lamp to the approaching engine. If all was well, he'd hang his lamp at the door of the hut and go to sleep.

He was just settling down on his cot for an afternoon nap when he saw the boy emerge from the tunnel. He waited until Suraj was only a few feet away and then said, 'Welcome, welcome, I don't often have visitors. Sit down for a while, and tell me why you were inspecting my tunnel.'

'Is it your tunnel?' asked Suraj.

'It is,' said the watchman. 'It is truly my tunnel, since no one else will have anything to do with it. I have only lent it to the government.'

Suraj sat down on the edge of the cot.

'I wanted to see the train come through,' he said. 'And then, when it had gone, I thought I'd walk through the tunnel.'

'And what did you find in it?'

'Nothing. It was very dark. But when I came out, I thought I saw an animal—up on the hill—but I'm not sure, it moved away very quickly.'

'It was a leopard you saw,' said the watchman. 'My leopard.'

'Do you own a leopard too?'

'I do.'

'And do you lend it to the government?'

'I do not.'

'Is it dangerous?'

'No, it's a leopard that minds its own business. It comes to this range for a few days every month.'

'Have you been here a long time?' asked Suraj.

'Many years. My name is Sunder Singh.'

'My name's Suraj.'

'There's one train during the day. And another during the night. Have you seen the night mail come through the tunnel?'

'No. At what time does it come?'

'About nine o'clock, if it isn't late. You could come and sit here with me, if you like. And after it has gone, I'll take you home.'

'I shall ask my parents,' said Suraj. 'Will it be safe?'

'Of course. It's safer in the jungle than in the town. Nothing happens to me out here, but last month when I went into the town, I was almost run over by a bus.'

Sunder Singh yawned and stretched himself out on the cot. 'And now I'm going to take a nap, my friend. It is too hot to be up and about in the afternoon.'

'Everyone goes to sleep in the afternoon,' complained Suraj. 'My father lies down as soon as he's had his lunch.'

'Well, the animals also rest in the heat of the day. It is only the tribe of boys who cannot, or will not, rest.'

Sunder Singh placed a large banana leaf over his face to keep away the flies, and was soon snoring gently. Suraj stood up, looking up and down the railway tracks. Then he began walking back to the village.

The following evening, towards dusk, as the flying foxes swooped silently out of the trees, Suraj made his way to the watchman's hut.

It had been a long hot day, but now the earth was cooling, and a light breeze was moving through the trees. It carried with it a scent of mango blossoms, the promise of rain.

Sunder Singh was waiting for Suraj. He had watered his small garden, and the flowers looked cool and fresh. A kettle was boiling on a small oil stove.

'I'm making tea,' he said. 'There's nothing like a glass of hot tea while waiting for a train.'

They drank their tea, listening to the sharp notes of the tailorbird and the noisy chatter of the seven sisters. As the brief twilight faded, most of the birds fell silent. Sunder Singh lit his oil lamp and said it was time for him to inspect the tunnel. He moved off towards the tunnel, while Suraj sat on the cot, sipping his tea. In the dark, the trees seemed to move closer to him. And the night life of the forest was conveyed on the breeze—the sharp call of a barking deer, the cry of a fox, the quaint *tonk-tonk* of a nightjar. There were some sounds that Suraj couldn't recognize—sounds that came from the trees, creakings and whisperings, as though the trees were coming alive, stretching their limbs in the dark, shifting a little, flexing their fingers.

Sunder Singh stood inside the tunnel, trimming his lamp. The night sounds were familiar to him and he did not give them much thought; but something else—a padded footfall, a rustle of dry leaves—made him stand alert for a few seconds, peering into the darkness. Then, humming softly to himself, he returned to where Suraj was waiting. Another ten minutes remained for the night mail to arrive.

As Sunder Singh sat down on the cot beside Suraj, a new sound reached both of them quite distinctly—a rhythmic sawing sound, as if someone was cutting through the branch of a tree.

'What's that?' whispered Suraj.

'It's the leopard,' said Sunder Singh. 'I think it's in the tunnel.'

'The train will soon be here,' reminded Suraj.

'Yes, my friend. And if we don't drive the leopard out of the tunnel, it will be run over and killed. I can't let that happen.'

'But won't it attack us if we try to drive it out?' asked Suraj, beginning to share the watchman's concern.

'Not this leopard. It knows me well. We have seen each other many times. It has a weakness for goats and stray dogs, but it won't harm us. Even so, I'll take my axe with me. You stay here, Suraj.'

'No, I'm going with you. It'll be better than sitting here alone in the dark!'

'All right, but stay close behind me. And remember, there's nothing to fear.'

Raising his lamp high, Sunder Singh advanced into the tunnel, shouting at the top of his voice to try and scare away the animal.

Suraj followed close behind, but he found he was unable to do any shouting. His throat was quite dry.

They had gone just about twenty paces into the tunnel when the light from the lamp fell upon the leopard. It was crouching between the tracks, only fifteen feet away from them. It was not a very big leopard, but it looked lithe and sinewy. Baring its teeth and snarling, it went down on its belly, tail twitching.

Suraj and Sunder Singh both shouted together. Their voices rang through the tunnel. And the leopard, uncertain as to how many terrifying humans were there in the tunnel with him, turned swiftly and disappeared into the darkness.

To make sure that it had gone, Sunder Singh and Suraj walked the length of the tunnel. When they returned to the entrance, the rails were beginning to hum. They knew the train was coming.

Suraj put his hand to the rails and felt its tremor. He heard the distant rumble of the train. And then the engine came round the bend, hissing at them, scattering sparks into the darkness, defying the jungle as it roared through the steep sides of the cutting. It charged straight at the tunnel, and into it, thundering past Suraj like the beautiful dragon of his dreams.

And when it had gone, the silence returned and the forest seemed to breathe, to live again. Only the rails still trembled with the passing of the train.

And they trembled to the passing of the same train, almost a week later, when Suraj and his father were both travelling in it.

Suraj's father was scribbling in a notebook, doing his accounts. Suraj sat at an open window staring out at the darkness. His father was going to Delhi on a business trip and had decided to take the boy along. ('I don't know where he gets to most of the time,' he'd complained. 'I think it's time he learnt something about my business.')

The night mail rushed through the forest with its hundreds of passengers. Tiny flickering lights came and went, as they passed small villages on the fringe of the jungle.

Suraj heard the rumble as the train passed over a small bridge. It was too dark to see the hut near the cutting, but he knew they must be approaching the tunnel. He strained his eyes looking out into the night; and then, just as the engine let out a shrill whistle, Suraj saw the lamp.

He couldn't see Sunder Singh, but he saw the lamp, and he knew that his friend was out there.

The train went into the tunnel and out again; it left the jungle behind and thundered across the endless plains; and Suraj stared out at the darkness, thinking of the lonely cutting in the forest, and the watchman with the lamp who would always remain a firefly for those travelling thousands, as he lit up the darkness for steam engines and leopards.

The Coral Tree

THE NIGHT had been hot, the rain frequent, and I had been sleeping on the verandah instead of in the house. I was in my twenties, had begun to earn a living and felt I had certain responsibilities.

In a short time, a tonga would take me to the railway station, and from there a train would take me to Bombay, and then a ship would take me to England. There would be work, interviews, a job, a different kind of life, so many things that this small bungalow of my grandfather would be remembered fitfully, in rare moments of reflection.

When I awoke on the veranda, I saw a grey morning, smelt the rain on the red earth and remembered that I had to go away. A girl was standing on the veranda porch, looking at me very seriously. When I saw her, I sat up in bed with a start.

She was a small dark girl, her eyes big and black, her pigtails tied up in a bright red ribbon, and she was fresh and clean like the rain and the red earth.

She stood looking at me and was very serious.

'Hullo,' I said, smiling and trying to put her at ease. But the girl was business-like and acknowledged my greeting with a brief nod.

'Can I do anything for you?' I asked, stretching my limbs. 'Do you stay nearby?'

With great assurance she said, 'Yes, but I can stay on my own.'

'You're like me,' I said, and for a while, forgot about being an old man of twenty. 'I like to be on my own but I'm going away today.'

'Oh,' she said, a little breathlessly.

'Would you care to go to England?'

'I want to go everywhere,' she said. 'To America and Africa and Japan and Honolulu.'

'Maybe you will,' I said. 'I'm going everywhere, and no one can stop me... But what is it you want, what did you come for?'

'I want some flowers but I can't reach them.' She waved her hand towards the garden, 'That tree, see?'

The coral tree stood in front of the house surrounded by pools of water and broken, fallen blossoms. The branches of the tree were thick with scarlet, pea-shaped flowers.

'All right, just let me get ready.'

The tree was easy to climb and I made myself comfortable on one of the lower branches, smiling down at the serious upturned face of the girl.

'I'll throw them down to you,' I said.

I bent a branch but the wood was young and green and I had to twist it several times before it snapped.

'I'm not sure I ought to do this,' I said as I dropped the flowering branch to the girl.

'Don't worry,' she said.

I felt a sudden nostalgic longing for childhood and an urge to remain behind in my grandfather's house with its tangled memories and ghosts of yesteryear. But I was the only one left and what could I do except climb tamarind and jackfruit trees?

'Have you many friends?' I asked.

'Oh yes.'

'And who is the best?'

'The cook. He lets me stay in the kitchen which is more interesting than the house. And I like to watch him cooking. And he gives me things to eat and tells me stories...'

'And who is your second best friend?'

She inclined her head to one side and thought very hard.

'I'll make you second best,' she said.

I sprinkled coral blossoms on her head. 'That's very kind of you. I'm happy to be second best.'

A tonga bell sounded at the gate and I looked out from the tree and said, 'It's come for me. I have to go now.'

I climbed down.

'Will you help me with my suitcases?' I asked, as we walked together towards the veranda. 'There's no one here to help me. I am the last to go. Not because I want to go but because I have to.'

I sat down on the cot and packed a few last things in my suitcase. All the doors of the house were locked. On my way to the station, I would leave the keys with the caretaker. I had already given instructions to the agent to try and sell the house. There was nothing more to be done. We walked in silence to the waiting tonga, thinking and wondering about each other. The girl stood at the side of the path, on the damp earth, looking at me.

'Thank you,' I said, 'I hope I shall see you again.'

'I'll see you in London,' she said. 'Or America or Japan, I want to go everywhere.'

'I'm sure you will,' I said. 'And perhaps I'll come back and we'll meet again in this garden. That would be nice, wouldn't it?'

She nodded and smiled. We knew it was an important moment. The tonga driver spoke to his pony and the carriage set off down the gravel path, rattling a little. The girl and I waved to each other. In the girl's hand was a spring of coral blossom. As she waved, the blossoms fell apart and danced lightly in the breeze.

'Goodbye!' I called.

'Goodbye!' called the girl.

The ribbon had come loose from her pigtail and lay on the ground with the coral blossoms.

And she was fresh and clean like the rain and the red earth.

The Night the Roof Blew off

WE ARE used to sudden storms up here on the first range of the Himalayas. The old building in which we live has, for more than a hundred years, received the full force of the wind as it sweeps across the hills from the east.

We'd lived in the building for more than ten years without a disaster. It had even taken the shock of a severe earthquake. As my granddaughter Dolly said, 'It's difficult to tell the new cracks from the old!'

It's a two-storey building, and I live on the upper floor with my family: my three grandchildren and their parents. The roof is made of corrugated tin sheets, the ceiling of wooden boards. That's the traditional Mussoorie roof.

Looking back at the experience, it was the sort of thing that should have happened in a James Thurber story, like the dam that burst or the ghost who got in. But I wasn't thinking of Thurber at the time, although a few of his books were among the many I was trying to save from the icy rain pouring into my bedroom.

Our roof had held fast in many a storm, but the wind that night was really fierce. It came rushing at us with a high-pitched, eerie wail. The old roof groaned and protested. It took a battering for several hours while the rain lashed against the windows and the lights kept coming and going.

There was no question of sleeping, but we remained in bed for warmth and comfort. The fire had long since gone out as the chimney had collapsed, bringing down a shower of sooty rainwater.

After about four hours of buffeting, the roof could take it no longer. My bedroom faces east, so my portion of the roof was the first to go.

The wind got under it and kept pushing until, with a ripping, groaning sound, the metal sheets shifted and slid off the rafters, some of them dropping with claps like thunder on to the road below.

So that's it, I thought. Nothing worse can happen. As long as the ceiling stays on, I'm not getting out of bed. We'll collect our roof in the morning.

Icy water splashing down on my face made me change my mind in a hurry. Leaping from the bed, I found that much of the ceiling had gone, too. Water was pouring on my open typewriter as well as on the bedside radio and bed cover.

Picking up my precious typewriter (my companion for forty years) I stumbled into the front sitting room (and library), only to find a similar situation there. Water was pouring through the slats of the wooden ceiling, raining down on the open bookshelves.

By now I had been joined by the children, who had come to my rescue. Their section of the roof hadn't gone as yet. Their parents were struggling to close a window against the driving rain.

'Save the books!' shouted Dolly, the youngest, and that became our rallying cry for the next hour or two.

Dolly and her brother Mukesh picked up armfuls of books and carried them into their room. But the floor was awash, so the books had to be piled on their beds. Dolly was helping me gather some of my papers when a large field rat jumped on to the desk in front of her. Dolly squealed and ran for the door.

'It's all right,' said Mukesh, whose love of animals extends even to field rats. 'It's only sheltering from the storm.'

Big brother Rakesh whistled for our dog, Tony, but Tony wasn't interested in rats just then. He had taken shelter in the kitchen, the only dry spot in the house.

Two rooms were now practically roofless, and we could see the sky lit up by flashes of lightning.

There were fireworks indoors, too, as water spluttered and crackled along a damaged wire. Then the lights went out altogether.

Rakesh, at his best in an emergency, had already lit two kerosene lamps. And by their light we continued to transfer books, papers, and clothes to the children's room.

We noticed that the water on the floor was beginning to subside a little.

'Where is it going?' asked Dolly.

'Through the floor,' said Mukesh. 'Down to the flat below!'

Cries of concern from our downstairs neighbours told us that they were having their share of the flood.

Our feet were freezing because there hadn't been time to put on proper footwear. And besides, shoes and slippers were awash by now. All chairs and tables were piled high with books. I hadn't realized the extent of my library until that night!

The available beds were pushed into the driest corner of the children's room, and there, huddled in blankets and quilts, we spent the remaining hours of the night while the storm continued.

Towards morning the wind fell, and it began to snow. Through the door to the sitting room I could see snowflakes drifting through the gaps in the ceiling, settling on picture frames. Ordinary things like a glue bottle and a small clock took on a certain beauty when covered with soft snow.

Most of us dozed off.

When dawn came, we found the windowpanes encrusted with snow and icicles. The rising sun struck through the gaps in the ceiling and turned everything golden. Snow crystals glistened on the empty bookshelves. But the books had been saved.

Rakesh went out to find a carpenter and tinsmith, while the rest of us started putting things in the sun to dry. By evening, we'd put much of the roof back on.

It's a much-improved roof now, and we look forward to the next storm with confidence!

Mussoorie's Landour Bazaar

As in most north Indian bazaars, here too there is a clock tower. And, like most clocks in clock towers, this one works in fits and starts; listless in summer, sluggish during the monsoon, stopping altogether when it snows in January. Almost every year the tall brick structure gets a coat of paint. It was pink last year. Now it's a livid purple.

From the clock tower at one end to the mule sheds at the other, this old Mussoorie bazaar is a mile long. The tall, shaky, three-storey buildings cling to the mountainside, shutting out the sunlight. They are even shakier now that heavy trucks have started rumbling down the narrow street, originally made for nothing heavier than a rickshaw. The street is narrow and damp, retaining all the bazaar smells; sweetmeats frying, smoke from wood or charcoal fires, the sweat and urine of mules, petrol fumes, all of which mingle with the smell of mist and old building and distant pines.

The bazaar sprang up about 150 years ago to serve the needs of British soldiers who were sent to the Landour convalescent depot to recover from sickness or wounds. The old military hospital, built in 1827, now houses the Defence Institute of Management.

The Landour bazaar today serves the local population. There are a number of silversmiths in Landour. They fashion silver nose rings, earrings, bracelets and anklets, which are bought by the women from the surrounding Jaunpuri village. One silversmith had a chestfull of old silver rupees. These rupees are sometimes hung on thin silver chains and worn as pendants.

At the other extreme there are the kabari shops, where you can pick up almost anything—a tape recorder discarded by a Woodstock student, or a piece of furniture from grandmother's time in the hill station. Old clothes, Victorian bric-a-brac, and bite of modern gadgetry vie for your attention.

The old clothes are often more reliable than the new. Last winter I bought a pullover marked 'Made in Nepal' from a Tibetan pavement vendor. I was wearing it on the way home when it began to rain. By the time I reached my cottage, the pullover had shrunk inches and I had some difficulty getting out of it! It was now just the right size for Bijju, the milkman's twelve-year-old son. But it continued to shrink at every wash, and it is now being worn by Teju, Bijju's younger brother, who is eight.

At the dark, windy corner in the bazaar, one always found an old man bent over his charcoal fire, roasting peanuts. He was probably quite tall, but I never saw him standing up. One judged his height from his long, loose limbs. He was very thin, probably tubercular, and the high cheekbones added to the tautness of his tightly stretched skin.

His peanuts were always fresh, crisp and hot. They were popular with small boys who had a few coins to spend on their way to and from school.

No one seemed to know the old man's name. One just took his presence for granted. He was as fixed a landmark as the clock tower or the old cherry tree that grew crookedly from the hillside. He seemed less perishable than the tree, more dependable than the clock. He had no family, but in a way all the world was his family because he was in continuous contact with people. And yet he was a remote sort of being; always polite, even to children, but never familiar. He was seldom alone, but he must have been lonely.

Summer nights he rolled himself up in a thin blanket and slept on the ground beside the dying embers of his fire. During winter, he waited until the last cinema show was over before retiring to the rickshaw coolies' shelter where there was protection from the freezing wind.

He died last summer.

That corner remained very empty, very dark, and every time I passed it, I was haunted by visions of the old peanut vendor, troubled by the questions I did not ask; and I wondered if he was really as indifferent to life as he appeared to be.

Then, a few weeks ago, there was a new occupant of the corner, a new seller of peanuts. No relative of the old man, but a boy of thirteen or fourteen. The human personality can impose its own nature on its surroundings. In the old man's time it seemed a dark, gloomy corner. Now it's lit up by sunshine—a sunny personality, smiling, chattering. Old age gives way to youth; and I'm glad I won't be alive when the new peanut vendor grows old. One shouldn't see too many people grow old.

Leaving the main bazaar behind, I walk some way down the Mussoorie-Tehri road, a fine road to walk on, in spite of the dust from an occasional bus or jeep. From Mussoorie to Chamba, a distance of some thirty-five miles, the road seldom descends below 7,000 feet and there is a continual vista of the snow range to the north and valleys and rivers to the south. Dhanaulti is one of the lovelier spots, and the Garhwal Mandal Vikas Nigam has a rest house here, where one can spend an idyllic weekend.

Leaving the Tehri Road, one can also trek down to the little Aglar river and then up to Nag Tibba, 9,000 feet, which has an oak forest and animals ranging from the barking deer to the Himalayan Bear; but this is an arduous trek and you must be prepared to spend the night in the open.

On this particular day I reach Suakholi, and rest in a teashop, a loose stone structure with a tin roof held down by stones. It serves the bus passengers, mule drivers, milkmen and others who use this road.

I find a couple of mules tethered to a pine tree. The mule drivers, handsome men in tattered clothes, sit on a bench in the shade of the tree, drinking tea from brass tumblers. The shopkeeper, a man of indeterminate age—the cold dry winds from the mountain passes having crinkled his face like a walnut—greets me enthusiastically. He even produces a chair, which looks a survivor from one of Wilson's rest houses and may even be a Sheration. Fortunately, the Mussoorie kabaris do not know about it or they'd have snapped it up long ago. In any case, the stuffing has come out of the seat. The shopkeeper apologizes for its condition: 'The rats were nesting in it.' And then, to reassure me: 'But they have gone now.'

I would just as soon be on the bench with the Jaunpuri mule drivers, but I do not wish to offend Mela Ram, the teashop owner, so I take his chair.

'How long have you kept this shop?'

'Oh, ten-fifteen years, I do not remember.'

He hasn't bothered to count the years. Why should he, outside the towns in the isolation of the hills, life is simply a matter of yesterday, today and tomorrow.

Unlike Mela Ram, the mule drivers have somewhere to go and something to deliver: sacks of potatoes! From Jaunpur to Jaunsar, the potato is probably the crop best suited to these stony, terraced fields. They have to deliver their potatoes in Landour Bazaar and return to their village before nightfall; and soon they lead their pack animals away, along the dusty road to Mussoorie.

'Tea or lassi?' Mela Ram offers me a choice, and I choose the curd preparation, which is sharp and sour and very refreshing. The wind sighs gently in the upper branches of the pine trees, and I relax in my Sheration chair like some eighteenth-century nawab who has brought his own furniture into the wilderness.

Having wandered some way down the Tehri road, it is quite late by the time I return to the Landour Bazaar. Lights still twinkle on the hills, but shop fronts are shuttered and the little bazaar is silent. The people living on either side of the narrow street can hear my footsteps, and I hear their casual remarks, music, a burst of laughter.

Through a gap in the rows of buildings, I can see Pari Tibba outlined in the moonlight. A greenish phosphorescent glow appears to move here and there about the hillside. This is the 'fairy light' that gives the hill its name Pari Tibba—Fairy Hill. I have no explanation for it, and I don't know anyone else who has been able to explain it satisfactorily; but often from my window I see this greenish light zigzagging about the hill.

A three-quarter moon is up, and the tin roofs of the bazaar, drenched with drew, glisten in the moonlight. Although the street is unlit, I need no torch. I can see every step of the way. I can even read the headlines on the discarded newspaper lying in the gutter.

Although I am alone on the road, I am aware of the life pulsating around me. It is a cold night, doors and windows are shut; but through the many chinks, narrow fingers of light reach out into the night. Who could still be up? A shopkeeper going through his accounts, a college student preparing for his exams, someone coughing and groaning in the dark.

A jackal slinks across the road, looking right and left he knows his road drill to make sure the dogs have gone; a field rat wriggles through a hole in a rotting plank on its nightly foray among sacks of grain and pulses.

Yes, this is an old bazaar. The bakers, tailors, silversmith and wholesale merchants are the grandsons of those who followed the mad sahibs to this hilltop in the thirties and fourties of the last century. Most of them are plainsmen, quite prosperous even though many of their houses are crooked and shaky.

Although the shopkeepers and tradesmen are fairly prosperous, the hill people, those who come from the surrounding Tehri and Jaunpur villages, are usually poor. Their small holdings and rocky fields do not provide them with much of a living, and men and boys often have to come into the hill station or go down to the cities in search of a livelihood. They pull rickshaws or work in hotels and restaurants. Most of them have somewhere to stay.

But as I pass along the deserted street, under the shadow of the clock tower, I find a boy huddled in a recess, a thin shawl wrapped around his shoulders. He is wide awake and shivering.

I pass by, my head down, my thoughts already on the warmth of my small cottage only a mile away. And then I stop. It is almost as though the bright moonlight has stopped me, holding my shadow in thrall.

'If I am not for myself,
who will be for me?
And if I am not for others,
what am I?
And if not now, when?'

The words of an ancient sage beat upon my mind. I walk back to the shadows where the boy crouches. He does not say anything, but he looks up at me, puzzled and apprehensive. All the warnings of well-wishers crowd in upon me—stories of crime by night, of assault and robber, 'ill met by moonlight'.

But this is not Northern Ireland or the Lebanon or the streets of New York. This is Landour in the Garhwal Himalayas. And the boy is no criminal. I can tell from his features that he comes from the hills beyond Tehri. He has come here looking for work and he has yet to find any.

'Have you somewhere to stay?' I asked.

He shakes his head; but something about my tone of voice has given him confidence, because there is a glimmer of hope, a friendly appeal in his eyes.

I have committed myself. I cannot pass on. A shelter for the night—that's the very least one human should be able to expect from another.

'If you can walk some way,' I offer, 'I can give you a bed and blanket.'

He gets up immediately, a thin boy, wearing only a shirt and part of an old track-suit. He follows me without any hesitation. I cannot now betray his trust. Nor can I fail to trust him.

Visitors from the forest

WHEN MIST fills the Himalayan valleys, and heavy monsoon rain sweeps across the hills, it is natural for wild creatures to seek shelter. And sometimes my cottage in the forest is the most convenient refuge.

There is no doubt I make things easier for all concerned by leaving most of my windows open. I like plenty of fresh air indoors, and if a few birds, beasts and insects come in too, they're welcome, provided they don't make too much of a nuisance of themselves.

I must confess, I did lose patience with a bamboo beetle who blundered in the other night and fell into the water jug. I rescued him and pushed him out of the window. A few seconds later he came whirring in again, and with unerring accuracy landed with a plop in the same jug. I fished him out once more and offered him the freedom of the night. But attracted no doubt by the light and warmth of my small sitting room, he came buzzing back, circling the room like a helicopter looking for a place to land. Quickly I covered the water jug. He landed in a bowl of wild dahlias, and I allowed him to remain there, comfortably curled up in the hollow of a flower.

Sometimes during the day, a bird visits me—a deep blue whistling thrush, hopping about on long, dainty legs, too nervous to sing. She perches on the windowsill, looking out at the rain. She does not permit any familiarity. But if I sit quietly in my chair she will sit quietly on my windowsill, glancing quickly at me now and then to make sure I am keeping my distance. When the rain stops, she glides away, and it is only then, confident in her freedom, that she bursts into full-throated song, her broken but haunting melody echoing down the ravine.

A squirrel comes sometimes, when his home in the oak tree gets waterlogged. Apparently he is a bachelor; anyway, he lives alone. He knows me well, this squirrel, and is bold enough to climb on to the dining table looking for titbits which he always finds because I leave them there deliberately. Had I met him when he was a youngster, he would have learnt to eat from my hand; but I have only been here for a few months. I like it this way. I am not looking for pets; these are simply guests.

Last week, as I was sitting down at my desk to write a long-deferred article, I was startled to see an emerald-green praying mantis sitting on my writing pad. He peered at me with his protuberant glass-bead eyes, and I stared down at him through my glasses. When I gave him a prod, he moved off in a leisurely way. Later, I found him examining the binding of *Leaves of Grass*; perhaps he had found a succulent bookworm. He disappeared for a couple of days, and then I found him on my dressing table, preening himself before the mirror.

Out in the garden, I spotted another mantis, perched on the jasmine bush. Its arms were raised like a boxer's. Perhaps they are a pair, I thought, and went indoors, fetched my mantis and placed him on the jasmine bush opposite his fellow insect. He did not like what he saw—no comparison with his own image!—and made off in a hurry.

My most interesting visitor comes at night, when the lights are still burning—a tiny bat who prefers to fly in through the open door, and will use the window only if there is no alternative. His object is to snap up the moths who cluster round the lamps.

All the bats I have seen fly fairly high, keeping near the ceiling;

but this particular bat flies in low like a dive bomber, zooming in and out of chair legs and under tables. Once he passed straight between my legs. Has his radar gone wrong, I wondered, or is he just plain mad?

I went to my shelves of natural history and looked up bats, but could find no explanation for this erratic behaviour. As a last resort, I turned to an ancient volume, Sterndale's *Indian Mammalia* (Calcutta, 1884), and in it, to my delight, found what I was looking for: 'A bat found near Mussoorie by Captain Hutton, on the southern range of hills at 1,800 metres; head and body about three centimetres, skims close to the ground, instead of flying high as bats generally do. Habitat, Jharipani, north-west Himalayas.' Apparently, the bat was rare even in 1884.

Perhaps I have come across one of the few surviving members of the species. Jharipani is only three kilometres from where I live. I am happy that this bat survives in my small corner of the woods, and I undertake to celebrate it in prose and verse. Once, I found it suspended upside down from the railing at the foot of my bed. I decided to leave it there. For a writer alone in the woods, even an eccentric bat is welcome company.

Gently Flows the Ganga

THE BHAGIRATHI is a beautiful river, gentle and caressing (as compared to the turbulent Alaknanda), and pilgrims and others have responded to it with love and respect. The god Shiva released the waters of Goddess Ganga from his locks, and she sped towards the plains in the tracks of Prince Bhagirath's chariot.

> *He held the river on his head*
> *And kept her wandering, where*
> *Dense as Himalaya's woods were spread*
> *The tangles of his hair.*

Revered by Hindus and loved by all, Goddess Ganga weaves her spell over all who come to her.

Some assert that the true Ganga (in its upper reaches) is the Alaknanda. Geographically, this may be so. But tradition carries greater weight in the abode of the Gods and, traditionally, the Bhagirathi is the Ganga. Of course, the two rivers meet at Devprayag, in the foothills, and this marriage of the waters settles the issue.

Here, at the source of the river, we come to the realization that we are at the very centre and heart of things. One has an almost primaeval sense of belonging to these mountains and to this valley in particular. For me, and for many who have been here, the Bhagirathi is the most beautiful of the four main river valleys of Garhwal.

The Bhagirathi seems to have everything—a gentle disposition, deep glens and forests, the ultravision of an open valley graced with tiers of cultivation leading up by degrees to the peaks and glaciers at its head.

At Tehri, the big dam slows down Prince Bhagirath's chariot. But upstream, from Bhatwari to Harsil, there are extensive pine forests. They fill the ravines and plateaus, before giving way to yew and cypress, oak and chestnut. Above 9,000 feet, the deodar (devdar, tree of the gods) is the principal tree. It grows to a little distance above Gangotri, and then gives way to the birch, which is found in patches to within half a mile of the glacier.

It was the valuable timber of the deodar that attracted the adventurer Frederick 'Pahari' Wilson to the valley in the 1850s. He leased the forests from the Raja of Tehri, and within a few years he had made a fortune. From his home and depot at Harsil, he would float the logs downstream to Tehri, where they would be sawn up and despatched to buyers in the cities.

Bridge building was another of Wilson's ventures. The most famous of these was a 350 feet suspension bridge at Bhaironghat, over 1,200 feet above the young Bhagirathi where it thunders through a deep defile. This rippling contraption was at first a source of terror to travellers, and only a few ventured across it. To reassure people, Wilson would mount his horse and gallop to and fro across the bridge. It has since collapsed, but local people will tell you that the ghostly hoof beats of Wilson's horse can still be heard on full moon nights. The supports of the old bridge were massive deodar trunks, and they can still be seen to one side of the new road bridge built by engineers of the Northern Railway.

Wilson married a local girl, Gulabi, the daughter of a drummer from Mukbha, a village a few miles above Harsil. He acquired properties in Dehradun and Mussoorie, and his wife lived there in some style, giving him three sons. Two died young. The third, Charlie Wilson, went through most of his father's fortune. His grave lies next to my grandfather's grave in the old Dehradun cemetery. Gulabi is buried in Mussoorie, next to her husband. I wrote this haiku for her:

> Her beauty brought her fame,
> But only the wild rose growing beside her grave
> Is there to hear her whispered name—
> Gulabi.

I remember old Mrs Wilson, Charlie's widow, when I was a boy in Dehra. She lived next door in what was the last of the Wilson properties. Her nephew, Geoffrey Davis, went to school with me in Shimla, and later joined the Indian Air Force. But luck never went the way of Wilson's descendants, and Geoffrey died when his plane crashed.

In the old days, before motorable roads opened up the border states, only the staunchest of pilgrims visited the shrines at Gangotri and elsewhere. The footpaths were rocky and dangerous, ascending and descending the faces of deep precipices and ravines, at times leading along banks of loose earth where landslides had swept the original path away. There are no big towns above Uttarkashi, and this absence of large centres of population could be the main reason why the forests are better preserved here than at lower altitudes.

Uttarkashi is a sizeable town but situated between two steep hills, it gives one a cramped, shut-in feeling. Fifteen years ago, it was devastated by a major earthquake, and in recent months it has suffered from repeated landslides. Somehow its situation seems far from ideal.

Gangotri, far more secure, is situated at just over 10,300 feet.

On the right bank of the river is the principal temple, a small neat shrine without much ornamentation. It was built by Amar Singh Thapa, a Nepali general, in the early 1800s. It was renovated by the Maharaja of Jaipur in 1920. The rock on which it stands is called Bhagirath Shila and is said to be the place where Prince Bhagirath did penance in order that Ganga be brought down from her abode of eternal snow.

Here the rocks are carved and polished by ice and water, so smooth that in places they look like rolls of silk. The fast-flowing waters of this mountain torrent look very different from the huge, sluggish river that joins the Yamuna at Allahabad.

The Ganga emerges from beneath a great glacier, thickly studded with enormous loose rocks and earth. The glacier is about a mile in width and extends upwards for many miles. The chasm in the glacier, from which the stream rushes forth into the light of day, is named Gaumukh, the cow's mouth, and is held in deepest reverence by Hindus. This region of eternal frost was the scene of many of their most sacred mysteries.

At Gangotri, the Ganga is no puny stream but is already a river thirty or forty yards wide. At Gauri Kund, below the temple, it falls over a rock of considerable height, and continues tumbling over a succession of small cascades until it enters the Bhaironghat gorge.

A night spent beside the river is an eerie experience. After some time it begins to sound, not like one fall but a hundred, and this sound is ever-present both in one's dreams and waking hours.

Rising early to greet the dawn proved rather pointless, as the surrounding peaks did not let the sun in till after 9 a.m. Everyone rushed about to keep warm, exclaiming delightedly at what they described as gulabi thand, literally 'rosy cold'. Guaranteed to turn the cheeks a rosy pink! A charming expression, but I prefer a rosy sunburn and remained beneath a heavy quilt until the sun came up over the mountain to throw its golden shafts across the river.

This is mid-October, and after Diwali the shrine and the small township will close for the winter, the pandits retreating to the relative warmth of Mukbha. Soon, snow will cover everything, and even the hardy purple plumaged whistling thrushes (known here as kastura), who are lovers of deep shade, will move further down the valley. And further down, below the forest line, the hardy Garhwali farmers will go about harvesting their terraced fields which form patterns of yellow, green and gold above the deep green of the river.

Yes, the Bhagirathi is a green river. Although deep and swift, it has a certain serenity. At no place does it look hurried or confused—unlike the turbulent Alaknanda, fretting and fuming as it crashes down its boulder-strewn bed. The Bhagirathi is free-flowing, at peace with itself and its devotees. At all times and places, it seems to find a true and harmonious balance.

Falling for Mandakini

A GREAT RIVER at its confluence with another great river is, for me, a special moment in time. And so it was with the Mandakini at Rudraprayag, where its waters joined the waters of the Alaknanda, the one having come from the glacial snows above Kedarnath, the other from the Himalayan heights beyond

Badrinath. Both sacred rivers, destined to become the holy Ganga further downstream.

I fell in love with the Mandakini at first sight. Or was it the valley that I fell in love with? I am not sure, and it doesn't really matter. The valley is the river.

While the Alaknanda valley, especially in its higher reaches, is a deep and narrow gorge where precipitous outcrops of rock hang threateningly over the traveller, the Mandakini valley is broader, gentler, the terraced fields wider, the banks of the river a green sward in many places. Somehow, one does not feel that one is at the mercy of the Mandakini whereas one is always at the mercy of the Alaknanda with its sudden floods.

Rudraprayag is hot. It is probably a pleasant spot in winter, but at the end of June, it is decidedly hot. Perhaps its chief claim to fame is that it gave its name to the dreaded man-eating leopard of Rudraprayag who, in the course of seven years (1918-25), accounted for more than 300 victims. It was finally shot by Jim Corbett, who recounted the saga of his long hunt for the killer in his fine book, *The Man-Eating Leopard of Rudraprayag.*

The place at which the leopard was shot was the village of Gulabrai, two miles south of Rudraprayag. Under a large mango tree stands a memorial raised to Jim Corbett by officers and men of the Border Roads Organization. It is a touching gesture to one who loved Garhwal and India. Unfortunately, several buffaloes are tethered close by, and one has to wade through slush and buffalo dung to get to the memorial stone. A board tacked on to the mango tree attracts the attention of motorists who might pass without noticing the memorial, which is off to one side.

The killer leopard was noted for its direct method of attack on humans, and, in spite of being poisoned, trapped in a cave, and shot at innumerable times, it did not lose its contempt for man. Two English sportsmen covering both ends to the old suspension bridge over the Alaknanda fired several times at the man-eater but to little effect.

It was not long before the leopard acquired a reputation among the hill folk for being an evil spirit. A sadhu was suspected of turning into the leopard by night, and was only saved from being lynched by the ingenuity of Philip Mason, then deputy commissioner of Garhwal. Mason kept the sadhu in custody until the leopard made his next attack, thus proving the man innocent. Years later, when Mason turned novelist and (using the pen name Philip Woodruffe) wrote *The Wild Sweet Witch,* he had one of the characters, a beautiful young woman who apparently turns into a man-eating leopard by night.

Corbett's host at Gulabrai was one of the few who survived an encounter with the leopard. It left him with a hole in his throat. Apart from being a superb storyteller, Corbett displayed great compassion for people from all walks of life and is still a legend in Garhwal and Kumaon amongst people who have never read his books.

In June, one does not linger long in the steamy heat of

Rudraprayag. But as one travels up the river, making a gradual ascent of the Mandakini valley, there is a cool breeze coming down from the snows, and the smell of rain is in the air.

The thriving little township of Agastmuni spreads itself along the wide river banks. Further upstream, near a little place called Chandrapuri, we cannot resist breaking our journey to sprawl on the tender green grass that slopes gently down to the swift flowing river. A small rest house is in the making. Around it, banana fronds sway and poplar leaves dance in the breeze.

This is no sluggish river of the plains, but a fast moving current, tumbling over rocks, turning and twisting in its efforts to discover the easiest way for its frothy snow-fed waters to escape the mountains. Escape is the word! For the constant plaint of many a Garhwali is that, while his hills abound in rivers, the water runs down and away, and little if any reaches the fields and villages above it. Cultivation must depend on the rain and not on the river.

The road climbs gradually, still keeping to the river. Just outside Guptakashi, my attention is drawn to a clump of huge trees sheltering a small but ancient temple. We stop here and enter the shade of the trees.

The temple is deserted. It is a temple dedicated to Shiva, and in the courtyard are several river-rounded stone lingams on which leaves and blossoms have fallen. No one seems to come here, which is strange, since it is on the pilgrim route. Two boys from a neighbouring field leave their yoked bullocks to come and talk to me, but they cannot tell me much about the temple except to confirm that it is seldom visited. 'The buses do not stop here.' That seems explanation enough. For where the buses go, the pilgrims go; and where the pilgrims go, other pilgrims will follow. Thus far and no further.

The trees seem to be magnolias. But I have never seen magnolia trees grow to such huge proportions. Perhaps they are something else. Never mind; let them remain a mystery.

Guptakashi in the evening is all a bustle. A coachload of pilgrims (headed for Kedarnath) has just arrived, and the tea shops near the bus stand are doing brisk business. Then the 'local' bus from Ukhimath, across the river arrives, and many of the passengers head for a tea shop famed for its samosas. The local bus is called the Bhook Hartal, the 'Hunger Strike' bus.

'How did it get that name?' I asked one of the samosa-eaters.

'Well, it's an interesting story. For a long time we had been asking the authorities to provide a bus service for the local people and for the villagers who live off the roads. All the buses came from Srinagar or Rishikesh, and were taken up by pilgrims. The locals couldn't find room in them. But our pleas went unheard until the whole town, or most of it, decided to go on hunger strike.'

'They nearly put me out of business, too,' said the tea shop owner cheerfully. 'Nobody ate any samosas for two days!'

There is no cinema or public place of entertainment at Guptakashi, and the town goes to sleep early. And wakes early.

At six, the hillside, green from recent rain, sparkles in the morning sunshine. Snowcapped Chaukhamba (7,140 metres) is dazzling. The air is clear; no smoke or dust up here. The climate, I am told, is mild all the year round judging by the scent and shape of the flowers, and the boys call them Champs, Hindi for champa blossom. Ukhimath, on the other side of the river, lies in the shadow. It gets the sun at nine. In winter, it must wait till afternoon.

Guptakashi has not yet been rendered ugly by the barrack-type architecture that has come up in some growing hill towns. The old double-storeyed houses are built of stone, with grey slate roofs. They blend well with the hillside. Cobbled paths meander through the old bazaar.

One of these takes up to the famed Guptakashi temple, tucked away above the old part of the town. Here, as in Benaras, Shiva is worshipped as Vishwanath, and two underground streams representing the sacred Jainuna and Bhagirathi rivers feed the pool sacred to the god. This temple gives the town its name, Guptakashi, the 'Invisible Benaras', just as Uttarkashi on the Bhagirathi is 'Upper Benaras.'

Guptakashi and its environs have so many lingams that the saying *'Jitne kankar utne shankar'*—'As many stones, so many Shivas'—has become a proverb to describe its holiness.

From Guptakashi, pilgrims proceed north to Kedarnath, and the last stage of their journey—about a day's march—must be covered on foot or horseback. The temple of Kedarnath, situated at a height of 11.753 feet, is encircled by snowcapped peaks, and Atkinson has conjectured that 'the symbol of the linga may have arisen from the pointed peaks around his (Lord Shiva's) original home.'

The temple is dedicated to Sadashiva, the subterranean form of the god, who, 'fleeing from the Pandavas took refuge here in the form of a he-buffalo and finding himself hard-pressed, dived into the ground leaving the hinder parts on the surface, which continue to be the subject of adoration.' (Atkinson).

The other portions of the god are worshipped as follows—the arms at Tungnath, at a height of 13,000 feet, the face at Rudranath (12,000 feet), the belly at Madrnaheshwar, eighteen miles northeast of Guptakashi; and the hair and head at Kalpeshwar, neai Joshimath. These five sacred shrines form the Panch Kedars (five Kedars).

We leave the Mandakini to visit Tungnath on the Chandrashila range. But I will return to this river. It has captured my mind and heart.

Breakfast Time

I like a good sausage, I do;
It's a dish for the chosen and few.
Oh, for sausage and mash,
And of mustard a dash,
And an egg nicely fried—maybe two?
At breakfast or lunch, or at dinner,
The sausage is always a winner;
If you want a good spread,
Go for sausage on bread,
And forget all your vows to be slimmer.

'In Praise of the Sausage'
(Written for Victor and Maya Banerjee,
who excel at making sausage breakfasts.)

THERE IS something to be said for breakfast.

If you take an early morning walk down Landour Bazaar, you might be fortunate enough to see a very large cow standing in the foyer of a hotel, munching on a succulent cabbage or cauliflower. The owner of the hotel has a soft spot for this particular cow, and invites it in for breakfast every morning. Having had its fill, the cow—very well-behaved—backs out of the shop and makes way for paying customers.

I am not one of them. I prefer to have my breakfast at home—a fried egg, two or three buttered toasts, a bit of bacon if I'm lucky, otherwise some fish pickle from the south, followed by a cup of strong coffee—and I'm a happy man and can take the rest of the day in my stride.

I don't think I have ever written a good story without a good breakfast. There are, of course, writers who do not eat before noon. Both they and their prose have a lean and hungry look. Dickens was good at describing breakfasts and dinners—especially Christmas repasts—and many of his most rounded characters were good-natured people who were fond of their food and drink—Mr Pickwick, the Cheeryble brothers, Mr Weller senior, Captain Cuttle—as opposed to the half-starved characters in the works of some other Victorian writers. And remember, Dickens had an impoverished childhood. So I took it as a compliment when a little girl came up to me the other day and said, 'Sir, you're Mr Pickwick!'

As a young man, I had a lean and hungry look. After all, I was often hungry. Now if I look like Pickwick, I take it as an achievement.

And all those breakfasts had something to do with it.

It's not only cows and early-to-rise writers who enjoy a good breakfast. Last summer, Colonel Solomon was out taking his pet Labrador for an early morning walk near Lal Tibba when a leopard sprang out of a thicket, seized the dog and made off with it down the hillside. The dog did not even have time to yelp. Nor did the Colonel. Suffering from shock, he left Landour the next day and has yet to return.

Another leopard—this time at the other end of Mussoorie—entered the Savoy hotel at dawn, and finding nothing in the kitchen except chicken's feathers, moved on to the billiard room and there vented its frustration on the cloth of the billiard table, clawing it to shreds. The leopard was seen in various parts of the hotel before it made off in the direction of the Ladies' Block.

Just a hungry leopard in search of a meal. But three days later,

Nandu Jauhar, the owner of the Savoy, found himself short of a lady housekeeper. Had she eloped with the laundryman, or had she become a good breakfast for the leopard? We do not know till this day.

English breakfasts, unlike continental breakfasts, are best enjoyed in India where you don't have to rush off to catch a bus or a train or get to your office in time. You can linger over your scrambled egg and marmalade on toast. What would breakfast be without some honey or marmalade? You can have an excellent English breakfast at the India International Centre, where I have spent many pleasant reflective mornings... And a super breakfast at the Raj Mahal Hotel in Jaipur. But some hotels give very inferior breakfasts, and I am afraid that certain Mussoorie establishments are great offenders, specializing in singed omelettes and burnt toasts.

Many people are under the erroneous impression that the days of the British Raj were synonymous with huge meals and unlimited food and drink. This may have been the case in the days of the East India Company, but was far from being so during the last decade of British rule. Those final years coincided with World War II, when food rationing was in force. At my boarding school in Shimla, omelettes were made from powdered eggs, and the contents of the occasional sausage were very mysterious—so much so, that we called our sausages 'sweet mysteries of life!' after a popular Nelson Eddy song.

Things were not much better at home. Just porridge (no eggs!) bread and jam (no butter!), and tea with *ghur* instead of refined sugar. The *ghur* was, of course, much healthier than sugar.

Breakfasts are better now, at least for those who can afford them. The jam is better than it used to be. So is the bread. And I can enjoy a fried egg, or even two, without feeling guilty about it. But good omelettes are still hard to come by. They shouldn't be made in a hurried or slapdash manner. Some thought has to go into an omelette. And a little love too. It's like writing a book—done much better with some feeling!

Trees by My Window

LIVING AT 7,000 feet, I am fortunate to have a big window that opens out on the forest so that the trees are almost within my reach. If I jumped, I could land quite neatly in the arms of an oak or horse chestnut. I have never made that leap, but the big langurs—silver-grey monkeys with long, swishing tails—often spring from the trees onto my corrugated tin roof, making enough noise to frighten all the birds away.

Standing on its own outside my window is a walnut tree, and truly this is a tree for all seasons. In winter the branches are bare, but beautifully smooth and rounded. In spring each limb produces a bright green spear of new growth, and by mid-summer the entire tree is in leaf. Toward the end of the monsoon the walnuts, encased in their green jackets, have reached maturity. When the jackets begin to split, you can see the hard brown shells of the nuts, and inside each shell is the delicious meat itself.

Every year this tree gives me a basket of walnuts. But last year the nuts were disappearing one by one, and I was at a loss as to who had been taking them. Could it have been the milkman's small son? He was an inveterate tree climber, but he was usually to be found on the oak trees, gathering fodder for his herd. He admitted that his cows had enjoyed my dahlias, which they had eaten the previous week, but he stoutly denied having fed them walnuts.

It wasn't the woodpecker either. He was out there every day, knocking furiously against the bark of the tree, trying to pry an insect out of a narrow crack, but he was strictly non-vegetarian. As for the langurs, they ate my geraniums but did not care for the walnuts.

The nuts seemed to disappear early in the morning while I was still in bed, so one day I surprised everyone, including myself, by getting up before sunrise. I was just in time to catch the culprit climbing out of the walnut tree. She was an old woman who sometimes came to cut grass on the hillside. Her face was as wrinkled as the walnuts she so fancied, but her arms and legs were very sturdy.

'And how many walnuts did you gather today, Grandmother?' I asked.

'Just two,' she said with a giggle, offering them to me on her open palm. I accepted one, and thus encouraged, she climbed higher into the tree and helped herself to the remaining nuts. It was impossible for me to object. I was taken with admiration for her agility. She must have been twice my age, but I knew I could never get up that tree. To the victor, the spoils!

Unlike the prized walnuts, the horse chestnuts are inedible. Even the rhesus monkeys throw them away in disgust. But the tree itself is a friendly one, especially in summer when it is in full leaf. The lightest breeze makes the leaves break into conversation, and their rustle is a cheerful sound. The spring flowers of the horse chestnut look like candelabra, and when the blossoms fall, they carpet the hillside with their pale pink petals.

Another of my favorites is the deodar. It stands erect and dignified and does not bend with the wind. In spring the new leaves, or needles, are a tender green, while during the monsoon the tiny young cones spread like blossoms in the dark green folds of the branches. The deodar enjoys the company of its own kind: where one deodar grows, there will be others. A walk in a deodar forest is awe-inspiring—

surrounded on all sides by these great sentinels of the mountains, you feel as though the trees themselves are on the march.

I walk among the trees outside my window often, acknowledging their presence with a touch of my hand against their trunks. The oak has been there the longest, and the wind has bent its upper branches and twisted a few so that it looks shaggy and undistinguished. But it is a good tree for the privacy of birds. Sometimes it seems completely uninhabited until there is a whirring sound, as of a helicopter approaching, and a party of Long-Tailed Blue Magpies flies across the forest glade.

Most of the pines near my home are on the next hillside. But there is a small Himalayan Blue a little way below the cottage, and sometimes I sit beneath it to listen to the wind playing softly in its branches.

When I open the window at night, there is almost always something to listen to: the mellow whistle of a pygmy owlet, or the sharp cry of a barking deer. Sometimes, if I am lucky, I will see the moon coming up over the next mountain, and two distant deodars in perfect silhouette.

Some night sounds outside my window remain strange and mysterious. Perhaps they are the sounds of the trees themselves, stretching their limbs in the dark, shifting a little, flexing their fingers, whispering to one another. These great trees of the mountains, I feel they know me well, as I watch them and listen to their secrets, happy to rest my head beneath their outstretched arms.

Some Hill Station Ghosts

SHIMLA HAS its phantom rickshaw and Lansdowne its headless horseman. Mussoorie has its woman in white. Late at night, she can be seen sitting on the parapet wall on the winding road up to the hill station. Don't stop to offer her a lift. She will fix you with her evil eye and ruin your holiday.

The Mussoorie taxi drivers and other locals call her Bhoot Aunty. Everyone has seen her at some time or the other. To give her a lift is to court disaster. Many accidents have been attributed to her baleful presence. And when people pick themselves up from the road (or are picked up by concerned citizens), Bhoot Aunty is nowhere to be seen, although survivors swear that she was in the car with them.

Ganesh Saili, Abha and I were coming back from Dehradun late one night when we saw this woman in white sitting on the parapet by the side of the road. As our headlights fell on her, she turned her face away, Ganesh, being a thorough gentleman, slowed down and offered her a lift. She turned towards us then, and smiled a wicked smile. She seemed quite attractive except that her canines protruded slightly in vampire fashion.

'Don't stop!' screamed Abha. 'Don't even look at her! It's Bhoot Aunty!'

Ganesh pressed down on the accelerator and sped past her. Next day we heard that a tourist's car had gone off the road and the occupants had been severely injured. The accident took place shortly after they had stopped to pick up a woman in white who had wanted a lift. But she was not among the injured.

Miss Ripley Bean, an old English lady who was my neighbour when I lived near Wynberg-Allen school, told me that her family was haunted by a malignant phantom head that always appeared before the death of one of her relatives.

She said her brother saw this apparition the night before her mother died, and both she and her sister saw it before the death of their father. The sister slept in the same room. They were both awakened one night by a curious noise in the cupboard facing their beds. One of them began getting out of bed to see if their cat was in the room, when the cupboard door suddenly opened and a luminous head appeared. It was covered with matted hair and appeared to be in an advanced stage of decomposition. Its fleshless mouth grinned at the terrified sisters. And then as they crossed themselves, it vanished. The next day they learned that their father, who was in Lucknow, had died suddenly, at about the time that they had seen the death's head.

Everyone likes to hear stories about haunted houses; even sceptics will listen to a ghost story, while casting doubts on its veracity.

Rudyard Kipling wrote a number of memorable ghost stories set in India—*Imray's Return, The Phantom Rickshaw, The Mark of the Beast, The End of the Passage*—his favorite milieu being the haunted dak bungalow. But it was only after his return to England that he found himself actually having to live in a haunted house. He writes about it in his autobiography, *Something of Myself*:

'The spring of '96 saw us in Torquay, where we found a house for our heads that seemed almost too good to be true. It was large and bright, with big rooms each and all open to the sun, the ground embellished with great trees and the warm land dipping southerly to the clean sea under the Mary Church cliffs. It had been inhabited for thirty years by three old maids.

The revelation came in the shape of a growing depression which enveloped us both—a gathering blackness of mind and sorrow of the heart, that each put down to the new, soft climate and, without telling the other, fought against for long weeks. It was the Feng-shui—the Spirit of the house itself—that darkened the sunshine and fell upon us every time we entered, checking the very words on our lips... We paid forfeit and fled. More than thirty years later we returned down the steep little road to that house, and found, quite unchanged, the same brooding spirit of deep despondency within the rooms.'

Again, thirty years later, he returned to this house in his short story, 'The House Surgeon', in which two sisters cannot come to terms with the suicide of a third sister, and brood upon the tragedy day and night until their thoughts saturate every room of the house.

Many years ago, I had a similar experience in a house in Dehradun, in which an elderly English couple had died from neglect and starvation. In 1947, when many European residents were leaving the town and emigrating to the UK, this poverty-stricken old couple, sick and friendless, had been forgotten. Too ill to go out for food or medicine, they had died in their beds, where they were discovered several days later by the landlord's munshi.

The house stood empty for several years. No one wanted to live in it. As a young man, I would sometimes roam about the neglected grounds or explore the cold, bare rooms, now stripped of furniture, doorless and windowless, and I would be assailed by a feeling of deep gloom and depression. Of course I knew what had happened there, and that may have contributed to the effect the place had on me. But when I took a friend, Jai Shankar, through the house, he told me he felt quite sick with apprehension and fear. 'Ruskin, why have you brought me to this awful house?' he said. 'I'm sure it's haunted.' And only then did I tell him about the tragedy that had taken place within its walls.

Today, the house is used as a government office. No one lives in it at night except for a Gurkha chowkidar, a man of strong nerves who sleeps in the back verandah. The atmosphere of the place doesn't bother him, but he does hear strange sounds in the night. 'Like someone crawling about on the floor above,' he tells me. 'And someone groaning. These old houses are noisy places...'

A morgue is not a noisy place, as a rule. And for a morgue attendant, corpses are silent companions.

Old Mr Jacob, who lives just behind the cottage, was once a morgue attendant for the local mission hospital. In those days it was situated at Sunny Bank, about a hundred metres up the hill from here. One of the outhouses served as the morgue: Mr Jacob begs me not to identify it.

He tells me of a terrifying experience he went through when he was doing night duty at the morgue.

'The body of a young man was found floating in the Aglar river, behind Landour, and was brought to the morgue while I was on night duty. It was placed on the table and covered with a sheet.

'I was quite accustomed to seeing corpses of various kinds and did not mind sharing the same room with them, even after dark. On this occasion a friend had promised to join me, and to pass the time I strolled around the room, whistling a popular tune. I think it was 'Danny Boy', if I remember right. My friend was a long time coming, and I soon got tired of whistling and sat down on the bench beside the table. The night was very still, and I began to feel uneasy. My thoughts went to the boy who had drowned and I wondered what he had been like when he was alive. Dead bodies are so impersonal...

'The morgue had no electricity, just a kerosene lamp, and after some time I noticed that the flame was very low. As I was about to turn it up, it suddenly went out. I lit the lamp again, after extending the wick. I returned to the bench, but I had not been sitting there for long when the lamp again went out, and something moved very softly and quietly past me.

'I felt quite sick and faint, and could hear my heart pounding away. The strength had gone out of my legs, otherwise I would have fled from the room. I felt quite weak and helpless, unable even to call out...

'Presently the footsteps came nearer and nearer. Something cold and icy touched one of my hands and felt its way up towards my neck and throat. It was behind me, then it was before me. Then it was *over* me. I was in the arms of the corpse!

'I must have fainted, because when I woke up I was on the floor, and my friend was trying to revive me. The corpse was back on the table.'

'It may have been a nightmare,' I suggested. 'Or you allowed your imagination to run riot.'

'No,' said Mr Jacobs. 'There were wet, slimy marks on my clothes. And the feet of the corpse matched the wet footprints on the floor.'

After this experience, Mr Jacobs refused to do any more night duty at the morgue.

From Herbertpur near Paonta you can go up to Kalsi, and then up the hill road to Chakrata.

Chakrata is in a security zone, most of it off limits to tourists, which is one reason why it has remained unchanged in 150 years of its existence. This small town's population of 1,500 is the same today as it was in 1947—probably the only town in India that hasn't shown a population increase.

Courtesy a government official, I was fortunate enough to be able to stay in the forest rest house on the outskirts of the town. This is a new building, the old rest house—a little way downhill—having fallen into disuse. The chowkidar told me the old rest house was haunted, and that this was the real reason for its having been abandoned. I was a bit sceptical about this, and asked him what kind of haunting took place in it. He told me that he had himself gone through a frightening experience in the old house, when he had gone there to light a fire for some forest officers who were expected that night. After lighting the fire, he looked round and saw a large black animal, like a wild cat, sitting on the wooden floor and gazing into the fire. 'I called out to it, thinking it was someone's pet. The creature turned, and looked full at me with *eyes that were human,* and a face which was the *face of an ugly woman!* The creature snarled at me, and the snarl became an angry howl. Then it vanished!'

'And what did you do?' I asked.

'I vanished too,' said the chowkidar. 'I haven't been down to that house again.'

I did not volunteer to sleep in the old house but made myself comfortable in the new one, where I hoped I would not be troubled by any phantom. However, a large rat kept me company, gnawing away at the woodwork of a chest of drawers. Whenever I switched on the light it would be silent, but as soon as the light was off, it would start gnawing away again.

This reminded me of a story old Miss Kellner (of my Dehra childhood) told me, of a young man who was desperately in love with a girl who did not care for him. One day, when he was following her in the street, she turned on him and, pointing to a rat which some boys had just killed, said, 'I'd as soon marry that rat as marry you.' He took her cruel words so much to heart that he pined away and died. After his death, the girl was haunted at night by a rat and occasionally she would be bitten. When the family decided to emigrate, they travelled down to Bombay in order to embark on a ship sailing for London. The ship had just left the quay when shouts and screams were heard from the pier. The crowd scattered, and a huge rat with fiery eyes ran down to the end of the quay. It sat there, screaming with rage, then jumped into the water and disappeared. After that (according to Miss Kellner), the girl was not haunted again.

Old dak bungalows and forest rest houses have a reputation for being haunted. And most hill stations have their resident ghosts—and ghost writers! But I will not extend this catalogue of ghostly hauntings and visitations as I do not want to discourage tourists from visiting Landour and Mussoorie. In some countries, ghosts are an added attraction for tourists. Britain boasts of hundreds of haunted castles and stately homes, and visitors to Romania seek out Transylvania and Dracula's castle. So do we promote Bhoot Aunty as a tourist attraction? Only if she reforms and stops sending vehicles off those hairpin bends that lead to Mussoorie.

The Bat

Most bats fly high,
Swooping only
To take some insect on the wing;
But there's a bat I know,
Who flies so low,
He skims the floor;
He does not enter at the window,
But flies in at the door,
Does stunts beneath the furniture...
Is his radar wrong,
Or does he just prefer
Being different from other bats?
And when sometimes,
He settles upside down,
At the foot of my bed,
I let him be.
On lonely nights, even a crazy bat
Is company.

Our Great Escape

IT HAD been a lonely winter for a fourteen-year-old. I had spent the first few weeks of the vacation with my mother and stepfather in Dehra. Then they left for Delhi, and I was pretty much on my own. Of course, the servants were there to take care of my needs, but there was no one to keep me company. I would wander off in the mornings, taking some path up the hills, come back home for lunch, read a bit and then stroll off again till it was time for dinner. Sometimes I walked up to my grandparents' house, but it seemed so different now, with people I didn't know occupying the house.

The three-month winter break over, I was almost eager to return to my boarding school in Shimla.

It wasn't as though I had many friends at school. I needed a friend but it was not easy to find one among a horde of rowdy, pea-shooting eighth formers, who carved their names on desks and stuck chewing gum on the class teacher's chair. Had I grown up with other children, I might have developed a taste for schoolboy anarchy; but in sharing my father's loneliness after his separation from my mother, and in being bereft of any close family ties, I had turned into a premature adult.

After a month in the eighth form, I began to notice a new boy, Omar, and then only because he was a quiet, almost taciturn person who took no part in the form's feverish attempt to imitate the Marx Brothers at the circus. He showed no resentment at the prevailing anarchy, nor did he make a move to participate in it. Once he caught me looking at him, and he smiled ruefully, tolerantly. Did I sense another adult in the class? Someone who was a little older than his years?

Even before we began talking to each other, Omar and I developed an understanding of sorts, and we'd nod almost respectfully to each other when we met in the classroom corridors or the environs of the dining hall or the dormitory. We were not in the same house. The house system practised its own form of apartheid, whereby a member of one house was not expected to fraternize with someone belonging to another. Those public schools certainly knew how to clamp you into compartments. However, these barriers vanished when Omar and I found ourselves selected for the School Colts' hockey team, Omar as a full-back, I as the goalkeeper.

The taciturn Omar now spoke to me occasionally, and we combined well on the field of play. A good understanding is needed between a goalkeeper and a full-back. We were on the same wavelength. I anticipated his moves, he was familiar with mine. Years later, when I read Conrad's *The Secret Sharer*, I thought of Omar.

It wasn't until we were away from the confines of school, classroom and dining hall that our friendship flourished. The hockey team travelled to Sanawar on the next mountain range, where we were to play a couple of matches against our old rivals, the Lawrence Royal Military School. This had been my father's old school, so I was keen to explore its grounds and peep into its classrooms.

Omar and I were thrown together a good deal during the visit to Sanawar, and in our more leisurely moments, strolling undisturbed around a school where we were guests and not pupils, we exchanged life histories and other confidences. Omar, too, had lost his father— had I sensed that before?—shot in some tribal encounter on the Frontier, for he hailed from the lawless lands beyond Peshawar.

A wealthy uncle was seeing to Omar's education.

We wandered into the school chapel, and there I found my father's name—A. A. Bond—on the school's roll of honour board: old boys who had lost their lives while serving during the two World Wars.

'What did his initials stand for?' asked Omar.

'Aubrey Alexander.'

'Unusual names, like yours. Why did your parents call you Rusty?'

'I am not sure.' I told him about the book I was writing. It was my first one and was called *Nine Months* (the length of the school term, not a pregnancy), and it described some of the happenings at school and lampooned a few of our teachers. I had filled three slim exercise books with this premature literary project, and I allowed Omar to go through them. He must have been my first reader and critic.

'They're very interesting,' he said, 'but you'll get into trouble if someone finds them, especially Mr Fisher.'

I have to admit it wasn't great literature. I was better at hockey and football. I made some spectacular saves, and we won our matches against Sanawar. When we returned to Shimla, we were school heroes for a couple of days and lost some of our reticence; we were even a little more forthcoming with other boys. And then Mr Fisher, my housemaster, discovered my literary opus, *Nine Months*, under my mattress, and took it away and read it (as he told me later) from cover to cover. Corporal punishment then being in vogue, I was given six of the best with a springy Malacca cane, and my manuscript was torn up and deposited in Mr Fisher's wastepaper basket. All I had to show for my efforts were some purple welts on my bottom. These were proudly displayed to all who were interested, and I was a hero for another two days.

'Will you go away too when the British leave India?' Omar asked me one day.

'I don't think so,' I said. 'I don't have anyone to go back to in

England, and my guardian, Mr Harrison, too seems to have no intention of going back.'

'Everyone is saying that our leaders and the British are going to divide the country. Shimla will be in India, Peshawar in Pakistan!'

'Oh, it won't happen,' I said glibly. 'How can they cut up such a big country?' But even as we chatted about the possibility, Nehru, Jinnah and Mountbatten, and all those who mattered, were preparing their instruments for major surgery.

Before their decision impinged on our lives and everyone else's, we found a little freedom of our own, in an underground tunnel that we discovered below the third flat.

It was really part of an old, disused drainage system, and when Omar and I began exploring it, we had no idea just how far it extended. After crawling along on our bellies for some twenty feet, we found ourselves in complete darkness. Omar had brought along a small pencil torch, and with its help we continued writhing forward (moving backwards would have been quite impossible) until we saw a glimmer of light at the end of the tunnel. Dusty, musty, very scruffy, we emerged at last on to a grassy knoll, a little way outside the school boundary.

It's always a great thrill to escape beyond the boundaries that adults have devised. Here we were in unknown territory. To travel without passports—that would be the ultimate in freedom!

But more passports were on their way—and more boundaries.

Lord Mountbatten, viceroy and governor-general-to-be, came for our Founder's Day and gave away the prizes. I had won a prize for something or the other, and mounted the rostrum to receive my book from this towering, handsome man in his pinstripe suit. Bishop Cotton's was then the premier school of India, often referred to as the 'Eton of the East'. Viceroys and governors had graced its functions. Many of its boys had gone on to eminence in the civil services and armed forces. There was one 'old boy' about whom they maintained a stolid silence—General Dyer, who had ordered the massacre at Amritsar and destroyed the trust that had been building up between Britain and India.

Now Mountbatten spoke of the momentous events that were happening all around us—the War had just come to an end, the United Nations held out the promise of a world living in peace and harmony, and India, an equal partner with Britain, would be among the great nations...

A few weeks later, Bengal and the Punjab provinces were bisected. Riots flared up across northern India, and there was a great exodus of people crossing the newly-drawn frontiers of Pakistan and India. Homes were destroyed, thousands lost their lives.

The common room radio and the occasional newspaper kept us abreast of events, but in our tunnel, Omar and I felt immune from all that was happening, worlds away from all the pillage, murder and revenge. And outside the tunnel, on the pine knoll below the school, there was fresh untrodden grass, sprinkled with clover and daisies; the only sounds we heard were the hammering of a woodpecker and the distant insistent call of the Himalayan Barbet. Who could touch us there?

'And when all the wars are done,' I said, 'a butterfly will still be beautiful.'

'Did you read that somewhere?'

'No, it just came into my head.'

'Already you're a writer.'

'No, I want to play hockey for India or football for Arsenal. Only winning teams!'

'You can't win forever. Better to be a writer.'

When the monsoon arrived, the tunnel was flooded, the drain choked with rubble. We were allowed out to the cinema to see Laurence Olivier's *Hamlet*, a film that did nothing to raise our spirits on a wet and gloomy afternoon; but it was our last picture that year, because communal riots suddenly broke out in Shimla's Lower Bazaar, an area that was still much as Kipling had described it—'a man who knows his way there can defy all the police of India's summer capital'—and we were confined to school indefinitely.

One morning after prayers in the chapel, the headmaster announced that the Muslim boys—those who had their homes in what was now Pakistan—would have to be evacuated, sent to their homes across the border with an armed convoy.

The tunnel no longer provided an escape for us. The bazaar was out of bounds. The flooded playing field was deserted. Omar and I sat on a damp wooden bench and talked about the future in vaguely hopeful terms, but we didn't solve any problems. Mountbatten and Nehru and Jinnah were doing all the solving.

It was soon time for Omar to leave—he left along with some fifty other boys from Lahore, Pindi and Peshawar. The rest of us—Hindus, Christians, Parsis—helped them load their luggage into the waiting trucks. A couple of boys broke down and wept. So did our departing school captain, a Pathan who had been known for his stoic and unemotional demeanour. Omar waved cheerfully to me and I waved back. We had vowed to meet again some day.

The convoy got through safely enough. There was only one casualty—the school cook, who had strayed into an off-limits area in the foothill town of Kalika and been set upon by a mob. He wasn't seen again.

Towards the end of the school year, just as we were all getting ready to leave for the school holidays, I received a letter from Omar. He told me something about his new school and how he missed my company and our games and our tunnel to freedom. I replied and gave him my home address, but I did not hear from him again.

Some seventeen or eighteen years later, I did get news of Omar, but in an entirely different context. India and Pakistan were at war, and in a bombing raid over Ambala, not far from Shimla, a Pakistani plane was shot down. Its crew died in the crash. One of them, I learnt later, was Omar.

Did he, I wonder, get a glimpse of the playing fields we knew so well as boys? Perhaps memories of his schooldays flooded back as he flew over the foothills. Perhaps he remembered the tunnel through which we were able to make our little escape to freedom.

But there are no tunnels in the sky.

The Eyes of the Eagle

IT WAS a high, piercing sound, almost like the yelping of a dog. Jai stopped picking the wild strawberries that grew in the grass around him, and looked up at the sky. He had a dog—a shaggy guard dog called Motu—but Motu did not yet yelp, he growled and barked. The strange sound came from the sky, and Jai had heard it before. Now, realizing what it was, he jumped to his feet, calling to his dog, calling his sheep to start for home. Motu came bounding towards him, ready for a game.

'Not now, Motu!' said Jai. 'We must get the lambs home quickly.' Again he looked up at the sky.

He saw it now, a black speck against the sun, growing larger as it circled the mountain, coming lower every moment—a Golden Eagle, king of the skies over the higher Himalayas, ready now to swoop and seize its prey.

Had it seen a pheasant or a pine marten? Or was it after one of the lambs? Jai had never lost a lamb to an eagle, but recently some of the other shepherds had been talking about a golden eagle that had been preying on their flocks.

The sheep had wandered some way down the side of the mountain, and Jai ran after them to make sure that none of the lambs had gone off on its own.

Motu ran about, barking furiously. He wasn't very good at keeping the sheep together—he was often bumping into them and sending them tumbling down the slope—but his size and bear-like look kept the leopards and wolves at a distance.

Jai was counting the lambs; they were bleating loudly and staying close to their mothers. *One—two—three—four...*

There should have been a fifth. Jai couldn't see it on the slope below him. He looked up towards a rocky ledge near the steep path to the Tung temple. The golden eagle was circling the rocks.

The bird disappeared from sight for a moment, then rose again with a small creature grasped firmly in its terrible talons.

'It has taken a lamb!' shouted Jai. He started scrambling up the slope. Motu ran ahead of him, barking furiously at the big bird as it glided away over the tops of the stunted junipers to its eyrie on the cliffs above Tung.

There was nothing that Jai and Motu could do except stare helplessly and angrily at the disappearing eagle. The lamb had died the instant it had been struck. The rest of the flock seemed unaware of what had happened. They still grazed on the thick, sweet grass of the mountain slopes.

'We had better drive them home, Motu,' said Jai, and at a nod from the boy, the big dog bounded down the slope to take part in his favourite game of driving the sheep homewards. Soon he had them running all over the place, and Jai had to dash about trying to keep them together. Finally they straggled homewards.

'A fine lamb gone,' said Jai to himself gloomily. 'I wonder what Grandfather will say.'

Grandfather said, 'Never mind. It had to happen some day. That eagle has been watching the sheep for some time.'

Grandmother, more practical, said, 'We could have sold the lamb for three hundred rupees. You'll have to be more careful in future, Jai. Don't fall asleep on the hillside, and don't read storybooks when you are supposed to be watching the sheep!'

'I wasn't reading this morning,' said Jai truthfully, forgetting to mention that he had been gathering strawberries.

'It's good for him to read,' said Grandfather, who had never had the luck to go to school. In his days, there weren't any schools in the mountains. Now there was one in every village.

'Time enough to read at night,' said Grandmother, who did not think much of the little one-room school down at Maku, their home village.

'Well, these are the October holidays,' said Grandfather. 'Otherwise he would not be here to help us with the sheep. It will snow by the end of the month, and then we will move with the flock. You will have more time for reading then, Jai.'

At Maku, which was down in the warmer valley, Jai's parents tilled a few narrow terraces on which they grew barley, millets and potatoes. The old people brought their sheep up to the Tung meadows to graze during the summer months. They stayed in a small stone hut just off the path which pilgrims took to the ancient temple. At 12,000 feet above sea level, it was the highest Hindu temple on the inner Himalayan ranges.

The following day Jai and Motu were very careful. The did not let the sheep out of sight even for a minute. Nor did they catch sight of the golden eagle. 'What if it attacks again?' wondered Jai. 'How will I stop it?'

The great eagle, with its powerful beak and talons, was more than a match for boy or dog. Its hind claw, four inches round the curve, was its most dangerous weapon. When it spread its wings, the distance from tip to tip was more than eight feet.

The eagle did not come that day because it had fed well and was now resting in its eyrie. Old bones, which had belonged to pheasants, snow cocks, pine martens and even foxes, were scattered about the rocks which formed the eagle's home. The eagle had a mate, but it was not the breeding season and she was away on a scouting expedition of her own.

The golden eagle stood on its rocky ledge, staring majestically across the valley. Its hard, unblinking eyes missed nothing. Those strange orange-yellow eyes could spot a field rat or a mouse hare more than a hundred yards below.

There were other eagles on the mountain, but usually they kept to their own territory. And only the bolder ones went for lambs, because the flocks were always protected by men and dogs.

The eagle took off from its eyrie and glided gracefully, powerfully over the valley, circling the Tung mountain.

Below lay the old temple, built from slabs of grey granite. A line of pilgrims snaked up the steep, narrow path. On the meadows below the peak, the sheep grazed peacefully, unaware of the presence of the eagle. The great bird's shadow slid over the sunlit slopes.

The eagle saw the boy and the dog, but he did not fear them. He had his eye on a lamb that was frisking about on the grass, a few feet away from the other grazing sheep.

Jai did not see the eagle until it swept round an outcrop of rocks about a hundred feet away. It moved silently, without any movement of its wings, for it had already built up the momentum for its dive. Now it came straight at the lamb.

Motu saw the bird in time. With a low growl he dashed forward and reached the side of the lamb at almost the same instant that the eagle swept in.

There was a terrific collision. Feathers flew. The eagle screamed with rage. The lamb tumbled down the slope, and Motu howled in pain as the huge beak struck him high on the leg.

The big bird, a little stunned by the clash, flew off rather unsteadily, with a mighty beating of its wings.

Motu had saved the lamb. It was frightened but unhurt. Bleating loudly, it joined the other sheep, who took up the bleating. Jai ran up to Motu, who lay whimpering on the ground. There was no sign of the eagle. Quickly he removed his shirt and vest; then he wrapped his vest round the dog's wound, tying it in position with his belt.

Motu could not get up, and he was much too heavy for Jai to carry. Jai did not want to leave his dog alone, in case the eagle returned to attack.

He stood up, cupped his hand to his mouth, and began calling for his grandfather.

'Dada, dada!' he shouted, and presently Grandfather heard him and came stumbling down the slope. He was followed by another shepherd, and together they lifted Motu and carried him home.

Motu had a bad wound, but Grandmother cleaned it and applied a paste made of herbs. Then she laid strips of carrot over the wound—an old mountain remedy—and bandaged the leg. But it would be some time before Motu could run about again. By then it would probably be snowing and time to leave these high-altitude pastures and return to the valley. Meanwhile, the sheep had to be taken out to graze, and Grandfather decided to accompany Jai for the remaining period.

They did not see the golden eagle for two or three days, and, when they did, it was flying over the next range. Perhaps it had found some other source of food, or even another flock of sheep. 'Are you afraid of the eagle?' Grandfather asked Jai.

'I wasn't before,' said Jai. 'Not until it hurt Motu. I did not know it could be so dangerous. But Motu hurt it too. He banged straight into it!'

'Perhaps it won't bother us again,' said Grandfather thoughtfully. 'A bird's wing is easily injured—even an eagle's.'

Jai wasn't so sure. He had seen it strike twice, and he knew that it was not afraid of anyone. Only when it learnt to fear his presence would it keep away from the flock.

The next day Grandfather did not feel well; he was feverish and kept to his bed. Motu was hobbling about gamely on three legs; the wounded leg was still very sore.

'Don't go too far with the sheep,' said Grandmother. 'Let them graze near the house.'

'But there's hardly any grass here,' said Jai.

'I don't want you wandering off while that eagle is still around.'

'Give him my stick,' said Grandfather from his bed. Grandmother took it from the corner and handed it to the boy.

It was an old stick, made of wild cherry wood, which Grandfather often carried around. The wood was strong and well-seasoned; the stick was stout and long. It reached up to Jai's shoulders.

'Don't lose it,' said Grandfather. 'It was given to me many years ago by a wandering scholar who came to the Tung temple. I was going to give it to you when you got bigger, but perhaps this is the right time for you to have it. If the eagle comes near you, swing the stick around your head. That should frighten it off!'

Clouds had gathered over the mountains, and a heavy mist hid the Tung temple. With the approach of winter, the flow of pilgrims had been reduced to a trickle. The shepherds had started leaving the lush meadows and returning to their villages at lower altitudes. Very soon the bears and the leopards and the golden eagles would have the high ranges all to themselves.

Jai used the cherry wood stick to prod the sheep along the path until they reached the steep meadows. The stick would have to be a substitute for Motu. And they seemed to respond to it more readily than they did to Motu's mad charges.

Because of the sudden cold and the prospect of snow, Grandmother had made Jai wear a rough woollen jacket and a pair of high boots bought from a Tibetan trader. He wasn't used to the boots—he wore sandals at other times—and had some difficulty in climbing quickly up and down the hillside. It was tiring work, trying to keep the flock together. The cawing of some crows warned Jai that the eagle might be around, but the mist prevented him from seeing very far.

After some time the mist lifted and Jai was able to see the temple and the snow peaks towering behind it. He saw the golden eagle, too. It was circling high overhead. Jai kept close to the flock—one eye on the eagle, one eye on the restless sheep.

Then the great bird stooped and flew lower. It circled the temple and then pretended to go away. Jai felt sure it would be back. And a few minutes later it reappeared from the other side of the mountain. It was much lower now, wings spread out and back, taloned feet to the fore, piercing eyes fixed on its target—a small lamb that had suddenly gone frisking down the slope, away from Jai and the flock.

Now it flew lower still, only a few feet off the ground, paying no attention to the boy.

It passed Jai with a great rush of air, and as it did so the boy struck out with his stick and caught the bird a glancing blow.

The eagle missed its prey, and the tiny lamb skipped away.

To Jai's amazement, the bird did not fly off. Instead it landed on the hillside and glared at the boy, as a king would glare at a humble subject who had dared to pelt him with a pebble.

The golden eagle stood almost as tall as Jai. Its wings were still outspread. Its fierce eyes seemed to be looking through and through the boy.

Jai's first instinct was to turn and run. But the cherry wood stick was still in his hands, and he felt sure there was power in it. He saw that the eagle was about to launch itself again at the lamb. Instead of running away, he ran forward, the stick raised above his head.

The eagle rose a few feet off the ground and struck out with its huge claws.

Luckily for Jai, his heavy jacket took the force of the blow. A talon ripped through the sleeve, and the sleeve fell away. At the same time the heavy stick caught the eagle across its open wing. The bird gave a shrill cry of pain and fury. Then it turned and flapped heavily away, flying unsteadily because of its injured wing.

Jai still clutched the stick because he expected the bird to return; he did not even glance at his torn jacket. But the golden eagle had alighted on a distant rock and was in no hurry to return to the attack.

Jai began driving the sheep home. The clouds had become heavy and black, and presently the first snowflakes began to fall.

Jai saw a hare go lolloping done the hill. When it was about fifty yards away, there was a rush of air from the eagle's beating wings, and Jai saw the bird approaching the hare in a sidelong drive.

'So it hasn't been badly hurt,' thought Jai, feeling a little relieved, for he could not help admiring the great bird. 'Now it has found something else to chase for its dinner.'

The hare saw the eagle and dodged about, making for a clump of junipers. Jai did not know if it was caught or not, because the snow and sleet had increased and both bird and hare were lost in the gathering snowstorm.

The sheep were bleating behind him. One of the lambs looked tired, and he stooped to pick it up. As he did so, he heard a thin, whining sound. It grew louder by the second. Before he could look up, a huge wing caught him across the shoulders and sent him sprawling. The lamb tumbled down the slope with him, into a thorny bilberry bush.

The bush saved them. Jai saw the eagle coming in again, flying low. It was another eagle! One had been vanquished, and now here was another, just as big and fearless, probably the mate of the first eagle.

Jai had lost his stick and there was no way by which he could fight the second eagle. So he crept further into the bush, holding the lamb beneath him. At the same time he began shouting at the top of his voice—both to scare the bird away and to summon help. The eagle could not easily get at them now; but the rest of the flock was exposed on the hillside. Surely the eagle would make for them.

Even as the bird circled and came back in another dive, Jai heard fierce barking. The eagle immediately swung away and rose skywards.

The barking came from Motu. Hearing Jai's shouts and sensing that something was wrong, he had come limping out of the house, ready to do battle. Behind him came another shepherd and—most wonderful of all—Grandmother herself, banging two frying-pans together. The barking, the banging and the shouting frightened the eagles away. The sheep scattered, too, and it was some time before they could all be rounded up. By then it was snowing heavily.

'Tomorrow, we must all go down to Maku,' said the shepherd.

'Yes, it's time we went,' said Grandmother. 'You can read your storybooks again, Jai.'

'I'll have my own story to tell,' said Jai.

When they reached the hut and Jai saw Grandfather, he said, 'Oh, I've forgotten your stick!'

But Motu had picked it up. Carrying it between his teeth, he brought it home and sat down with it in the open doorway. He had decided the cherry wood was good for his teeth and would have chewed it up if Grandmother hadn't taken it from him.

'Never mind,' said Grandfather, sitting up on his cot. 'It isn't the stick that matters. It's the person who holds it.'

Grandpa Fights an Ostrich

BEFORE MY grandfather joined the Indian Railways, he worked for a few years on the East African Railways, and it was during that period that he had his now famous encounter with the ostrich. My childhood was frequently enlivened by this oft-told tale of his, and I give it here in his own words—or as well as I can remember them!

While engaged in the laying of a new railway line, I had a miraculous escape from an awful death. I lived in a small township, but my work lay some twelve miles away, and I had to go to the work site and back on horseback.

One day, my horse had a slight accident, so I decided to do the journey on foot, being a great walker in those days. I also knew of a short cut through the hills that would save me about six miles.

This short cut went through an ostrich farm—or 'camp', as it was called. It was the breeding season. I was fairly familiar with the ways of ostriches, and knew that male birds were very aggressive in the breeding season, ready to attack on the slightest provocation, but I also knew that my dog would scare away any bird that might try to attack me. Strange though it may seem, even the biggest ostrich (and some of them grow to a height of nine feet) will run faster than a racehorse at the sight of even a small dog. So, I felt quite safe in the company of my dog, a mongrel who had adopted me some two months previously.

On arrival at the 'camp', I climbed through the wire fencing and, keeping a good look out, dodged across the open spaces between the thorn bushes. Now and then I caught a glimpse of the birds feeding some distance away.

I had gone about half a mile from the fencing when up started a hare. In an instant my dog gave chase. I tried calling him back, even though I knew it was hopeless. Chasing hares was that dog's passion.

I don't know whether it was the dog's bark or my own shouting, but what I was most anxious to avoid immediately happened. The ostriches were startled and began darting to and fro. Suddenly, I saw a big male bird emerge from a thicket about a hundred yards away. He stood still and stared at me for a few moments. I stared back. Then, expanding his short wings and with his tail erect, he came bounding towards me.

As I had nothing, not even a stick, with which to defend myself, I turned and ran towards the fence. But it was an unequal race. What were my steps of two or three feet against the creature's great strides of sixteen to twenty feet? There was only one hope: to get behind a large bush and try to elude the bird until help came. A dodging game was my only chance.

And so, I rushed for the nearest clump of thorn bushes and waited for my pursuer. The great bird wasted no time—he was immediately upon me.

Then the strangest encounter took place. I dodged this way and that, taking great care not to get directly in front of the ostrich's deadly kick. Ostriches kick forward, and with such terrific force that if you were struck, their huge chisel-like nails would cause you much damage.

I was breathless, and really quite helpless, calling wildly for help as I circled the thorn bush. My strength was ebbing. How much longer could I keep going? I was ready to drop from exhaustion.

As if aware of my condition, the infuriated bird suddenly doubled back on his course and charged straight at me. With a desperate effort

I managed to step to one side. I don't know how, but I found myself holding on to one of the creature's wings, quite close to its body.

It was now the ostrich's turn to be frightened. He began to turn, or rather waltz, moving round and round so quickly that my feet were soon swinging out from his body, almost horizontally! All the while the ostrich kept opening and shutting his beak with loud snaps.

Imagine my situation as I clung desperately to the wing of the enraged bird. He was whirling me round and round as though he were a discus-thrower—and I the discus! My arms soon began to ache with the strain, and the swift and continuous circling was making me dizzy. But I knew that if I relaxed my hold, even for a second, a terrible fate awaited me.

Round and round we went in a great circle. It seemed as if that spiteful bird would never tire. And, I knew I could not hold on much longer. Suddenly the ostrich went into reverse! This unexpected move made me lose my hold and sent me sprawling to the ground. I landed in a heap near the thorn bush and in an instant, before I even had time to realize what had happened, the big bird was upon me. I thought the end had come. Instinctively I raised my hands to protect my face. But the ostrich did not strike.

I moved my hands from my face and there stood the creature with one foot raised, ready to deliver a deadly kick! I couldn't move. Was the bird going to play cat-and-mouse with me and prolong the agony?

As I watched, frightened and fascinated, the ostrich turned his head sharply to the left. A second later, he jumped back, turned, and made off as fast as he could go. Dazed, I wondered what had happened to make him beat so unexpected a retreat.

I soon found out. To my great joy, I heard the bark of my truant dog, and the next moment he was jumping around me, licking my face and hands. Needless to say, I returned his caresses most affectionately! And I took good care to see that he did not leave my side until we were well clear of that ostrich 'camp'.

At Sea with Uncle Ken

WITH UNCLE Ken you had always to expect the unexpected. Even in the most normal circumstances, something unusual would happen to him and to those around him. He was a catalyst for confusion.

My mother should have known better than to ask him to accompany me to England the year after I'd finished school. She felt that a boy of sixteen was a little too young to make the voyage on his own; I might get lost or lose my money or fall overboard or catch some dreadful disease. She should have realized that Uncle Ken, her only brother (well spoilt by his five sisters), was more likely to do all these things.

Anyway, he was put in charge of me and instructed to deliver me safely to my aunt in England, after which he could either stay there or return to India, whichever he preferred. Granny had paid for his ticket; so in effect he was getting a free holiday which included a voyage on a posh P&O liner.

Our train journey to Bombay passed off without incident, although Uncle Ken did manage to misplace his spectacles, getting down at the station wearing someone else's. This left him a little short-sighted, which might have accounted for his mistaking the stationmaster for a porter and instructing him to look after our luggage.

We had two days in Bombay before boarding the *S. S. Strathnaver* and Uncle Ken vowed that we would enjoy ourselves. However, he was a little constrained by his budget and took me to a rather seedy hotel on Lamington Road, where we had to share a toilet with over twenty other people.

'Never mind,' he said. 'We won't spend much time in this dump.' So he took me to Marine Drive and the Gateway of India and to an Irani restaurant in Colaba, where we enjoyed a super dinner of curried prawns and scented rice. I don't know if it was the curry, the prawns or the scent, but Uncle Ken was up all night, running back and forth to that toilet, so that no one else had a chance to use it. Several dispirited travellers simply opened their windows and ejected into space, cursing Uncle Ken all the while.

He had recovered by morning and proposed a trip to the Elephanta Caves. After a breakfast of fish pickle, Malabar chilli chutney and sweet Gujarati puris, we got into a launch, accompanied by several other tourists and set off on our short cruise. The sea was rather choppy and we hadn't gone far before Uncle Ken decided to share his breakfast with the fishes of the sea. He was as green as a seaweed by the time we went ashore. Uncle Ken collapsed on the sand and refused to move, so we didn't see much of the caves. I brought him some coconut water and he revived a bit and suggested we go on a fast until it was time to board our ship.

We were safely on board the following morning, and the ship sailed majestically out from Ballard Pier, Bombay, and India receded into the distance, quite possibly forever as I wasn't sure that I would ever return. The sea fascinated me and I remained on deck all day, gazing at small crafts, passing steamers, sea birds, the distant shoreline, salt water smells, the surge of the waves and, of course, my fellow passengers. I could well understand the fascination it held for writers such as Conrad, Stevenson, Maugham and others.

Uncle Ken, however, remained confined to his cabin. The rolling of the ship made him feel extremely ill. If he had been looking green in Bombay, he was looking yellow at sea. I took my meals in the dining saloon, where I struck up an acquaintance with a well-known palmist and fortune teller who was on his way to London to make his fortune. He looked at my hand and told me I'd never be rich, but that I'd help other people get rich!

When Uncle Ken felt better (on the third day of the voyage), he struggled up on the deck, took a large lungful of sea air and subsided into a deck chair. He dozed the day away, but was suddenly wide awake when an attractive blonde strode past us on her way to the lounge. After some time we heard the tinkling of a piano. Intrigued, Uncle Ken rose and staggered into the lounge. The girl was at the piano, playing something classical which wasn't something that Uncle Ken normally enjoyed, but he was smitten by the girl's good looks and stood enraptured, his eyes brightly gleaming, his jaw sagging. With his nose pressed against the glass of the lounge door, he reminded me of a goldfish who had fallen in love with an angel fish that had just been introduced into the tank.

'What is she playing?' he whispered, aware that I had grown up on my father's classical record collection.

'Rachmaninoff,' I made a guess. 'Or maybe Rimsky Korsakov.'

'Something easier to pronounce,' he begged.

'Chopin,' I said.

'And what's his most famous composition?'

'Polonaise in E flat. Or may be it's E minor.'

He pushed open the lounge door, walked in, and when the girl had finished playing, applauded loudly. She acknowledged his applause with a smile and then went on to play something else. When she had finished he clapped again and said, 'Wonderful! Chopin never sounded better!'

'Actually, it's Tchaikovsky,' said the girl. But she didn't seem to mind.

Uncle Ken would turn up at all her practice sessions and very soon they were strolling the decks together. She was Australian, on her way to London to pursue a musical career as a concert pianist. I don't know what she saw in Uncle Ken, but he knew all the right people. And he was quite good looking in an effete sort of way.

Left to my own devices, I followed my fortune-telling friend around and watched him study the palms of our fellow passengers. He foretold romance, travel, success, happiness, health, wealth and longevity, but never predicted anything that might upset anyone. As he did not charge anything (he was, after all, on holiday) he proved to be a popular passenger throughout the voyage. Later he was to become quite famous as a palmist and mind reader, an Indian 'Cheiro', much in demand in the capitals of Europe.

The voyage lasted eighteen days, with stops for passengers and cargo at Aden, Port Said and Marseilles, in that order. It was at Port Said that Uncle Ken and his friend went ashore, to look at the sights and do some shopping.

'You stay on the ship,' Uncle Ken told me. 'Port Said isn't safe for young boys.'

He wanted the girl all to himself, of course. He couldn't have shown off with me around. His 'man of the world' manner would not have been very convincing in my presence.

The ship was due to sail again that evening and passengers had to be back on board an hour before departure. The hours passed easily enough for me as the little library kept me engrossed. If there are books around, I am never bored. Towards evening, I went up on deck and saw Uncle Ken's friend coming up the gangway; but of Uncle Ken there was no sign.

'Where's Uncle?' I asked her.

'Hasn't he returned? We got separated in a busy marketplace and I thought he'd get here before me.'

We stood at the railings and looked up and down the pier, expecting to see Uncle Ken among the other returning passengers. But he did not turn up.

'I suppose he's looking for you,' I said. 'He'll miss the boat if he doesn't hurry.'

The ship's hooter sounded. 'All aboard!' called the captain on his megaphone. The big ship moved slowly out of the harbour. We were on our way! In the distance I saw a figure that looked like Uncle Ken running along the pier, frantically waving his arms. But there was no turning back.

A few days later my aunt met me at Tilbury Dock.

'Where's your Uncle Ken?' she asked.

'He stayed behind at Port Said. He went ashore and didn't get back in time.'

'Just like Ken. And I don't suppose he has much money with him. Well, if he gets in touch we'll send him a postal order.'

But Uncle Ken failed to get in touch. He was a topic of discussion for several days, while I settled down in my aunt's house and looked for a job. At sixteen, I was working in an office, earning a modest salary and contributing towards my aunt's housekeeping expenses. There was no time to worry about Uncle Ken's whereabouts.

My readers know that I longed to return to India, but it was nearly four years before that became possible. Finally I did come home and as the train drew into Dehra's little station, I looked out of the window and saw a familiar figure on the platform. It was Uncle Ken!

He made no reference to his disappearance at Port Said, and greeted me as though we had last seen each other the previous day.

'I've hired a cycle for you,' he said. 'Feel like a ride?'

'Let me get home first, Uncle Ken. I've got all this luggage.'

The luggage was piled into a tonga, I sat on top of everything and we went clip-clopping down an avenue of familiar lichi trees (all gone now, I fear). Uncle Ken rode behind the tonga, whistling cheerfully.

'When did you get back to Dehra?' I asked.

'Oh, a couple of years ago. Sorry I missed the boat. Was the girl upset?'

'She said she'd never forgive you.'

'Oh well, I expect she's better off without me. Fine piano player. Chopin and all that stuff.'

'Did Granny send you the money to come home?'

'No, I had to take a job working as a waiter in a Greek restaurant. Then I took tourists to look at the pyramids. I'm an expert on pyramids now. Great place, Egypt. But I had to leave when they found I had no papers or permit. They put me on a boat to Aden. Stayed in Aden six months teaching English to the son of a shiekh. Shiekh's son went to England, I came back to India.'

'And what are you doing now, Uncle Ken?'

'Thinking of starting a poultry farm. Lots of space behind your Gran's house. Maybe you can help with it.'

'I couldn't save much money, Uncle.'

'We'll start in a small way. There is a big demand for eggs, you know. Everyone's into eggs—scrambled, fried, poached, boiled. Egg curry for lunch. Omelettes for dinner. Egg sandwiches for tea. How do you like your egg?'

'Fried,' I said. 'Sunny side up.'

'We shall have fried eggs for breakfast. Funny side up!'

The poultry farm never did happen, but it was good to be back in Dehra, with the prospect of limitless bicycle rides with Uncle Ken.

My Failed Omelettes and Other Disasters

IN NEARLY fifty years of writing for a living, I have never succeeded in writing a bestseller. And now I know why. I can't cook.

Had I been able to do so, I could have turned out a few of those sumptuous-looking cookery books that brighten up the bookstore windows before being snapped up by folk who can't cook either.

As it is, if I were forced to write a cook book, it would probably be called *Fifty Different Ways of Boiling An Egg and Other Disasters*.

I used to think that boiling an egg would be a simple undertaking. But when I came to live at 7,000 feet in the Himalayan foothills, I found that just getting the water to boil was something of an achievement. I don't know if it's the altitude or the density of the water, but it just won't come to a boil in time for breakfast. As a result, my eggs are only half-boiled. 'Never mind,' I tell everyone, 'half-boiled eggs are more nutritious than full-boiled eggs.'

'Why boil them at all?' asks my five-year-old grandson, Gautam, who is my Mr Dick, always offering good advice. 'Raw eggs are probably healthier.'

'Just you wait and see,' I told him. 'I'll make you a cheese omelette you'll never forget.' And I did. It was a bit messy, as I was over-generous with the tomatoes, but I thought it tasted rather good. Gautam, however, pushed his plate away, saying, 'You forgot to put in the egg.'

101 Failed Omelettes might well be the title of my bestseller.

I love watching other people cook—a habit that I acquired at a young age, when I would watch my Granny at work in the kitchen, turning out delicious curries, koftas and custards. I would try helping her, but she soon put a stop to my feeble contributions. On one occasion she asked me to add a cup of spices to a large curry dish she was preparing, and absent-mindedly I added a cup of sugar. The result—a very sweet curry! Another invention of mine.

I was better at remembering Granny's kitchen proverbs. Here are some of them:

'There is skill in all things, even in making porridge.'

'Dry bread at home is better then curried prawns abroad.'

'Eating and drinking should not keep men from thinking.'

'Better a small fish than an empty dish.'

And her favourite maxim, with which she reprimanded me whenever I showed signs of gluttony: 'Don't let your tongue cut your throat.'

And as for making porridge, it's certainly no simple matter. I made one or two attempts, but it always came out lumpy.

'What's this?' asked Gautam suspiciously, when I offered him some.

'Porridge!' I said enthusiastically. 'It's eaten by those brave Scottish Highlanders who were always fighting the English!'

'And did they win?' he asked.

'Well—er—not usually. But they were outnumbered!'

He looked doubtfully at the porridge. 'Some other time,' he said.

So why not take the advice of Thoreau and try to simplify life?

Simplify, simplify! Or simply sandwiches...

These shouldn't be too difficult, I decided. After all, they are basically bread and butter. But have you tried cutting bread into thin slices? Don't. It's highly dangerous. If you're a pianist, you could be putting your career at great risk.

You must get your bread ready sliced. Butter it generously. Now add your fillings. Cheese, tomato, lettuce, cucumber, whatever. Gosh, I was really going places! Slap another slice of buttered bread over this mouth-watering assemblage. Now cut in two. Result: Everything spills out at the sides and on to the tablecloth.

'Now look what you've gone and done,' says Gautam, in his best Oliver Hardy manner.

'Never mind,' I tell him. 'Practice makes perfect!'

And one of these days you're going to find *Bond's Book of Better Sandwiches* up there on the bestseller lists.

The Earthquake

IF EVER there's a calamity,' Grandmother used to say, 'it will find Grandfather in his bath.' Grandfather loved his bath—which he took in a large round aluminum tub—and sometimes spent as long as an hour in it, 'wallowing' as he called it, and splashing around like a boy.

He was in his bath during the earthquake that convulsed Bengal and Assam on 12 June 1897—an earthquake so severe that even today, the region of the great Brahmaputra river basin hasn't settled down. Not long ago, it was reported that the entire Shillong Plateau had moved an appreciable distance away from the Geological Survey of India; this shift has been taking place gradually over the past eighty years.

Had Grandfather been alive, he would have added one more clipping to his scrapbook on earthquakes. The clipping goes in anyway, because the scrapbook is now with his children. More than newspaper accounts of the disaster, it was Grandfather's own letters and memoirs that made the earthquake seem recent and vivid; for he, along with Grandmother and two of their children (one of them my father), was living in Shillong, a picturesque little hill station in Assam, when the earth shook and the mountains heaved.

As I have mentioned, Grandfather was in his bath, splashing about, and did not hear the first rumbling. But Grandmother was in the garden hanging out or taking in the washing (she could never remember which) when, suddenly, the animals began making a hideous noise—a sure intimation of a natural disaster, for animals sense the approach of an earthquake much more quickly than humans.

The crows all took wing, wheeling wildly overhead and cawing loudly. The chickens flapped in circles, as if they were being chased. Two dogs sitting on the verandah suddenly jumped up and ran out with their tails between their legs. Within half a minute of her noticing the noise made by the animals, Grandmother heard a rattling, rumbling noise, like the approach of a train.

The noise increased for about a minute, and then there was the first trembling of the ground. The animals by this time all seemed to have gone mad. Treetops lashed backwards and forwards, doors banged and windows shook, and Grandmother swore later that the house actually swayed in front of her. She had difficulty in standing straight, though this could have been more due to the trembling of her knees than to the trembling of the ground.

The first shock lasted for about a minute and a half. 'I was in my tub having a bath,' Grandfather wrote for posterity, 'which for the first time in the last two months I had taken in the afternoon instead of in the morning. My wife and children and the maid were downstairs. Then the shock came and a quaking, which increased in intensity every second. It was like putting so many shells in a basket, and shaking them up with a rapid sifting motion from side to side.

'At first I did not realize what it was that caused my tub to sway about and the water to splash. I rose up, and found the earth heaving, while the washstand basin, ewer, cups and glasses danced and rocked about in the most hideous fashion. I rushed to the inner door to open it and search for my wife and children but could not move the dratted door as boxes, furniture and plaster had come up against it. The back door was the only way of escape. I managed to open it and, thank God, was able to get out. All the sections of the thatched roof had slithered down on the four sides like a pack of cards and blocked all the exits and entrances.

'With only a towel wrapped around my waist, I ran into the open to the front of the house, but found only my wife there. The whole front of the house was blocked by the fallen section of thatch from the roof. Through this I broke my way under the iron railings and extricated the others. The bearer had pluckily borne the weight of the whole thatched roof section on his back, and in this way saved the maid and children from being crushed beneath it.'

After the main shock of the earthquake had passed, minor shocks took place at regular intervals of five minutes or so, all through the night. But during that first shakeup, the town of Shillong was reduced to ruin and rubble. Everything made of masonry was brought to the ground. Government House, the post office, the jail, all tumbled down. When the jail fell, the prisoners, instead of making their escape, sat huddled on the road waiting for the superintendent to come to their aid.

'The ground began to heave and shake,' wrote a young girl in a newspaper called *The Englishman*. 'I stayed on my bicycle for a second, and then fell off and got up and tried to run, staggering about from side to side of the road. To my left I saw great clouds of dust, which I afterwards discovered to be houses falling and the earth slipping from the sides of the hills. To my right I saw the small dam at the end of the lake torn asunder and the water rushing out, the wooden bridge across the lake break in two and the sides of the lake falling in; and at my feet the ground cracking and opening. I was wild with fear and didn't know which way to turn.'

The lake rose up like a mountain, and then totally disappeared, leaving only a swamp of red mud. Not a house was left standing. People were rushing about, wives looking for husbands, parents looking for children, not knowing whether their loved ones were alive or dead. A crowd of people had collected on the cricket ground, which was considered the safest place; but Grandfather and the family took shelter in a small shop on the road outside his house. The shop was a rickety wooden structure, which had always looked as though it would fall down in a strong wind. But it withstood the earthquake.

And then the rain came and it poured. This was extraordinary, because before the earthquake there wasn't a cloud to be seen; but five minutes after, the shock was felt for more than a hundred miles on the Assam-Bengal Railway. A train overturned at Shamshernagar; another was derailed at Mantolla. Over a thousand people lost lives in the Cherrapunji Hills, and in other areas, too, the death toll was heavy.

The Brahmaputra burst its banks and many cultivators were drowned in the flood. A tiger was found drowned. And in North Bhagalpur, where the earthquake started, two elephants sat down in the bazaar and refused to get up until the following morning.

Over a hundred men, who were at work in Shillong's government printing press, were caught in the building when it collapsed, and though the men of Gurkha regiment did splendid rescue work, only a few were brought out alive. One of those killed in Shillong was Mr McCabe, a British official. Grandfather described the ruins of Mr McCabe's house: 'Here a bedpost, there a sword, a broken desk or chair, a bit of torn carpet, a well-known hat with its Indian Civil Service colours, battered books, speaking reminiscenes of the man we mourn.'

While most houses collapsed where they stood, Government House, it seems, fell backwards. The church was a mass of red stones in an ugly disorder. The organ was a tortured wreck.

A few days later, the family, with other refugees, were making their way to Calcutta to stay with friends or relatives. It was a slow, tedious journey with many interruptions, for the roads and railway lines had been badly damaged, and passengers had often to be transported in trolleys. Grandfather was rather struck at the stoicism displayed by an assistant engineer. At one station, a telegram was handed to the engineer informing him that his bungalow had been destroyed. 'Beastly nuisance,' he observed with an aggrieved air. 'I've seen it cave in during a storm, but this is the first time it has played me such a trick on account of an earthquake.'

The family got to Calcutta to find the inhabitants of the capital in a panic; for they too had felt the quake and were expecting it to recur. The damage in Calcutta was slight compared to the devastation elsewhere, but nerves were on the edge, and people slept in the open or in carriages. Cracks and fissures had appeared in a number of old buildings, and Grandfather was among the many who were worried at the proposal to fire a salute of sixty guns on Jubilee Day (the Diamond Jubilee of Queen Victoria). They felt the gunfire would bring down a number of shaky buildings. Obviously Grandfather did not wish to be caught in his bath a second time. However, Queen Victoria was not to be deprived of her salute. The guns were duly fired, and Calcutta remained standing.

Escape from Java

'No one, it seemed, was interested in defending Java, only in getting out as fast as possible.'

IT ALL happened within the space of a few days. The cassia tree had barely come into flower when the first bombs fell on Batavia (now called Jakarta) and the bright pink blossoms lay scattered over the wreckage in the streets.

News had reached us that Singapore had fallen to the Japanese. My father said: 'I expect it won't be long before they take Java. With the British defeated, how can the Dutch be expected to win?' He did not mean to be critical of the Dutch; he knew they did not have the backing of an Empire such as Britain then had. Singapore had been called the Gibraltar of the East. After its surrender there could only be retreat, a vast exodus of Europeans from Southeast Asia.

It was World War II. What the Javanese thought about the war is now hard for me to say, because I was only nine at the time and knew little of worldly matters. Most people knew they would be exchanging their Dutch-rulers for Japanese rulers; but there were also many who spoke in terms of freedom for Java when the war was over.

Our neighbor, Mr Hartono, was one of those who looked ahead to a time when Java, Sumatra, and the other islands would make up one independent nation. He was a college professor and spoke Dutch, Chinese, Javanese and a little English. His son, Sono, was about my age. He was the only boy I knew who could talk to me in English, and as a result we spent a lot of time together. Our favourite pastime was flying kites in the park.

The bombing soon put an end to kite flying. Air raid alerts sounded at all hours of the day and night, and although in the beginning most of the bombs fell near the docks, a couple of miles from where we lived, we had to stay indoors. If the planes sounded very near, we dived under beds or tables. I don't remember if there were any trenches. Probably there hadn't been time for trench digging, and now there was time only for digging graves. Events had moved all too swiftly, and everyone (except, of course, the Javanese) was anxious to get away from Java.

'When are you going?' asked Sono, as we sat on the veranda steps in a pause between air raids.

'I don't know,' I said. 'It all depends on my father.'

'My father says the Japs will be here in a week. And if you're still here then, they'll put you to work building a railway.'

'I wouldn't mind building a railway,' I said.

'But they won't give you enough to eat. Just rice with worms in it. And if you don't work properly they'll shoot you.'

'They do that to soldiers,' I said. 'We're civilians.'

'They do it to civilians, too,' said Sono.

What were my father and I doing in Batavia, when our home had been first in India and then in Singapore? He worked for a firm dealing in rubber, and six months earlier he had been sent to Batavia to open a new office in partnership with a Dutch business house. Although I was so young, I accompanied my father almost everywhere. My mother had died when I was very small, and my father had always looked after me. After the war was over, he was going to take me to England.

'Are we going to win the war?' I asked.

'It doesn't look it from here,' he said.

No, it didn't look as though we were winning. Standing at the docks with my father, I watched the ships arrive from Singapore, crowded with refugees—men, women and children all living on the decks in the hot tropical sun; they looked pale and worn out and worried. They were on their way to Colombo or Bombay. No one came ashore at Batavia. It wasn't British territory; it was Dutch, and everyone knew it wouldn't be Dutch for long.

'Aren't we going too?' I asked. 'Sono's father says the Japs will be here any day.'

'We've still got a few days,' said my father. He was a short, stocky man who seldom got excited. If he was worried, he didn't show it. 'I've got to wind up a few business matters, and then we'll be off.'

'How will we go? There's no room for us on those ships.'

'There certainly isn't. But we'll find a way, lad, don't worry.'

I didn't worry. I had complete confidence in my father's ability to find a way out of difficulties. He used to say, 'Every problem has a solution hidden away somewhere, and if only you look hard enough enough you will find it.'

There were British soldiers in the streets but they did not make us feel much safer. They were just waiting for troop ships to come and take them away. No one, it seemed, was interested in defending Java, only in getting out as fast as possible.

Although the Dutch were unpopular with the Javanese people, there was no ill-feeling against individual Europeans. I could walk safely through the streets. Occasionally, small boys in the crowded Chinese quarter would point at me and shout, '*Orang Balandi!*' (Dutchman!) but they did so in good humour, and I didn't know the language well enough to stop and explain that the English weren't Dutch. For them, all white people were the same, and understandably so.

My father's office was in the commercial area, along the canal banks. Our two-storied house, about a mile away, was an old building with a roof of red tiles and a broad balcony which had stone dragons at either end. There were flowers in the garden almost all the year round. If there was anything in Batavia more regular than the bombing, it was the rain, which came pattering down on the roof and on the banana fronds almost every afternoon. In the hot and steamy atmosphere of Java, the rain was always welcome.

There were no anti-aircraft guns in Batavia—at least we never heard any—and the Jap bombers came over at will, dropping their bombs by daylight. Sometimes bombs fell in the town. One day the building next to my father's office received a direct hit and tumbled into the river. A number of office workers were killed.

One day Sono said, 'The bombs are falling on Batavia, not in the countryside. Why don't we get cycles and ride out of town?'

I fell in with the idea at once. After the morning all-clear had sounded, we mounted our cycles and rode out of town. Mine was a hired cycle, but Sono's was his own. He'd had it since the age of five, and it was constantly in need of repairs. 'The soul has gone out of it,' he used to say.

Our fathers were at work; Sono's mother had gone out to do her shopping (during air raids she took shelter under the most convenient shop counter) and wouldn't be back for at least an hour. We expected to be back before lunch.

We were soon out of town, on a road that passed through rice fields, pineapple orchards and cinchona plantations. On our right lay dark green hills; on our left, groves of coconut palms, and beyond them, the sea. Men and women were working in the rice fields, knee-deep in mud, their broad-brimmed hats protecting them from the fierce sun. Here and there a buffalo wallowed in a pool of brown water, while a naked boy lay stretched out on the animal's broad back.

We took a bumpy track through the palms. They grew right down to the edge of the sea. Leaving our cycles on the shingle, we ran down a smooth, sandy beach and into the shallow water.

'Don't go too far in,' warned Sono. 'There may be sharks about.'

Wading in amongst the rocks, we searched for interesting shells, then sat down on a large rock and looked out to sea, where a sailing ship moved placidly on the crisp blue waters. It was difficult to imagine that half the world was at war, and that Batavia, two or three miles away, was right in the middle of it.

On our way home we decided to take a short cut through the rice fields, but soon found that our tires got bogged down in the soft mud. This delayed our return; and to make things worse, we got the roads mixed up and reached an area of the town that seemed unfamiliar. We had barely entered the outskirts when the siren sounded, to be followed soon after by the drone of approaching aircraft.

'Should we get off our cycles and take shelter somewhere?' I called out.

'No, let's race home!' shouted Sono. 'The bombs won't fall here.'

But he was wrong. The planes flew in very low. Looking up for a moment, I saw the sun blotted out by the sinister shape of a Jap fighter-bomber. We pedalled furiously, but we had barely covered fifty yards when there was a terrific explosion on our right, behind some houses. The shock sent us spinning across the road. We were flung from our cycles. And the cycles, still propelled by the blast, crashed into a wall.

I felt a stinging sensation in my hands and legs, as though scores of little insects had bitten me. Tiny droplets of blood appeared here and there on my flesh. Sono was on all fours, crawling beside me, and I saw that he too had the same small scratches on his hands and forehead, made by tiny shards of flying glass.

We were quickly on our feet, and then we began running in the general direction of our homes. The twisted cycles lay forgotten in the road.

'Get off the street, you two!' shouted someone from a window;

but we weren't going to stop running until we got home. And we ran faster than we'd ever run in our lives.

My father and Sono's parents were themselves running about the street, calling for us, when we came rushing around the corner and tumbled into their arms.

'Where have you been?'

'What happened to you?'

'How did you get those cuts?'

All superfluous questions; but before we could recover our breath and start explaining, we were bundled into our respective homes. My father washed my cuts and scratches, dabbed at my face and legs with iodine—ignoring my yelps—and then stuck plaster all over my face.

Sono and I had both had a fright, and we did not venture far from the house again.

That night my father said, 'I think we'll able to leave in a day or two.'

'Has another ship come in?'

'No.'

'Then how are we going? By plane?'

'Wait and see, lad. It isn't settled yet. But we won't be able to take much with us—just enough to fill a couple of travelling bags.'

'What about the stamp collection?' I asked.

My father's stamp collection was quite valuable, and filled several volumes.

'I'm afraid we'll have to leave most of it behind,' he said. 'Perhaps Mr Hartono will keep it for me, and when the war is over—if it's ever over—we'll come back for it.'

'But we can cake one or two albums with us, can't we?'

'I'll take one. There'll be room for one. Then if we're short of money in Bombay, we can sell the stamps.'

'Bombay? That's in India. I thought we were going back to England.'

'First we must go to India.'

The following morning I found Sono in the garden, patched up like me, and with one foot in a bandage. But he was as cheerful as ever and gave me his usual wide grin.

'We're leaving tomorrow,' I said.

The grin left his face.

'I will be sad when you go,' he said. 'But I will be glad, too, because then you will be able to escape from the Japs.'

'After the war, I'll come back.'

'Yes, you must come back. And then, when we are big, we will go round the world together. I want to see England and America and Africa and India and Japan. I want to go everywhere.'

'We can't go everywhere.'

'Yes, we can. No one can stop us!'

We had to be up very early the next morning. Our bags had been packed late at night. We were taking a few clothes, some of my father's business papers, a pair of binoculars, one stamp album, and several bars of chocolate. I was pleased about the stamp album and the chocolates, but I had to give up several of my treasures—favourite books, the gramophone and records, an old Samurai sword, a train set and a dartboard. The only consolation was that Sono, and not a stranger, would have them.

In the first faint light of dawn a truck drew up in front of the house. It was driven by a Dutch businessman, Mr Hookens, who worked with my father. Sono was already at the gate, waiting to say goodbye.

'I have a present for you,' he said.

He took me by the hand and pressed a smooth, hard object into my palm. I grasped it and then held it up against the light. It was a beautiful little sea horse, carved out of pale blue jade.

'It will bring you luck,' said Sono.

'Thank you,' I said. 'I will keep it forever.'

And I slipped the little sea horse into my pocket.

'In you get, lad,' said my father, and I got up on the front seat between him and Mr Hookens.

As the truck started up, I turned to wave to Sono. He was sitting on his garden wall, grinning at me. He called out, 'We will go everywhere, and no one can stop us!'

He was still waving when the truck took us round the bend at the end of the road.

We drove through the still, quiet streets of Batavia, occasionally passing burnt-out trucks and shattered buildings. Then we left the sleeping city far behind and were climbing into the forested hills. It had rained during the night, and when the sun came up over the green hills, it twinkled and glittered on the broad, wet leaves. The light in the forest changed from dark green to greenish gold, broken here and there by the flaming red or orange of a trumpet-shaped blossom. It was impossible to know the names of all those fantastic plants! The road had been cut through dense tropical forest, and on either side, the trees jostled each other, hungry for the sun; but they were chained together by the liana creepers and vines that fed upon the same struggling trees.

Occasionally a Jelarang, a large Javan squirrel, frightened by the passing of the truck, leapt through the trees before disappearing into the depths of the forest. We saw many birds: peacocks, jungle fowl, and once, standing majestically at the side of the road, a crowned pigeon, its great size and splendid crest making it a striking object even at a distance. Mr Hookens slowed down so that we could look at the bird. It bowed its head so that its crest swept the ground; then it emitted a low, hollow boom rather like the call of a turkey.

When we came to a small clearing, we stopped for breakfast. Butterflies—black, green and gold—flitted across the clearing. The silence of the forest was broken only by the drone of airplanes, Japanese Zeros heading for Batavia on another raid. I thought about

Sono, and wondered what he would be doing at home: probably trying out the gramophone!

We ate boiled eggs and drank tea from a thermos, then got back into the truck and resumed our journey.

I must have dozed off soon after because the next thing I remember is that we were going quite fast down a steep, winding road, and in the distance I could see a calm blue lagoon.

'We've reached the sea again,' I said.

'That's right,' said my father. 'But we're now nearly a hundred miles from Batavia, in another part of the island. You're looking out over the Sunda Straits.'

Then he pointed towards a shimmering white object resting on the waters of the lagoon.

'There's our plane,' he said.

'A seaplane!' I exclaimed. 'I never guessed. Where will it take us?'

'To India, I hope. There aren't many other places left to go to!'

It was a very old seaplane, and no one, not even the captain—the pilot was called the captain—could promise that it would take off. Mr Hookens wasn't coming with us; he said the plane would be back for him the next day. Besides my father and me, there were four other passengers, and all but one were Dutch. The odd man out was a Londoner, a motor mechanic who'd been left behind in Java when his unit was evacuated. (He told us later that he'd fallen asleep at a bar in the Chinese quarter, waking up some hours after his regiment had moved off!) He looked rather scruffy. He'd lost the top button of his shirt, but instead of leaving his collar open, as we did, he'd kept it together with a large safety pin, which thrust itself out from behind a bright pink tie.

'It's a relief to find you here, guvnor,' he said, shaking my father by the hand. 'Knew you for a Yorkshireman the minute I set eyes on you. It's the *song fried* that does it, if you know what I mean.' (He meant *sang froid*, French for a 'cool look.') 'And here I was, with all these flippin' forriners, and me not knowing a word of what they've been yattering about. Do you think this old tub will get us back to Blighty?'

'It does look a bit shaky,' said my father. 'One of the first flying boats, from the looks of it. If it gets us to Bombay, that's far enough.'

'Anywhefe out of Java's good enough for me,' said our new companion. 'The name's Muggeridge.'

'Pleased to know you, Mr Muggeridge,' said my father. 'I'm Bond. This is my son.'

Mr Muggeridge rumpled my hair and favoured me with a large wink.

The captain of the seaplane was beckoning to us to join him in a small skiff which was about to take us across a short stretch of water to the seaplane.

'Here we go,' said Mr Muggeridge. 'Say your prayers and keep your fingers crossed.'

The seaplane was a long time getting airborne. It had to make several runs before it finally took off; then, lurching drunkenly, it rose into the clear blue sky.

'For a moment I thought we were going to end up in the briny,' said Mr Muggeridge, untying his seat belt. 'And talkin' of fish, I'd give a week's wages for a plate of fish an' chips and a pint of beer.'

'I'll buy you a beer in Calcutta,' said my father.

'Have an egg,' I said, remembering we still had some boiled eggs in one of the travelling bags.

'Thanks, mate,' said Mr Muggeridge, accepting an egg with alacrity. 'A real egg, too! I've been livin' on egg powder these last six months. That's what they give you in the army. And it ain't hens' eggs they make it from, let me tell you. It's either gulls' or turtles' eggs!'

'No,' said my father with a straight face. 'Snakes' eggs.'

Mr Muggeridge turned a delicate shade of green; but he soon recovered his poise, and for about an hour kept talking about almost everything under the sun, including Churchill, Hitler, Roosevelt, Mahatma Gandhi and Betty Grable. (The last-named was famous for her beautiful legs.) He would have gone on talking all the way to India had he been given a chance, but suddenly a shudder passed through the old plane, and it began lurching again.

'I think an engine is giving trouble,' said my father.

When I looked through the small glassed-in window, it seemed as though the sea was rushing up to meet us.

The co-pilot entered the passenger cabin and said something in Dutch. The passengers looked dismayed, and immediately began fastening their seat belts.

'Well, what did the blighter say?' asked Mr Muggeridge.

'I think he's going to have to ditch the plane,' said my father, who knew enough Dutch to get the gist of anything that was said.

'Down in the drink!' exclaimed Mr Muggeridge. 'Gawd 'elp us! And how far are we from India, guv?'

'A few hundred miles,' said my father.

'Can you swim, mate?' asked Mr Muggeridge looking at me.

'Yes,' I said. 'But not all the way to Bombay. How far can you swim?'

'The length of a bathtub,' he said.

'Don't worry,' said my father. 'Just make sure your life jacket's properly tied.'

We looked to our life jackets; my father checked mine twice, making sure that it was properly fastened.

The pilot had now cut both engines, and was bringing the plane down in a circling movement. But he couldn't control the speed, and it was tilting heavily to one side. Instead of landing smoothly on its belly, it came down on a wing tip, and this caused the plane to swivel violently around in the choppy sea. There was a terrific jolt when the plane hit the water, and if it hadn't been for the seat belts, we'd have been flung from our seats. Even so, Mr Muggeridge struck his head against the seat in front, and he was now holding a bleeding nose and using some shocking language.

As soon as the plane came to a standstill, my father undid my seat belt. There was no time to lose. Water was already filling the cabin, and all the passengers—except one, who was dead in his seat with a broken neck—were scrambling for the exit hatch. The co-pilot pulled a lever and the door fell away to reveal high waves slapping against the sides of the stricken plane.

Holding me by the hand, my father was leading me towards the exit.

'Quick, lad,' he said. 'We won't stay afloat for long.'

'Give us a hand!' shouted Mr Muggeridge, still struggling with his life jacket. 'First this bloody bleedin' nose, and now something's gone and stuck.'

My father helped him fix the life jacket, then pushed him out of the door ahead of us.

As we swam away from the seaplane (Mr Muggeridge splashing furiously alongside us), we were aware of the other passengers in the water. One of them shouted to us in Dutch to follow him.

We swam after him towards the dinghy, which had been released the moment we hit the water. That yellow dinghy, bobbing about on the waves, was as welcome as land.

All who had left the plane managed to climb into the dinghy. We were seven altogether—a tight fit. We had hardly settled down in the well of the dinghy when Mr Muggeridge, still holding his nose, exclaimed, 'There she goes!' And as we looked on helplessly, the seaplane sank swiftly and silently beneath the waves.

The dinghy had shipped a lot of water, and soon everyone was busy bailing it out with mugs (there were a couple in the dinghy), hats and bare hands. There was a light swell, and every now and then water would roll in again and half fill the dinghy. But within half an hour, we had most of the water out, and then it was possible to take turns, two men doing the bailing while the others rested. No one expected me to do this work, but I took a hand anyway, using my father's sola-topee for the purpose.

'Where are we?' asked one of the passengers.

'A long way from anywhere,' said another.

'There must be a few islands in the Indian Ocean.'

'But we may be at sea for days before we come to one of them.'

'Days or even weeks,' said the captain. 'Let us look at our supplies.'

The dinghy appeared to be fairly well provided with emergency rations: biscuits, raisins, chocolates (we'd lost our own), and enough water to last a week. There was also a first-aid box, which was put to immediate use, as Mr Muggeridge's nose needed attention. A few others had cuts and bruises. One of the passengers had received a hard knock on the head and appeared to be suffering from loss of memory. He had no idea how we happened to be drifting about in the middle of the Indian Ocean; he was convinced that we were on a pleasure cruise a few miles off Batavia.

The unfamiliar motion of the dinghy, as it rose and fell in the troughs between the waves, resulted in almost everyone getting seasick. As no one could eat anything, a day's rations were saved.

The sun was very hot, but my father covered my head with a large spotted handkerchief. He'd always had a fancy for bandana handkerchiefs with yellow spots, and seldom carried fewer than two on his person; so he had one for himself too. The sola topee, well soaked in seawater, was being used by Mr Muggeridge.

It was only when I had recovered to some extent from my seasickness that I remembered the valuable stamp album, and sat up, exclaiming, 'The stamps! Did you bring the stamp album, Dad?'

He shook his head ruefully. 'It must be at the bottom of the sea by now,' he said. 'But don't worry, I kept a few rare stamps in my wallet.' And looking pleased with himself, he tapped the pocket of his bush shirt.

The dinghy drifted all day, with no one having the least idea where it might be taking us.

'Probably going round in circles,' said Mr Muggeridge pessimistically.

There was no compass and no sail, and paddling wouldn't have got us far even if we'd had paddles; we could only resign ourselves to the whims of the current and hope it would take us towards land or at least to within hailing distance of some passing ship.

The sun went down like an overripe tomato dissolving slowly in the sea. The darkness pressed down on us. It was a moonless night, and all we could see was the white foam on the crests of the waves. I lay with my head on my father's shoulder, and looked up at the stars which glittered in the remote heavens.

'Perhaps your friend Sono will look up at the sky tonight and see those same stars,' said my father. 'The world isn't so big after all.'

'All the same, there's a lot of sea around us,' said Mr Muggeridge from out of the darkness.

Remembering Sono, I put my hand in my pocket and was reassured to feel the smooth outline of the jade seahorse.

'I've still got Sono's seahorse,' I said, showing it to my father.

'Keep it carefully,' he said. 'It may bring us luck.'

'Are seahorses lucky?'

'Who knows? But he gave it to you with love, and love is like a prayer. So keep it carefully.'

I didn't sleep much that night. I don't think anyone slept. No one spoke much either, except of course Mr Muggeridge, who kept muttering something about cold beer and salami.

I didn't feel so sick the next day. By ten o'clock I was quite hungry; but breakfast consisted of two biscuits, a piece of chocolate, and a little drinking water. It was another hot day, and we were soon very thirsty, but everyone agreed that we should ration ourselves strictly.

Two or three still felt ill, but the others, including Mr Muggeridge, had recovered their appetites and normal spirits, and there was some discussion about the prospects of being picked up.

'Are there any distress-rockets in the dinghy?' asked my father. 'If we see a ship or a plane, we can fire a rocket and hope to be spotted. Otherwise there's not much chance of our being seen from a distance.'

A thorough search was made in the dinghy, but there were no rockets.

'Someone must have used them last Guy Fawkes Day,' commented Mr Muggeridge.

'They don't celebrate Guy Fawkes Day in Holland,' said my father. 'Guy Fawkes was an Englishman.'

'Ah,' said Mr Muggeridge, not in the least put out. 'I've always said, most great men are Englishmen. And what did this chap Guy Fawkes do?'

'Tried to blow up Parliament,' said my father.

That afternoon we saw our first sharks. They were enormous creatures, and as they glided backward and forward under the boat it seemed they might hit and capsize us. They went away for some time, but returned in the evening.

At night, as I lay half asleep beside my father, I felt a few drops of water strike my face. At first I thought it was the seaspray; but when the sprinkling continued, I realized that it was raining lightly.

'Rain!' I shouted, sitting up. 'It's raining!'

Everyone woke up and did their best to collect water in mugs, hats or other containers. Mr Muggeridge lay back with his mouth open, drinking the rain as it fell.

'This is more like it,' he said. 'You can have all the sun an' sand in the world. Give me a rainy day in England!'

But by early morning the clouds had passed, and the day turned out to be even hotter than the previous one. Soon we were all red and raw from sunburn. By midday even Mr Muggeridge was silent. No one had the energy to talk.

Then my father whispered, 'Can you hear a plane, lad?'

I listened carefully, and above the hiss of the waves I heard what sounded like the distant drone of a plane; but it must have been very far away, because we could not see it. Perhaps it was flying into the sun, and the glare was too much for our sore eyes; or perhaps we'd just imagined the sound.

Then the Dutchman who'd lost his memory thought he saw land, and kept pointing towards the horizon and saying, 'That's Batavia, I told you we were close to shore!' No one else saw anything. So my father and I weren't the only ones imagining things.

Said my father, 'It only goes to show that a man can see what he wants to see, even if there's nothing to be seen!'

The sharks were still with us. Mr Muggeridge began to resent them. He took off one of his shoes and hurled it at the nearest shark; but the big fish ignored the shoe and swam on after us.

'Now, if your leg had been in that shoe, Mr Muggeridge, the shark might have accepted it,' observed my father.

'Don't throw your shoes away,' said the captain. 'We might land on a deserted coastline and have to walk hundreds of miles!'

A light breeze sprang up that evening, and the dinghy moved more swiftly on the choppy water.

'At last we're moving forward,' said the captain.

'In circles,' said Mr Muggeridge.

But the breeze was refreshing; it cooled our burning limbs and helped us to get some sleep. In the middle of the night, I woke up feeling very hungry.

'Are you all right?' asked my father, who had been awake all the time.

'Just hungry,' I said.

'And what would you like to eat?'

'Oranges!'

He laughed. 'No oranges on board. But I kept a piece of my chocolate for you. And there's a little water, if you're thirsty.'

I kept the chocolate in my mouth for a long time, trying to make it last. Then I sipped a little water.

'Aren't you hungry?' I asked.

'Ravenous! I could eat a whole turkey. When we get to Calcutta or Madras or Colombo, or wherever it is we get to, we'll go to the best restaurant in town and eat like—like—'

'Like shipwrecked sailors!' I said.

'Exactly.'

'Do you think we'll ever get to land, Dad?'

'I'm sure we will. You're not afraid, are you?'

'No. Not as long as you're with me.'

Next morning, to everyone's delight, we saw seagulls. This was a sure sign that land couldn't be far away; but a dinghy could take days to drift a distance of thirty or forty miles. The birds wheeled noisily above the dinghy. Their cries were the first familiar sounds we had heard for three days and three nights, apart from the wind and the sea and our own weary voices.

The sharks had disappeared, and that too was an encouraging sign. They didn't like the oil slicks that were appearing in the water.

But presently the gulls left us, and we feared we were drifting away from land.

'Circles,' repeated Mr Muggeridge. 'Circles.'

We had sufficient food and water for another week at sea; but no one even wanted to think about spending another week at sea.

The sun was a ball of fire. Our water ration wasn't sufficient to quench our thirst. By noon, we were without much hope or energy.

My father had his pipe in his mouth. He didn't have any tobacco, but he liked holding the pipe between his teeth. He said it prevented his mouth from getting too dry.

The sharks came back.

Mr Muggeridge removed his other shoe and threw it at them.

'Nothing like a lovely wet English summer,' he mumbled.

I fell asleep in the well of the dinghy, my father's large handkerchief spread over my face. The yellow spots on the cloth seemed to grow into enormous revolving suns.

When I woke up, I found a huge shadow hanging over us. At first I thought it was a cloud. But it was a shifting shadow. My father took the handkerchief from my face and said, 'You can wake up now, lad. We'll be home and dry soon.'

A fishing boat was beside us, and the shadow came from its wide flapping sail. A number of bronzed, smiling, chattering fishermen— Burmese, as we discovered later—were gazing down at us from the deck of their boat.

A few days later, my father and I were in Calcutta.

My father sold his rare stamps for over a thousand rupees, and we were able to live in a comfortable hotel. Mr Muggeridge was flown back to England. Later we got a postcard from him saying the English rain was awful!

'And what about us?' I asked. 'Aren't we going back to England?'

'Not yet,' said my father. 'You'll be going to a boarding school in Shimla until the war's over.'

'But why should I leave you?' I asked.

'Because I've joined the R.A.F.,' he said. 'Don't worry, I'm being posted in Delhi. I'll be able to come up to see you sometimes.'

A week later I was on a small train which went chugging up the steep mountain track to Shimla. Several Indian, Anglo-Indian and English children tumbled around in the compartment. I felt quite out of place among them, as though I had grown out of their pranks. But I wasn't unhappy. I knew my father would be coming to see me soon. He'd promised me some books, a pair of rollerskates and a cricket bat, just as soon as he got his first month's pay.

Meanwhile, I had the jade seahorse which Sono had given me.

And I have it with me today.

King Bharata

1

King bharata ruled over all the world. He was a thoughtful and religious man, and he looked upon the whole world as evidence of the supreme spirit of God.

He worshipped God in the form of Vishnu, the Preserver, and was full of devotion, ruling the earth for one hundred thousand years. He had five sons, amongst whom he divided all his kingdom, and went at last into the forests near the river Gandak, where he lived alone, praying and meditating.

His worship consisted of offering fresh flowers, tender leaves, and wild fruits and roots. He controlled all his senses and never grew weary. There was no one to disturb him, no one to take his mind off the worship of God. He bathed three times a day, and worshipped Vishnu in the golden sun.

One day, while Bharata was bathing in the river, he heard a lion roaring, and saw a deer, which was about to give birth to a fawn, fleeing from the lion and splashing across the river. As it reached the other side, it gave birth to the fawn and then died. Bharata saw the helpless little fawn struggling in the water. Being moved with compassion, he took it in his hands and saved it. Then he took the fawn home and cared for it, and soon began to love it. He became so attached to it that little by little he began neglecting his services to God; but he was quite unaware that this was happening.

'There is no one to care for this deer,' he said to himself, 'and so I will look after it and bring it up. The great teachers say that to help the helpless is a virtue.'

His love for the deer grew, and he used to bring it tender grass to eat, and he would bathe it and keep it near him. Sometimes he would hold it in his arms or on his lap. He loved its company. Often, when performing some ceremony, he would break off in the middle to look for the deer.

But one day, the deer disappeared.

Bharata was overcome with grief and a terrible sense of loss.

'Did I not take care of you in every way?' he mused. 'Now I do not know if some animal has killed you, or if you will one day return to gladden my heart. I remember how you used to touch me gently with your horns as I sat in meditation. I remember how you would playfully trample on the things I brought for worship, and if I spoke to you in anger, you would stand at a distance till I called you again. The other hermits looked upon you as a holy animal. Perhaps the moon has taken you.'

Unable to get over his sorrow, he neglected the religious ceremonies he usually performed. He had renounced his family and his kingdom in order to obtain the spiritual freedom of the hermit. Now, because of his attachment to the deer, all his strivings appeared to have been futile.

Then one day, the deer returned.

Bharata was overcome with joy. He treated it as though it were his own son, and devoted the rest of his days to its welfare.

In his last days, on his death bed, his thoughts were only of the deer; and so, upon his soul leaving his body, he was reborn as a deer. But the memory of his past life remained with him. He felt sorry that he had neglected his duties to God, and regretted his former attachment to the deer. He did not mingle with the rest of the herd, and at last left them and went away alone to his old place, where he had formerly lived and worshipped; and there he remained, bathing in the river and grazing on its banks; and so much did he desire to be freed from the body of a deer that, when he died, he was able to be born again into a Brahmin family.

2

Born to a Brahmin father, Bharata was brought up well; but remembering his former lives, he kept aloof from other people, so that many thought he was half-witted. When his parents died, his brother forced him to do menial work. People made fun of him, but he paid no attention, and took everything that came his way, good and bad. He cared neither for cold nor heat, going without clothes and sleeping on the bare ground, so that his sacred thread became black with dirt.

In spite of these hardships, he remained sturdy and strong.

One day, the king of the country decided to offer a human sacrifice to the Goddess Kali, and hearing from his servants that Bharata was a useless fellow, seized him as being perfectly suitable for the sacrifice.

After a ceremonial bath, Bharata was given fine clothes and decorated with jewels. He was given rich food. Burning camphor and perfumes were placed before him. Then, accompanied by dancers and musicians, he was taken to the temple of Kali.

At the temple the king himself led Bharata to a raised platform. Sword in hand, he was about to cut off Bharata's head when Kali, seeing Bharata and recognizing him immediately as a man of God—a man without hatred in his heart, and with love for all living creatures—was afraid to receive such a sacrifice.

The goddess grew angry with the king. She became visible, and so terrifying was her aspect that the king and his followers fell dead on the spot.

Then Kali turned to Bharata and said, 'No deity will allow any harm to come to you.'

She disappeared, and Bharata, who feared neither the sword nor Kali, remained standing, his mind steadfast in God.

The people who had gathered to watch the sacrifice became greatly afraid. They made way for Bharata, and he returned to watch the fields as before.

Nala and Damayanti

LONG AGO, there reigned in Berar a famous king named Bhima. His chief claim to fame was that he had a beautiful daughter named Damayanti. She was waited upon day and night by a band of handmaids of great beauty, but she shone among them like the moon among the stars, and her hand was sought, we are told, by both gods and mortals.

Nala, King of Nishada, came to hear of Damayanti's loveliness and her many accomplishments, and was struck with passion for her. She, in turn, had heard that Nala was brave and handsome, well-read and skilled in arms. They loved each other upon the mere fame of their respective virtues, and Damayanti pined for the presence of her unknown lover.

One day, while Nala was seated in a grove dreaming of his beloved, he saw a flock of swans, with wings all flecked with gold, come to rest close by him.

Nala crept up to the leader of the flock and seized him.

'O mighty king,' said the swan, 'set me free, and I will do your bidding, whatever it might be.'

'If a bird can do a mortal any service,' said Nala, 'fly to my love, Damayanti, and tell her how much I love her!' He released the bird, and it flew off to Berar, rejoicing in its freedom.

When the bird arrived in King Bhima's kingdom, it found Damayanti reclining in her garden, surrounded by her charming handmaids.

'What a lovely bird!' she cried when she saw the swan. 'And look at its wings, all edged with gold!'

The swan came close to her and allowed itself to be made captive.

'Sweet princess,' said the swan, 'I come to you as a messenger of love from Nala, King of Nishada. He is as wonderful to look upon as the God of Love, and has no equal amongst mortals. The union of such a youth and maiden would be a union of perfection.'

Damayanti was struck with wonder at the bird's story, and she set him free, saying, 'Sweet bird! Speak to Nala on my behalf in like manner.' And the swan flew back to Nala with an answering message of love.

Before long, a swayamvara was held for Damayanti.

This was an ancient Hindu rite by which a princess might choose her husband from an assembly of suitors come from all parts to take their chance in the selection. The heroes submitted themselves in silent rivalry to inspection as the princess walked along their line to select from the throng the favoured suitor by presenting him with a garland, or a cup of water, or some such token of regard.

Many were the princes who came to woo Damayanti, attracted by the stories of her beauty. More wonderful still, some of the gods, equally enamoured of her charms, came down to earth to woo her. Most prominent among them were the four great guardians of the world: Indra, God of Heaven; Agni, God of Fire; Varuna, God of the Waters; and Yama, God of Death. What chance did Nala, a mere mortal, have in this assembly?

Damayanti stepped into the swayamvara hall, bejewelled from head to foot, bearing a garland of flowers to place round the neck of the one she would choose for her husband. She was taken round to each of the assembled princes, until she came to where her lover,

Nala, was seated; but great was her dismay when she saw not one but five Nalas, each indistinguishable from the other! The gods had assumed his shape to baffle her.

But Damayanti, garland in hand, did not pause for long. She had noticed that the gods cast no shadows, because they were spirits; and that their eyes never winked, because they were the ever-wakeful Guardian Gods; and that their garlands were fresher than most, being woven of the unfading blooms of Heaven. By these tokens did Damayanti tell the gods from her lover; and she threw her garland round the neck of her beloved, the real Nala.

Then, turning to the gods, she said, 'Forgive me, O mighty gods, that I have not chosen my husband from among you. I have long since pledged my heart to this prince, and the vow so pledged is sacred. Forgive me, therefore, for choosing an earthly lord and not one of the rulers of Heaven.'

In this way did Damayanti, the lovely, the peerless, choose Nala for her husband, with the gods themselves as witnesses.

The happy pair then did homage before the gods, and these great guardians of the earth bestowed upon them divine blessings in reward for their constancy.

The Ugly Prince and the Heartless Princess

IN THE kingdom of Malla, there was once a young prince named Kusa, who was famed for his great kindness and wisdom, but unfortunately, he was very ugly.

In spite of his ugliness, everyone in the kingdom was extremely fond of the prince, but Kusa himself was sensitive about his appearance, and when his father, King Okkaka, urged him to marry, he said, 'Don't ask me to get married. How could a beautiful princess love such an ugly fellow?'

But the king insisted, and at last Kusa grew so tired of refusing to choose a bride, that he hit upon a scheme by which he hoped to free himself for ever from the problem of his marriage. He was very skilful with his hands, and he fashioned a golden image, and showing the king his handiwork, he said, 'If a princess as beautiful as this image can be found for me, I will make her my bride. Otherwise I will remain single.'

Kusa felt sure that there was no princess who could compare with his statue, but the king was determined to find such a beauty, and he sent messengers far and wide.

The messengers visited many kingdoms, carrying the statue with them. Whenever they arrived at a city or a village, they asked the inhabitants whether they knew of anyone who resembled the golden image. But nowhere was such a beauty to be found until the messengers reached the kingdom of Madda.

The King of Madda had eight lovely daughters, and the eldest of them, Pabhavati, bore an extraordinary resemblance to the golden image. When the messengers saw her, they went straight to the king and said that they had come to ask the hand of Princess Pabhavati for Prince Kusa, the son of King Okkaka.

The King of Madda knew that Okkaka was a rich and powerful king, and he was pleased at the idea of being allied to him through marriage.

'If King Okkaka will visit me,' he said, 'I will give him the hand of Princess Pabhavati for his son, Prince Kusa.'

The messengers hurried back to Malla with the good news, and King Okkaka was delighted at the outcome of their mission; but poor Kusa was dismayed.

'But, my dear Father,' he said to the king, 'how will such a beautiful princess behave when she sees how ugly I am? She will surely flee from me at once.'

'Do not worry, my son,' said King Okkaka. 'I will revive an ancient custom in order to protect you. According to this custom, a bride may not look upon the face of her husband until one year after the marriage. Therefore, for one whole year, you must only meet your bride in a darkened room.'

'But how will that help me in the end?' asked Kusa doubtfully. 'My looks will not have improved by the end of the year. She will have to see me some day.'

'True, but during that year your bride will have learned to love you so much that, when she sees you at last, you will not be ugly in her eyes!'

Prince Kusa still had his doubts, but the king was insistent and wasted no time in visiting the kingdom of Madda and returning with the beautiful Princess Pabhavati. Soon after, the marriage ceremony was performed in a darkened chamber, by order of the king.

Princess Pabhavati was surprised to discover that she was not to look upon the face of her husband for one year after the marriage had taken place.

This is a strange custom, she thought, but she accepted the condition without protest, and settled down in a magnificent suite of apartments, one room of which was always to be kept in complete darkness.

Kusa came daily to this room to visit his bride, and as his voice and manners were kind and gentle, Pabhavati soon grew to love him, although she did not get a glimpse of his face. He spent many hours playing to her upon his sitar, and she would listen to him, enthralled.

Was there ever a prince like this husband of mine? she thought. How I long for the day when I shall see his face! Surely he must be as handsome as he is kind and wise.

All might have been well if Pabhavati had been content to wait for a year; but, after she had been married for only a month, she grew impatient and found herself constantly wondering about Prince Kusa's appearance. During the second month she could conceal her curiosity no longer. One day, when Kusa was with her in the darkened room, she said: 'Dear husband, it makes me sad that I must wait so long before I can look upon your face. I beg you to meet me in the light of day.'

'No, Pabhavati, that is impossible,' said the prince. 'I cannot disobey my father, the king. Be patient a little longer. The months will pass quickly.'

But the quality of patience was absent in the princess, and soon she began to question the maidservants and others about her husband's appearance. As she never received a clear answer, she became even more curious. Finally, she bribed one of her attendants to help her obtain a glimpse of Kusa.

One day, when the prince was due to ride through the city at the head of a procession, the waiting woman concealed the princess in a corner room of the palace, a window of which looked out upon the highway.

When the procession came by, Pabhavati hurried to the window. She heard the sound of music and shouting, and saw gay banners and garlands thrown at the feet of the elephant upon which Prince Kusa was riding in state.

'Long live Kusa, our noble prince!' cried the people on the streets.

As the elephant passed beneath the window, Pabhavati caught a glimpse of the prince's face. She shrank back in horror.

'Oh, no!' she cried. 'Can that hideous creature be my husband? No, that is not Kusa!'

Her attendant assured her that it was indeed the prince, whereupon Pabhavati decided that she would flee instantly from such an ugly husband. She demanded that an escort be provided for her return to the kingdom of Madda, declaring that she would not be bound by marriage to a husband who was so different from the man she had imagined!

King Okkaka could have forced the princess to remain in the palace, but Kusa shook his head sadly and said, 'No, let her do as she wishes.'

Then, forgetful of all the love and tenderness that she had received from Kusa, and thinking only of his ugly face, Pabhavati left the palace and returned to her father's kingdom.

Prince Kusa was terribly unhappy; but one day, the thought occurred to him that if he were to visit Pabhavati in her own land, he might find that her attitude had changed. He changed his princely robes for simple clothes, and, taking his sitar, he set out on foot for the kingdom of Madda.

After a journey of several days, Kusa arrived one evening at the chief city of Madda.

It was midnight when he reached the royal palace. He crept beneath the walls, then began playing softly upon his sitar. He played so sweetly that the sleepers in the palace stirred and smiled in their dreams. But Pabhavati wakened with a start and tensed as she listened to the familiar music.

That is Kusa below, she thought, afraid and angry at the same time. If my father knows that he is here, I will be forced to return to that hideous husband.

But Kusa had no intention of appealing to the king. He would rather lose Pabhavati for ever than have her return against her will. He was determined to keep his presence in the city a secret from everyone except the princess.

When morning came he went to the chief potter in the city and asked to become his apprentice.

'If I do good work for you, will you display my wares in the palace?' asked Kusa.

'Certainly,' said the potter. 'But show me what you can do.'

Kusa set to work at the potter's wheel, and the bowls he produced were so beautifully formed that the potter was delighted.

'I am sure the king will purchase such dainty bowls for his daughters,' he said, and taking some of the bowls made by Kusa, he went straight to the palace.

The King took a great fancy to the potter's new wares. When he learned that they had been made by a new apprentice, he said, 'Give the young man a thousand gold pieces, and tell him that from now on he must work only for my daughters. Now take eight of these beautiful bowls to the princesses as my gifts to them.'

The potter did as he was told, and the king's daughters were thrilled with their presents; but Pabhavati knew in her heart that they had been fashioned by Kusa. She returned her bowl to the potter and said, 'Take this bowl back to your apprentice and tell him that it is as ugly as he is.'

When the potter passed on these remarks to Kusa, the prince sighed and thought, how can I touch her hard heart? If I could speak to her, it might make a difference. Tomorrow I will seek service in the palace.

He gave the potter the king's gold pieces and said goodbye; then, hearing that the palace cook needed an assistant, he presented himself at the royal kitchens.

The cook took Kusa into his service, and the prince proved to be as good a cook as he was a potter—so much so, that a dish specially prepared by him was sent straight to the king.

The king thoroughly enjoyed the dish, and when he heard that it had been prepared by the cook's new assistant, he said, 'Give him a thousand pieces of gold, and from now on let him prepare and serve all the food for myself and my daughters.'

Kusa was happy to give the king's gold pieces to the chief cook, then set to work to prepare a delicious meal.

At dinner, Pabhavati was horrified to see her husband, disguised as a cook, stagger into the banquet hall with a heavy load of dishes. He gave no sign of recognition, but the princess was angry and, staring at him with contempt, said, 'I do not care for these dishes. Bring me food that someone else has prepared.'

Her sisters protested, crying out that they had never tasted such delicious cooking. But although Kusa came day after day, serving a variety of tasty dishes, Pabhavati would not touch any of them.

At last, the prince decided that there was no way in which he could touch the heart of the princess.

Nothing that I do pleases her, he thought. Now I must leave her for ever.

While he was preparing to leave the palace, he heard that the King of Madda was greatly troubled. The king had received news that seven kings were riding towards the city with seven armies, and that each of these kings, having heard of the beauty of Pabhavati, was anxious to make her his wife.

The king was in a quandary, because he felt sure that if he chose one of these kings as the husband of Pabhavati, the other six would attack his kingdom in revenge.

If only Pabhavati had not left her rightful husband, thought the king, these troubles would not have arisen.

Realizing that it was useless to spend his time in regrets, the king summoned his advisers and asked them which king he should choose for the princess.

'Not one of them alone,' declared the wise men. 'The princess has endangered the kingdom. Therefore she must suffer the consequences. She must be executed, her body divided into seven pieces, and one portion presented to each of the seven kings. Only in this way can a terrible war be avoided.'

The king was horrified by this advice from his men of wisdom; but while he was sitting alone, deep in thought, Kusa, still in the guise of a cook, came to him and said, 'Your Majesty, let me deal with these kings. Give me your army, and I will crush them or die in the attempt.'

'What!' cried the astonished king. 'Shall a cook do battle with kings?'

'If a cook knows how to fight, why not? But I must confess that I am not really a servant, but Prince Kusa, to whom you once entrusted your daughter. Although she has rejected me, I still love her, and it is only right that I should deal with these suitors.'

The king could hardly believe that it was Kusa who stood before him. He had Pabhavati brought to him, and when she admitted that the cook's apprentice was her royal husband, he cried, 'You should be ashamed, daughter, for allowing your husband to be treated as a servant in the palace.'

202 ❧ RUSKIN BOND

He dismissed Pabhavati from his presence, and begged Kusa's pardon for the way in which he had been insulted.

Kusa replied that all he wanted was freedom to deal with the seven invading kings, and the king immediately placed him at the head of an army. The fate of the kingdom lay in Kusa's hands.

The seven kings were taken by surprise when they saw Kusa and his forces advancing towards them, for they had not expected any resistance. In spite of their superior numbers, they were soon routed by an inspired force under Kusa's command. They laid down their arms and surrendered, and the Prince led them as captives to the king.

'Deal with these prisoners as you will,' said Kusa.

'They are your captives,' said the king. 'It is for you to decide their fate.'

'Then,' said the prince, 'since each of these kings wishes to marry a beautiful princess, why do you not marry them all to the sisters of Pabhavati?'

The king was delighted with this solution to his problem; it would guarantee the safety of his kingdom for ever. The seven kings were bowled over by the beauty and grace of Pabhavati's sisters. And the seven sisters thought their prospective husbands looked very handsome indeed.

But Pabhavati sat alone, weeping bitter tears. She now realized how heartlessly she had treated Kusa, and what a noble man and lover she had scorned.

He will never forgive me, she thought sadly.

She went to him, and threw herself at his feet, crying, 'Forgive me, my husband, and take me back, even if you decide to treat me as a slave.'

Kusa raised her gently from the ground.

'Do you really wish to return to me?' he asked. 'Look at me, Pabhavati. I am still as ugly as when you ran away from me.' Pabhavati gazed at him steadfastly, and instead of the loathing which Kusa had seen in her eyes before, he now saw only wonder and tenderness.

'You have changed!' she cried. 'You are no longer ugly!'

'No,' said Kusa. 'I haven't changed. It is you who has changed.'

A Demon for Work

IN A VILLAGE in South India there lived a very rich landlord who owned several villages and many fields; but he was such a great miser that he found it difficult to find tenants who would willingly work on his land, and those who did, gave him a lot of trouble. As a result, he left all his fields unfilled, and even his tanks and water channels dried up. This made him poorer day by day. But he made no effort to obtain the goodwill of his tenants.

One day, a holy man paid him a visit. The landlord poured out his tale of woe.

'These miserable tenants won't do a thing for me,' he complained. 'All my lands are going to waste.'

'My dear good landlord,' said the holy man. 'I think I can help you, if you will repeat a mantra—a few magic words—which I will teach you. If you repeat it for three months, day and night, a wonderful demon will appear before you on the first day of the fourth month. He will willingly be your servant and take upon himself all the work that has been left undone by your wretched tenants. The demon will obey all your orders. You will find him equal to a hundred servants!'

The miserly landlord immediately fell at the feet of the holy man and begged for instruction. The sage gave him the magic words and · then went his way. The landlord, greatly pleased, repeated the mantra day and night, for three months, till, on the first day of the fourth month, a magnificent young demon stood before him.

'What can I do for you, master?' he said. 'I am at your command.'

The landlord was taken aback by the sight of the huge monster who stood before him, and by the sound of his terrible voice, but he summoned up enough courage to say, 'You can work for me provided—er—you don't expect any salary.'

'Very well,' said the demon, 'but I have one condition. You must give me enough work to keep me busy all the time. If I have nothing to do, I shall kill you and eat you. Juicy landlords are my favourite dish.'

The landlord, certain that there was enough work to keep several demons busy for ever, agreed to these terms. He took the demon to a large tank which had been dry for years, and said: 'You must deepen this tank until it is as deep as the height of two palm trees.'

'As you say, master,' said the demon, and set to work.

The landlord went home, feeling sure that the job would take several weeks. His wife gave him a good dinner, and he was just sitting down in his courtyard to enjoy the evening breeze when the demon arrived, casually remarking that the tank was ready.

'The tank ready!' exclaimed the astonished landlord. 'Why, I thought it would take you several weeks! How shall I keep him busy?' he asked, turning to his wife for aid. 'If he goes on at this rate, he'll soon have an excuse for killing and eating me!'

'You must not lose heart, my husband,' said the landlord's wife. 'Get all the work you can out of the demon. You'll never find such a good worker again. And when you have no more work for him, let me know—I'll find something to keep him busy.'

The landlord went out to inspect the tank and found that it had been completed to perfection. Then he set the demon to plough all his farm lands, which extended over a number of villages. This was done in two days. He next asked the demon to dig up all the waste land. This was done in less than a day.

'I'm getting hungry,' said the demon. 'Come on, master, give me more work, quickly!'

The landlord felt helpless. 'My dear friend,' he said, 'my wife says she has a little job for you. Do go and see what it is she wants done. When you have finished, you can come and eat me, because I just can't see how I can keep you busy much longer!'

The landlord's wife, who had been listening to them, now came out of the house, holding in her hands a long hair which she had just pulled out of her head.

'Well, my good demon,' she said. 'I have a very light job for you. I'm sure you will do it in a twinkling. Take this hair, and when you have made it perfectly straight, bring it back to me.'

The demon laughed uproariously, but took the hair and went away with it.

All night he sat in a peepul tree, trying to straighten the hair. He kept rolling it against his thighs and then lifting it up to see if it had become straight. But no, it would still bend! By morning the demon was feeling very tired.

Then he remembered that goldsmiths, when straightening metal wires, would heat them over a fire. So he made a fire and placed the hair over it, and in the twinkling of an eye it frizzled and burnt up.

The demon was horrified. He dared not return to the landlord's wife. Not only had he failed to straighten the hair, but he had lost it too. Feeling that he had disgraced himself, he ran away to another part of the land.

So the landlord was rid of his demon. But he had learnt a lesson. He decided that it was better to have tenants working for him than demons, even if it meant paying for their services.

The Lost Ruby

ONCE UPON a time there lived a king, who was a great and powerful monarch. One day he was very sad, and as he sat in his council hall surrounded by his ministers, the chief minister, who was a good and wise man, asked him, 'Defender of the World! Why is your spirit sad today? Your Majesty ought not to allow grief to trouble your mind.'

The king would not tell him his grief. On the contrary, he resented his good minister's concern for him. 'It is all very well for you to talk,' he said. 'But if you had reason to be sad, I am sure you would find it impossible to practise what you have just suggested.' And the king decided to put his chief minister to the test, and told him to wait at the royal palace after the council was dismissed.

The minister accordingly made his way to the royal apartments and awaited further orders. The king took out a ruby of great price from a beautiful ivory casket and, placing it in the minister's hand, told him to look after it with great care.

When the minister got home, he found his wife reclining on cushions, chewing scented paan. He gave her the ruby to keep. She dropped it in a partition of her cash box and thought no more about it.

No sooner had the wily king delivered the ruby to his minister than he employed female spies to follow him up and mark where he kept the jewel. After a few days he bribed the steward of the minister's household to steal it for him. The king was sitting on the balcony of his palace overlooking the river when the jewel was brought to him. Taking it from the hands of the steward, he deliberately threw it into the river.

The next morning, after dismissing his court, he asked the chief minister, 'Where is the ruby which I gave you to keep the other day?' The minister replied, 'I have got it, Defender of the World.'

'Well then,' said the king, 'go and fetch it, for I want it right now.'

Imagine the poor minister's amazement when, on going home, he understood that the ruby was nowhere to be found. He hurried back to the king and reported the loss. 'Your Majesty,' he said, 'if you will allow me a few days grace, I hope to find it and bring it back to you.'

'Very well,' said the king, laughing to himself. 'I give you three days in which to find the ruby. If, at the end of that time, you fail to find it, your life and the lives of all who are dear to you will be forfeit. And your house will be razed to the ground and ploughed up by donkeys!'

The minister left the palace with a heavy heart. He searched everywhere for the lost jewel, but because of its mysterious disappearance, he did not have much hope of finding it.

I have no one, he thought, to whom I can leave my riches and possessions. My wife is the only soul on earth who is dear to me, and it seems we must both die after three days. What could be better than for us to enjoy ourselves during this period? We'll make the most of the time that's left to us.

In this mood he reached home and told his wife about the king's decision.

'Let us spend our wealth liberally and freely,' he said, 'for soon we must die.'

His wife sighed deeply and only said, 'As you wish. Fate has dealt us a cruel blow. Let us take it with dignity and good cheer.'

That day saw the commencement of a period of great revelry in the chief minister's house. Musicians of all kinds were engaged, and the halls were filled with guests, who came wondering what great luck had come the way of the chief minister. Rich food was served, and night and day the sound of music and laughter filled the house.

In addition, large quantities of food were prepared and given to the poor. No one who came to the house was allowed to leave empty-handed. Tradesmen, when they brought their customary presents of fresh fruit, were rewarded with gold coins, and went away rejoicing.

In a village near by, there lived a poor flower seller and a fisherwoman—the two women were neighbours and close friends. The flower seller happened to be visiting the bazaar, where she heard of the grand doings at the minister's house. So she hurried there with a present of vegetables and garlands, and received a gold coin. Then she walked across to her friend's house and advised her to take a present of fish to the minister, who would reward her in the same manner.

The fisherwoman was very poor. Her husband used to go fishing daily, but he seldom was able to catch large fish; those that he caught were so small that they rarely fetched more than a few pice in the bazaar. So the fisherwoman said to herself: 'Those miserable fish that my husband brings home are hardly worth presenting to the minister—he'll only feel insulted,' and she thought no more about it.

But the following morning, as good luck would have it, her husband caught a large Rohu, the most delicious of Indian fresh-water fish. Delighted at his good fortune, he took it home to show his wife, who immediately placed the fish in a basket, covered it with a clean cloth, and hurried to the minister's house. The minister was really pleased to see such a fine large Rohu fish, and instead of giving her one gold coin, he gave her two. The fisherwoman was overjoyed. She ran home with her prize, which was enough to keep herself and her husband in comfort for many a month.

This happened on the third and last day of the minister's life;

the next day he and his wife were to be executed. Being very fond of fish curry, he said to his wife, 'Let's have one of your delightful fish curries for lunch today. We will never be able to enjoy it again. Now here's a fine Rohu. Let's take it to the kitchen and have it cleaned.'

He and his wife sat together to see the fish cut. The cook took out his kitchen knife and set to work.

As the cook thrust his knife into the fish's belly, out dropped the ruby which had been thrown into the river.

The minister and his wife were overcome with astonishment and joy. They washed the ruby in perfumed water, and then the minister hastened to restore it to the king.

The king was equally amazed to see the ruby which he had thrown into the river. He at once demanded an explanation for its recovery. The minister told him how he had decided to spend all his riches, and how he had received the present of a fish which, when it was cut, gave up the lost ruby.

The king then acknowledged the part he had played in the loss of the ruby. 'But I see that you took your own advice to me,' he said. 'Endure sorrow cheerfully!' He bestowed high honours on his minister, and commended his wisdom and understanding before all his courtiers and ministers.

And so the minister's evil fortune was changed to good.

'And may the Eternal Dispenser of all Good thus deal with his servants.'

The Tiger King's Gift

Long ago, in the days of the ancient Pandya kings of South India, a father and his two sons lived in a village near Madura. The father was an astrologer, but he had never become famous, and so was very poor. The elder son was called Chellan; the younger Gangan. When the time came for the father to put off his earthly body, he gave his few fields to Chellan, and a palm leaf with some words scratched on it to Gangan.

These were the words that Gangan read:

> 'From birth, poverty;
> For ten years, captivity;
> On the seashore, death.
> For a little while happiness shall follow.'

'This must be my fortune,' said Gangan to himself, 'and it doesn't seem to be much of a fortune. I must have done something terrible in a former birth. But I will go as a pilgrim to Papanasam and do penance. If I can expiate my sin, I may have better luck.'

His only possession was a water jar of hammered copper, which had belonged to his grandfather. He coiled a rope round the jar, in case he needed to draw water from a well. Then he put a little rice into a bundle, said farewell to his brother, and set out.

As he journeyed, he had to pass through a great forest. Soon he had eaten all his food and drunk all the water in his jar. In the heat of the day he became very thirsty.

At last he came to an old, disused well. As he looked down into it, he could see that a winding stairway had once gone round it down to the water's edge, and that there had been four landing places at different heights down this stairway, so that those who wanted to fetch water might descend the stairway to the level of the water and fill their water pots with ease, regardless of whether the well was full, or three-quarters full, or half full or only one-quarter full.

Now the well was nearly empty. The stairway had fallen away. Gangan could not go down to fill his water jar so he uncoiled his rope, tied his jar to it and slowly let it down. To his amazement, as it was going down past the first landing place, a huge striped paw shot out and caught it, and a growling voice called out: 'Oh Lord of Charity, have mercy! The stair is fallen. I die unless you save me! Fear me not. Though King of Tigers, I will not harm you.'

Gangan was terrified at hearing a tiger speak, but his kindness overcame his fear, and with a great effort, he pulled the beast up.

The Tiger King—for it was indeed the Lord of All Tigers—bowed his head before Gangan, and reverently paced around him thrice from right to left as worshippers do round a shrine.

'Three days ago,' said the Tiger King, 'a goldsmith passed by, and I followed him. In terror he jumped down this well and fell on the fourth landing place below. He is there still. When I leaped after him I fell on the first landing place. On the third landing is a rat who jumped in when a great snake chased him. And on the second landing, above the rat, is the snake who followed him. They will all clamour for you to draw them up.

'Free the snake, by all means. He will be grateful and will not harm you. Free the rat, if you will. But do not free the goldsmith, for he cannot be trusted. Should you free him, you will surely repent of your kindness. He will do you an injury for his own profit. But remember that I will help you whenever you need me.'

Then the Tiger King bounded away into the forest.

Gangan had forgotten his thirst while he stood before the Tiger King. Now he felt it more than before, and again let down his water jar.

As it passed the second landing place on the ruined staircase, a huge snake darted out and twisted itself round the rope. 'Oh, Incarnation of Mercy, save me!' it hissed. 'Unless you help me, I must die here, for I cannot climb the sides of the well. Help me, and I will always serve you!'

Gangan's heart was again touched, and he drew up the snake. It glided round him as if he were a holy being. 'I am the Serpent King,' it said. 'I was chasing a rat. It jumped into the well and fell on the third landing below. I followed, but fell on the second landing. Then the goldsmith leaped in and fell on the fourth landing place, while the tiger fell on the top landing. You saved the Tiger King. You have saved me. You may save the rat, if you wish. But do not free the goldsmith. He is not to be trusted. He will harm you if you help him. But I will not forget you, and will come to your aid if you call upon me.'

Then the King of Snakes disappeared into the long grass of the forest.

Gangan let down his jar once more, eager to quench his thirst. But as the jar passed the third landing, the rat leaped into it.

'After the Tiger King, what is a rat?' said Gangan to himself, and pulled the jar up.

Like the tiger and the snake, the rat did reverence, and offered his services if ever they were needed. And like the tiger and the snake, he warned Gangan against the goldsmith. Then the Rat

King—for he was none other—ran off into a hole among the roots of a banyan tree.

By this time, Gangan's thirst was becoming unbearable. He almost flung the water jar down the well. But again the rope was seized, and Gangan heard the goldsmith beg piteously to be hauled up.

'Unless I pull him out of the well, I shall never get any water,' groaned Gangan. 'And after all, why not help the unfortunate man?' So with a great struggle—for he was a very fat goldsmith—Gangan got him out of the well and on to the grass beside him.

The goldsmith had much to say. But before listening to him, Gangan let his jar down into the well a fifth time. And then he drank till he was satisfied.

'Friend and deliverer!' cried the goldsmith. 'Don't believe what those beasts have said about me! I live in the holy city of Tenkasi, only a day's journey north of Papanasam. Come and visit me whenever you are there. I will show you that I am not an ungrateful man.' And he took leave of Gangan and went his way.

'*From birth, poverty.*'

Gangan resumed his pilgrimage, begging his way to Papanasam. There he stayed many weeks, performing all the ceremonies which pilgrims should perform, bathing at the waterfall, and watching the Brahmin priests feeding the fishes in the sacred stream. He visited other shrines, going as far as Cape Comorin, the southernmost tip of India, where he bathed in the sea. Then he came back through the jungles of Travancore.

He had started on his pilgrimage with his copper water jar and nothing more. After months of wanderings, it was still the only thing he owned. The first prophecy on the palm leaf had already come true: 'From birth, poverty.'

During his wanderings Gangan had never once thought of the

Tiger King and the others, but as he walked wearily along in his rags, he saw a ruined well by the roadside, and it reminded him of his wonderful adventure. And just to see if the Tiger King was genuine, he called out: 'Oh King of Tigers, let me see you!'

No sooner had he spoken than the Tiger King leaped out of the bushes, carrying in his mouth a glittering golden helmet, embedded with precious stones.

It was the helmet of King Pandya, the monarch of the land.

The king had been waylaid and killed by robbers, for the sake of the jewelled helmet; but they in turn had fallen prey to the tiger, who had walked away with the helmet.

Gangan, of course, knew nothing about all this, and when the Tiger King laid the helmet at his feet, he stood stupefied at its splendour and his own good luck.

After the Tiger King had left him, Gangan thought of the goldsmith. 'He will take the jewels out of the helmet, and I will sell some of them. Others I will take home.' So he wrapped the helmet in a rag and made his way to Tenkasi.

In the Tenkasi bazaar he soon found the goldsmith's shop. When they had talked a while, Gangan uncovered the golden helmet. The goldsmith—who knew its worth far better than Gangan—gloated over it, and at once agreed to take out the jewels and sell a few so that Gangan might have some money to spend.

'Now let me examine this helmet at leisure,' said the goldsmith. 'You go to the shrines, worship, and come back. I will then tell you what your treasure is worth.'

Gangan went off to worship at the famous shrines of Tenkasi. And as soon as he had gone, the goldsmith went off to the local magistrate.

'Did not the herald of King Pandya's son come here only yesterday and announce that he would give half his kingdom to anyone who discovered his father's murderer?' he asked. 'Well, I have found the killer. He has brought the king's jewelled helmet to me this very day.'

The magistrate called his guards, and they all hurried to the goldsmith's shop and reached it just as Gangan returned from his tour of the temples.

'Here is the helmet!' exclaimed the goldsmith to the magistrate. 'And here is the villain who murdered the king to get it!'

The guards seized poor Gangan and marched him off to Madura, the capital of the Pandya kingdom, and brought him before the murdered king's son. When Gangan tried to explain about the Tiger King, the goldsmith called him a liar, and the new king had him thrown into the death cell, a deep, well-like pit, dug into the ground in a courtyard of the palace. The only entrance to it was a hole in the pavement of the courtyard. Here Gangan was left to die of hunger and thirst.

At first Gangan lay helpless where he had fallen. Then, looking around him, he found himself on a heap of bones, the bones of those who before him had died in the dungeon; and he was watched by an army of rats who were waiting to gnaw his dead body. He remembered how the Tiger King had warned him against the goldsmith, and had promised help if ever it was needed.

'I need help now,' groaned Gangan, and shouted for the Tiger King, the Snake King, and the Rat King.

For some time nothing happened. Then all the rats in the dungeon suddenly left him and began burrowing in a corner between some of the stones in the wall. Presently Gangan saw that the hole was quite large, and that many other rats were coming and going, working at the same tunnel. And then the Rat King himself came through the little passage, and he was followed by the Snake King, while a great roar from outside told Gangan that the Tiger King was there.

'We cannot get you out of this place,' said the Snake King. 'The walls are too strong. But the armies of the Rat King will bring rice cakes from the palace kitchens, and sweets from the shops in the bazaars, and rags soaked in water. They will not let you die. And from this day on the tigers and the snakes will slay tenfold, and the rats will destroy grain and cloth as never before. Before long the people will begin to complain. Then, when you hear anyone passing in front of your cell, shout: 'These disasters are the results of your ruler's injustice! But I can save you from them!' At first they will pay no attention. But after some time they will take you out, and at your word we will stop the sacking and the slaughter. And then they will honour you.'

'For ten years, captivity.'

For ten years the tigers killed. The serpents struck. The rats destroyed. And at last the people wailed, 'The gods are plaguing us.'

All the while Gangan cried out to those who came near his cell, declaring that he could save them; they thought he was a madman. So ten years passed, and the second prophecy on the palm leaf was fulfilled.

At last, the Snake King made his way into the palace and bit the king's only daughter. She was dead in a few minutes.

The king called for all the snake-charmers and offered half his kingdom to any one of them who would restore his daughter to life. None of them was able to do so. Then the king's servants remembered the cries of Gangan and remarked that there was a madman in the dungeons who kept insisting that he could bring an end to all their troubles. The king at once ordered the dungeon to be opened. Ladders were let down. Men descended and found Gangan, looking more like a ghost than a man. His hair had grown so long that none could see his face. The king did not remember him, but Gangan soon reminded the king of how he had condemned him without enquiry, on the word of the goldsmith.

The king grovelled in the dust before Gangan, begged forgiveness, and entreated him to restore the dead princess to life.

'Bring me the body of the princess,' said Gangan.

Then he called on the Tiger King and the Snake King to come and give life to the princess. As soon as they entered the royal chamber, the princess was restored to life.

Glad as they were to see the princess alive, the king and his courtiers were filled with fear at the sight of the Tiger King and the Snake King. But the tiger and the snake hurt no one, and at a second prayer from Gangan, they brought life to all those they had slain.

And when Gangan made a third petition, the Tiger, the Snake and the Rat Kings ordered their subjects to stop pillaging the Pandya kingdom, so long as the king did no further injustice.

'Let us find that treacherous goldsmith and put him in the dungeon,' said the Tiger King.

But Gangan wanted no vengeance. That very day he set out for his village to see his brother, Chellan, once more. But when he left the Pandya king's capital, he took the wrong road. After much wandering, he found himself on the seashore.

Now it happened that his brother was also making a journey in those parts, and it was their fate that they should meet by the sea. When Gangan saw his brother, his gladness was so sudden and so great that he fell down dead.

And so the third prophecy was fulfilled:

'On the seashore, death.'

Chellan, as he came along the shore road, had seen a half-ruined shrine of Pillaiyar, the elephant-headed god of good luck. Chellan was a very devout servant of Pillaiyar, and, the day being a festival day, he felt it was his duty to worship the god. But it was also his duty to perform the funeral rites for his brother.

The seashore was lonely. There was no one to help him. It would take hours to collect fuel and driftwood enough for a funeral pyre. For a while Chellan did not know what to do. But at last he took up the body and carried it to Pillaiyar's temple.

Then he addressed the god. 'This is my brother's body,' he said. 'I am unclean because I have touched it. I must go and bathe in the sea. Then I will come and worship you, and afterwards I will burn my brother's body. Meanwhile, I leave it in your care.'

Chellan left, and the god told his attendant *Ganas* (goblins) to watch over the body. These *Ganas* are inclined to be mischievous, and when the god wasn't looking, they gobbled up the body of Gangan.

When Chellan came back from bathing, he reverently worshipped Pillaiyar. He then looked for his brother's body. It was not to be found. Anxiously he demanded it of the god. Pillaiyar called on his goblins to produce it. Terrified, they confessed to what they had done.

Chellan reproached the god for the misdeeds of his attendants. And Pillaiyar felt so much pity for him that by his divine power he restored dead Gangan's body to Chellan, and brought Gangan to life again.

The two brothers then returned to King Pandya's capital, where Gangan married the princess and became king when her father died.

And so the fourth prophecy was fulfilled:

'For a little while happiness shall follow.'

But there are wise men who say that the lines of the prophecy were wrongly read and understood, and that the whole should run:

'From birth, poverty;
For ten years, captivity;
On the seashore, death for a little while;
Happiness shall follow.'

220 ⅔ Ruskin Bond

It is the last two lines that are different. And this must be the correct version, because when happiness came to Gangan it was not 'for a little while.' When the goddess of good fortune did arrive, she stayed in his palace for many, many years.

Seven Brides for Seven Princes

A LONG TIME ago, there was a king who had seven sons—all of them brave, handsome and clever. The old king loved them equally, and the princes dressed alike and received the same amounts of pocket money. When they grew up they were given separate palaces, but the palaces were built and furnished alike, and if you had seen one palace you had seen the others.

When the princes were old enough to marry, the king sent his ambassadors all over the country to search out seven brides of equal beauty and talent. The ambassadors travelled everywhere and saw many princesses but could not find seven equally suitable brides. They returned to the king and reported their failure.

The king now became so despondent and gloomy that his chief minister decided that something had to be done to solve his master's problem.

'Do not be so downcast, Your Majesty,' he said. 'Surely it is impossible to find seven brides as accomplished as your seven sons. Let us trust chance, and then perhaps we shall find the ideal brides.'

The minister had thought out a scheme, and when the princes agreed to it, they were taken to the highest tower of the fort, which overlooked the entire city as well as the surrounding countryside. Seven bows and seven arrows were placed before them, and they were told to shoot in any direction they liked. Each prince had agreed to marry the girl upon whose house the arrow fell, be she daughter of prince or peasant.

The seven princes took up their bows and shot their arrows in different directions, and all the arrows except that of the youngest prince fell on the houses of well-known and highly respected families. But the arrow shot by the youngest brother went beyond the city and out of sight.

Servants ran in all directions looking for the arrow and, after a long search, found it embedded in the trunk of a great banyan tree, in which sat a monkey.

Great was the dismay and consternation of the king when he discovered that his youngest son's arrow had made such an unfortunate descent. The king and his courtiers and his minister held a hurried conference. They decided that the youngest prince should be given another chance with his arrow. But to everyone's surprise, the prince refused a second chance.

'No,' he said. 'My brothers have found beautiful and good brides, and that is their good fortune. But do not ask me to break the pledge I took before shooting my arrow. I know I cannot marry this monkey. But I will not marry anyone else! Instead I shall take the monkey home and keep her as a pet.'

The six lucky princes were married with great pomp. The city was ablaze with lights and fireworks, and there was music and dancing in the streets. People decorated their houses with the leaves of mango and banana trees. There was great rejoicing everywhere, except in the palace of the youngest prince. He had placed a diamond collar about the neck of his monkey and seated her on a chair cushioned with velvet. They both looked rather melancholy.

'Poor monkey,' said the prince. 'You are as lonely as I am on this day of rejoicing. But I shall make your stay here a happy one! Are you hungry?' And he placed a bowl of grapes before her, and persuaded her to eat a few. He began talking to the monkey and spending all his time with her. Some called him foolish, or obstinate; others said he wasn't quite right in the head.

The king was worried and discussed the situation with his minister and his other sons in a bid to find some way of bringing the prince to his senses and marrying him into a noble family. But he refused to listen to their advice and entreaties.

As the months passed, the prince grew even more attached to his monkey, and could be seen walking with her in the gardens of his palace.

Then one day the king called a meeting of all seven princes and said, 'My sons, I have seen you all settled happily in life. Even you, my youngest, appear to be happy with your strange companion. The happiness of a father consists in the happiness of his sons and daughters. Therefore, I wish to visit my daughters-in-law and give them presents.'

The eldest son immediately invited his father to dine at his palace, and the others did the same. The king accepted all their invitations, including that of the youngest prince. The receptions were very grand, and the king presented his daughters-in-law with precious jewels and costly dresses. Eventually it was the turn of the youngest son to entertain the king.

The youngest prince was very troubled. How could he invite his father to a house in which he lived with a monkey? He knew his monkey was more gentle and affectionate than some of the greatest ladies in the land; and he was determined not to hide her away as though she were someone to be ashamed of.

Walking beside his pet in the palace gardens, he said, 'What shall I do now, my friend? I wish you had a tongue with which to comfort me. All my brothers have shown their homes and wives to my father. They will ridicule me when I present you to him.'

The monkey had always been a silent and sympathetic listener when the prince spoke to her. Now he noticed that she was gesturing to him with her hands. Bending over her, he saw that she held a piece of broken pottery in her hand. The prince took the shard from her and saw that something was written on it. These were the words he read:

'Do not worry, sweet prince, but go to the place where you found me, and throw this piece of pottery into the hollow trunk of the banyan tree, and wait for a reply.'

The prince did as he was told. Going to the ancient banyan tree, he threw the shard of pottery into the hollow, and then stood back to see if anything would happen.

He did not have to wait long.

A beautiful fairy dressed in green stepped out of the hollow and asked the prince to follow her. She told him that the queen of the fairies wished to see him in person.

The prince climbed the tree, entered the hollow, and after groping about in the dark was suddenly led into a spacious and wonderful garden, at the end of which stood a beautiful palace. Between an avenue of trees flowed a crystal-clear stream, and on the bed of the stream, instead of pebbles, there were rubies and diamonds and sapphires. Even the light which lit up this new world was warmer and less harsh than the light of the world outside. The prince was led past a fountain of silver water, up steps of gold, and in through the mother-of-pearl doors of the palace. But the splendour of the room into which he was led seemed to fade before the exquisite beauty of the fairy princess who stood before him.

'Yes, prince, I know your message,' said the princess. 'Do not be anxious, but go home and prepare to receive your father the king and your royal guests tomorrow evening. My servants will see to everything.'

Next morning, when the prince awoke in his palace, an amazing sight met his eyes. The palace grounds teemed with life. The gardens were full of pomegranate trees, laden with fruit, and under the trees were gaily decorated stalls serving sweets, scented water and cooling sherbets. Children were playing on the lawns, and men and women were dancing or listening to music.

The prince was bewildered by what he saw, and he was even more amazed when he entered his banquet hall and found it full of activity. Tables groaned under the weight of delicious pillaus, curries and biryanis. Great chandeliers hung from the ceiling, bunches of roses filled the room with their perfume.

A servant came running to announce that the king and his courtiers were arriving. The prince hurried out to meet them. After dinner was served, everyone insisted on seeing the companion the prince had chosen for himself. They thought the monkey would make excellent entertainment after such a magnificent feast.

The prince could not refuse this request, and passed gloomily through his rooms in search of his monkey. He feared the ridicule that would follow. This, he knew, was his father's way of trying to cure him of his obstinacy.

He opened the door of his room and was almost blinded by a blaze of light. There, on a throne in the middle of the room, sat the fairy princess.

'Come, prince,' she said. 'I have sent away the monkey and I am here to offer you my hand.'

On hearing that his pet had gone, the prince burst into tears. 'What have you done?' he cried. 'It was cruel of you to take away my monkey. Your beauty will not compensate me for the loss of my companion.'

'If my beauty does not move you,' said the princess with a smile, 'let gratitude help you take my hand. See what pains I have taken to prepare this feast for your father and brothers. As my husband, you shall have all the riches and pleasures of the world at your command.'

The prince was indignant. 'I did not ask these things of you—nor do I know what plot has been afoot to deprive me of my monkey. Restore her to me, and I will be your slave!'

Then the fairy princess came down from her throne, and taking the prince by the hand, spoke to him with great love and respect.

'You see in me your friend and companion,' she said. 'Yes, it was I who took the form of a monkey to test your faith and sincerity. See, my monkey's skin lies there in the corner.'

The prince looked, and saw in a corner of the room the skin of his monkey.

He joined the fairy princess on her throne, and when she said 'Arise, arise, arise,' the throne rose in the air and floated into the hall where the guests had gathered.

The prince presented his bride to his father, who was of course delighted. The guests were a little disappointed to find that their hostess was not, after all, a monkey. But they had to admit that the prince and the princess made a most handsome couple.

A Battle of Wits

IN A VILLAGE in northern India, there lived a Bania (a merchant) whose shop kept the villagers supplied with their everyday necessities.

One day, on his way to a neighbouring town to make some purchases, he met a poor Jat, one of a tribe of farmers who was also going to town to pay the monthly instalment of a debt he owed to the local mahajan—the banker and moneylender.

The debt had actually been incurred by the Jat's great-grandfather and had in the beginning been only fifty rupees; but his great grandfather had been unable to repay it, and in the last fifty years, through interest and compound interest, the amount had grown to five hundred rupees.

The Jat was walking along, wondering if he would ever get out of the clutches of the mahajan, when the Bania caught up with him.

'Good day to you, Chowdhri,' said the Bania, who, though he had a poor opinion of the farmer's intelligence, was always polite to his customers. 'I see you are going to town to pay your instalment to the *mahajan*. Before long you will have to give up your lands. Can nothing be done to save them?'

'It is too late to do anything, Shahji,' said the Jat. He was much taller and stronger than the Bania; at the same time he was an easy-going, good-natured sort. The Bania thought he was simple-minded.

'Well, let us forget our worries,' said the Bania, 'and pass the time telling stories.'

'A good idea, Shahji! It will make the journey less tiresome. But let there be one condition. No matter how fantastic or silly the story, neither of us must call it untrue. Whoever does so must pay the other five hundred rupees!'

'Agreed,' said the Bania with a laugh. 'And let me begin my story first. My great-grandfather was the greatest of Banias, and tremendously rich.'

'True, oh Shahji, true!' said the Jat.

'At one time he possessed a fleet of forty ships with which he sailed to China, and traded there in rich jewels and costly silks.'

'True, oh Shahji, true!' said the Jat.

'Well, after making a huge fortune, my great-grandfather returned home with many unique and precious things. One was a statue of pure gold which was able to answer any question put to it.'

'True, oh Shahji, true!'

'When my great-grandfather came home, many people came to have their questions answered by his wonderful statue. One day *your* great-grandfather came with a question. He asked, "Who are the wisest of all men?" The statue replied, "The Banias, of course." Then he asked: "And who are the most foolish?" The statue replied: "The Jats." And then your great-grandfather asked, "Among the Jats, who is the most stupid?" The statue replied: "Why, you are, of course."'

'True, oh Shahji, true,' said the Jat, inwardly resolving to repay the Bania in his own coin.

'My father,' continued the Bania, 'was himself a great traveller, and during a tour of the world he saw many wonders. One day, a mosquito hovering near his ear threatened to bite him. My father, not wishing to kill the mosquito, requested it to leave. The mosquito was amazed at such gentlemanly conduct. It said, "Noble Shahji, you are the greatest man I ever met, and I mean to do you a great service." Saying this, the mosquito opened its mouth, and inside it my father saw a large palace with golden doors and windows. At one of the windows stood the most beautiful princess in the world. At the door of the palace he saw a peasant about to attack the princess. My father, who was very brave, at once jumped into the mouth of the mosquito and entered its stomach. He found it very dark inside.'

'True, oh Shahji, true!' said the Jat.

'Well, after some time my father grew used to the darkness and was able to make out the palace, the princess and the peasant. He at once fell upon the peasant, who happened to be *your* father. They fought for a year in the stomach of the mosquito. At the end of that time your father was defeated and became my father's servant. My father then married the princess and I was born from the union. But when I was fifteen years old, a heavy rain of boiling water fell on the palace, which collapsed, throwing us into a scalding sea. With great difficulty we swam ashore, where the four of us found ourselves in a kitchen, where a woman was shaking with terror at the sight of us.'

'True, oh Shahji, true!'

'When the woman, who was a cook, realized that we were men and not ghosts, she complained that we had spoilt her soup. "Why did you have to enter my pot of boiling water and frighten me like that?" she complained. We apologized, explaining that for fifteen years we had been living in the belly of a mosquito, and that it was not our fault that we had found ourselves in her cooking pot. "Ah! I remember now," she said. "A little while ago, a mosquito bit me on the arm. You must have been injected into my arm, for when I squeezed out the poison, a large black drop fell into the boiling water. I had no idea you were in it!"'

'True, oh Shahji, true!' said the Jat.

'Well, when we left the kitchen, we found ourselves in another country, which happened to be our present village. Here we took to shopkeeping. The princess, my mother, died many years ago. That,

Chowdhri, is my story. Improve upon it if you can!'

'A very true story,' said the Jat. 'My story, though no less true, is perhaps not as wonderful. But it is perfectly true, every word of it...'

'My great-grandfather was the wealthiest Jat in the village. His noble appearance and great wisdom brought praise from all who met him. At village meetings he was always given the best seat, and when he settled disputes no one questioned his good judgement. In addition, he was of great physical strength, and a terror to the wicked.'

'True, oh Chowdhri, true,' said the Bania.

'There was a time when a great famine came to our village. There was no rain, the rivers and wells dried up, the trees withered away. Birds and beasts died in thousands. When my great-grandfather saw that the village stores had been exhausted, and that the people would die of hunger if something was not done, he called the Jats together and said, "Brother Jats, God Indra is angry with us for some reason, because he has withheld the seasonal rains. But if you do what I tell you, I will supply you all with food until the scarcity is over. I want you to give your fields to me for six months." Without any hesitation the Jats gave my great-grandfather their fields. Then, stripping himself of his clothes, he gave one great heave and lifted the entire village of a thousand acres and placed it on his head!'

'True, oh Chowdhri, true!' exclaimed the Bania.

'Then my great-grandfather, carrying the village on his head, searched for rain. 'Wherever there was rain he took the village, so that the rainwater fell on the fields and collected in the wells. Then he told the Jats (who were, of course, still in the village on his head) to plough their land and sow their seed. The crops that came up had never been so wonderful, and the wheat and the maize rose to such a height that they touched the clouds.'

'True, oh Chowdhri, true,' said the Bania.

'Then my great-grandfather returned to his country and placed the village in its proper place. The farmers reaped a record harvest that year. Every grain of corn was as big as your head.'

'True, oh Chowdhri, true,' said the Bania, annoyed at the comparison but anxious not to lose his wager. By this time, they had reached the outskirts of the town, but the Jat had not finished his story.

'At that time, *your* great-grandfather was a very poor man,' said the Jat, 'and mine, who had made huge profits from his wonderful harvest, employed him as a servant to weigh out the grain for the customers.'

'True, oh Chowdhri, true,' said the Bania with a sour look.

'Being a blockhead, your ancestor often made mistakes for which he would receive thrashings from my great-grandfather.'

'True, oh Chowdhri, true!'

By this time they had entered the shop of the mahajan to whom the Jat was owing money. Bidding the banker good morning, they sat down on the floor in front of him. But the Jat, without speaking to the banker, continued his story.

'Well, Shahji, after my great-grandfather sold his harvest, he discharged your great-grandfather. But, before he went, your ancestor asked mine for a loan of fifty rupees, which was generously given to him.'

'True, oh Chowdhri, true!' said the Bania.

'Very good,' said the Jat, raising his voice so that the mahajan could also hear them. 'Your ancestor did not repay that debt. Nor did your grandfather, or your father, repay the debt. Neither have you repaid it up to this time.'

'True, oh Chowdhri, true!'

'Now that sum of fifty rupees, with interest and compound interest, amounts to exactly five hundred rupees, which sum you owe me!'

'True, oh Chowdhri, true!'

'So, as you have admitted the debt before the mahajan, kindly pay the amount to him so that I may have my lands released.'

This placed the Bania in a dilemma. He had admitted a debt before a third party. If he said that it was merely a story, and completely untrue, he would have to pay the Jat five hundred rupees according to the terms of the wager. If he said it was true, he would have to pay the amount to the mahajan. Either way he was the loser.

So the Bania paid up, and never again did he belittle the intelligence of his Jat neighbours.

The Song of
the Whistling Thrush

In THE wooded hills of western India lives 'The Idle Schoolboy'—a bird who cannot learn a simple tune, though he is gifted with one of the most beautiful voices in the forest. He whistles away in various sharps and flats, and sometimes, when you think he is really going to produce a melody, he breaks off in the middle of his song as though he had just remembered something very important.

Why is it that the Whistling Thrush can never remember a tune? The story goes that on a hot summer's afternoon, the young God Krishna was wandering along the banks of a mountain stream when he came to a small waterfall, shot through with sunbeams. It was a lovely spot, cool and inviting. Tiny fish flecked the pool at the foot of the waterfall, and a Paradise Flycatcher, trailing its silver tail, moved gracefully amongst the trees.

Krishna was enchanted. He threw himself down on a bed of moss and ferns, and began playing on his flute—the famous flute with which he had charmed all the creatures in the forest. A fat yellow lizard nodded its head in time to the music; the birds were hushed; and the shy mouse-deer approached silently on their tiny hooves to see who it was who played so beautifully.

Presently the flute slipped from Krishna's fingers, and the beautiful young god fell asleep. But it was not a restful sleep, for his dreams were punctuated by an annoying whistling, as though someone who didn't know much about music was practising on his flute in an attempt to learn the tune that Krishna had been playing.

Awake now, Krishna sat up and saw a ragged urchin standing ankle-deep in the pool, the sacred flute held to his lips!

Krishna was furious.

'Come here, boy!' he shouted. 'How dare you steal my flute and disturb my sleep! Don't you know who I am?'

The boy, instead of being afraid, was thrilled at the discovery that he stood before his hero, the young Krishna, whose exploits were famous throughout the land.

'I did not steal your flute, lord,' he said. 'Had that been my intention, I would not have waited for you to wake up. It was only my great love for your music that made me touch your flute. You will teach me to play, will you not? I will be your disciple.'

Krishna's anger melted away, and he was filled with compassion for the boy. But it was too late to do anything, for it is everlastingly decreed that anyone who touches the sacred property of the gods, whether deliberately or in innocence, must be made to suffer throughout his next ten thousand births.

When this was explained to the boy, he fell on his face and wept bitterly, crying, 'Have mercy on me, Krishna. Do with me as you will, but do not send me away from the beautiful forests I love.'

Swiftly, Krishna communed in spirit with Brahma the Creator. Here was a genuine case of a crime committed in ignorance. If it could not be forgiven, surely the punishment could be less severe?

Brahma agreed, and Krishna laid his hand on the boy's mouth, saying, 'For ever try to copy the song of the gods, but never succeed.' Then he touched the boy's clothes and said, 'Let the raggedness and dust disappear, and only the beautiful colours of Krishna remain.'

Immediately the boy was changed into the bird we know today as the Whistling Thrush of Malabar, with its dark body and brilliant blue patches on head and wings. In this guise, he still continues to live among the beautiful, forested valleys of the hills, where he tries unsuccessfully to remember the tune that brought about his strange transformation.

Children of India

THEY PASS me every day on their way to school—boys and girls from the surrounding villages and the outskirts of the hill station. There are no school buses plying for these children: they walk.

For many of them, it's a very long walk to school.

Ranbir, who is ten, has to climb the mountain from his village, four miles distant and two thousand feet below the town level. He comes in all weathers wearing the same pair of cheap shoes until they have almost fallen apart.

Ranbir is a cheerful soul. He waves to me whenever he sees me at my window. Sometimes he brings me cucumbers from his father's field. I pay him for the cucumbers; he uses the money for books or for small things needed at home.

Many of the children are like Ranbir—poor, but slightly better off than what their parents were at the same age. They cannot attend the expensive residential and private schools that abound here, but must go to the government-aided schools with only basic facilities. Not many of their parents managed to go to school. They spent their lives working in the fields or delivering milk in the hill station. The lucky ones got into the army. Perhaps Ranbir will do something different when he grows up.

He has yet to see a train but he sees planes flying over the mountains almost every day.

'How far can a plane go?' he asks.

'All over the world,' I tell him. 'Thousands of miles in a day. You can go almost anywhere.'

'I'll go round the world one day,' he vows. 'I'll buy a plane and go everywhere!'

And maybe he will. He has a determined chin and a defiant look in his eye.

The following lines in my journal were put down for my own inspiration or encouragement, but they will do for any determined young person:

We get out of life what we bring to it. There is not a dream which may not come true if we have the energy which determines our own fate. We can always get what we want if we will it intensely enough... So few people succeed greatly because so few people conceive a great end, working towards it without giving up. We all know that the man who works steadily for money gets rich; the man who works day and night for fame or power reaches his goal. And those who work for deeper, more spiritual achievements will find them too. It may come when we no longer have any use for it, but if we have been willing it long enough, it will come!

Up to a few years ago, very few girls in the hills or in the villages of India went to school. They helped in the home until they were old enough to be married, which wasn't very old. But there are now just as many girls as there are boys going to school.

Bindra is something of an extrovert—a confident fourteen year old who chatters away as she hurries down the road with her companions. Her father is a forest guard and knows me quite well: I meet him on my walks through the deodar woods behind Landour. And I had grown used to seeing Bindra almost every day. When she did not put in an appearance for a week, I asked her brother if anything was wrong.

'Oh, nothing,' he says, 'she is helping my mother cut grass. Soon the monsoon will end and the grass will dry up. So we cut it now and store it for the cows in winter.'

'And why aren't you cutting grass too?'

'Oh, I have a cricket match today,' he says, and hurries away to join his teammates. Unlike his sister, he puts pleasure before work!

Cricket, once the game of the elite, has become the game of the masses. On any holiday, in any part of this vast country, groups of boys can be seen making their way to the nearest field, or open patch of land, with bat, ball and any other cricketing gear that they can cobble together. Watching some of them play, I am amazed at the quality of talent, at the finesse with which they bat or bowl. Some of the local teams are as good, if not better, than any from the private schools, where there are better facilities. But the boys from these poor or lower middle-class families will never get the exposure that is necessary to bring them to the attention of those who select state or national teams. They will never get near enough to the men of influence and power. They must continue to play for the love of the game, or watch their more fortunate heroes' exploits on television.

As winter approaches and the days grow shorter, those children who live far away must quicken their pace in order to get home before dark. Ranbir and his friends find that darkness has fallen before they are halfway home.

'What is the time, uncle?' he asks, as he trudges up the steep road past Ivy Cottage.

One gets used to being called 'uncle' by almost every boy or girl one meets. I wonder how the custom began. Perhaps it has its origins in the folktale about the tiger who refrained from pouncing on you if you called him 'uncle'. Tigers don't eat their relatives! Or do they? The ploy may not work if the tiger happens to be a tigress. Would you call her 'aunty' as she (or your teacher!) descends on you?

It's dark at six and by then, Ranbir likes to be out of the deodar forest and on the open road to the village. The moon and the stars and the village lights are sufficient, but not in the forest, where it is dark even during the day. And the silent flitting of bats and flying foxes, and the eerie hoot of an owl, can be a little disconcerting for the hardiest of children. Once Ranbir and the other boys were chased by a bear.

When he told me about it, I said, 'Well, now we know you can run faster then a bear!'

'Yes, but you have to run downhill when chased by a bear.' He spoke as one having long experience of escaping from bears. 'They run much faster uphill!'

'I'll remember that,' I said, 'thanks for the advice.' And I don't suppose calling a bear 'uncle' would help.

Usually Ranbir has the company of other boys, and they sing most of the way, for loud singing by small boys will silence owls and frighten away the forest demons. One of them plays a flute, and flute music in the mountains is always enchanting.

Not only in the hills, but all over India, children are constantly making their way to and from school, in conditions that range from dust storms in the Rajasthan desert to blizzards in Ladakh and Kashmir. In the larger towns and cities, there are school buses, but in remote rural areas, getting to school can pose a problem.

Most children are more than equal to any obstacles that may arise. Like those youngsters in the Ganjam district of Orissa. In the absence of a bridge, they swim or wade across the Dhanei river everyday in order to reach their school. I have a picture of them in my scrapbook. Holding books or satchels aloft in one hand, they do the breast stroke or dog paddle with the other; or form a chain and help each other across.

Wherever you go in India, you will find children helping out with the family's source of livelihood, whether it be drying fish on the Malabar coast, or gathering saffron buds in Kashmir, or grazing camels or cattle in a village in Rajasthan or Gujarat.

Only the more fortunate can afford to send their children to English medium private or 'public' schools, and those children really are fortunate, for some of these institutions are excellent schools, as good, and often better, than their counterparts in Britain or USA. Whether it's in Ajmer or Bangalore, New Delhi or Chandigarh, Kanpur or Kolkata, the best schools set very high standards. The growth of a prosperous middle-class has led to an ever-increasing demand for quality education. But as private schools proliferate, standards suffer, too, and many parents must settle for the second-rate.

The great majority of our children still attend schools run by the state or municipality. These vary from the good to the bad to the ugly, depending on how they are run and where they are situated. A classroom without windows, or with a roof that lets in the monsoon rain, is not uncommon. Even so, children from different communities learn to live and grow together. Hardship makes brothers of us all.

The census tells us that two in every five of the population is in the age group of five to fifteen. Almost half our population is on the way to school!

And here I stand at my window, watching some of them pass by—boys and girls, big and small, some scruffy, some smart, some mischievous, some serious, but all going somewhere—hopefully towards a better future.

And Now We Are Twelve

People often ask me why I've chosen to live in Mussoorie for so long—almost forty years without any significant breaks.

'I forgot to go away,' I tell them, but of course, that isn't the real reason.

The people here are friendly, but then people are friendly in a great many other places. The hills, the valleys are beautiful; but they are just as beautiful in Kulu or Kumaon.

'This is where the family has grown up and where we all live,' I say, and those who don't know me are puzzled because the general impression of the writer is of a reclusive old bachelor.

Unmarried I may be, but single I am not. Not since Prem came to live and work with me in 1970. A year later, he was married. Then his children came along and stole my heart; and when they grew up, their children came along and stole my wits. So now I'm an enchanted bachelor, head of a family of twelve. Sometimes I go out to bat, sometimes to bowl, but generally I prefer to be twelfth man, carrying out the drinks!

In the old days, when I was a solitary writer living on baked beans, the prospect of my suffering from obesity was very remote. Now there is a little more of author than there used to be, and the other day, five-year-old Gautam patted me on my tummy (or balcony, as I prefer to call it) and remarked, 'Dada, you should join the WWF.'

'I'm already a member,' I said. 'I joined the World Wildlife Fund years ago.'

'Not that,' he said. 'I mean the World Wrestling Federation.'

If I have a tummy today, it's thanks to Gautam's grandfather and now his mother who, over the years, have made sure that I am well-fed and well-proportioned.

Forty years ago, when I was a lean young man, people would look at me and say, 'Poor chap, he's definitely undernourished. What on earth made him take up writing as a profession?' Now they look at me and say, 'You wouldn't think he was a writer, would you? Too well nourished!'

It was a cold, wet and windy March evening when Prem came back from the village with his wife and first-born child, then just four months old. In those days, they had to walk to the house from the bus stand; it was a half-hour walk in the cold rain, and the baby was all wrapped up when they entered the front room. Finally, I got a glimpse of him, and he of me, and it was friendship at first sight. Little Rakesh (as he was to be called) grabbed me by the nose and held on. He did not have much of a nose to grab, but he had a dimpled chin and I played with it until he smiled.

The little chap spent a good deal of his time with me during those first two years of his in Maplewood—learning to crawl, to toddle, and then to walk unsteadily about the little sitting room. I would carry him into the garden, and later, up the steep gravel path to the main road. Rakesh enjoyed these little excursions, and so did I, because in pointing out trees, flowers, birds, butterflies, beetles, grasshoppers, et al, I was giving myself a chance to observe them better instead of just taking them for granted.

In particular, there was a pair of squirrels that lived in the big oak tree outside the cottage. Squirrels are rare in Mussoorie, though common enough down in the valley. This couple must have come up for the summer. They became quite friendly, and although they never got around to taking food from our hands, they were soon entering the house quite freely. The sitting room window opened directly on to the oak tree whose various denizens—ranging from stag beetles to small birds and even an acrobatic bat—took to darting in and out of the cottage at various times of the day or night.

Life at Maplewood was quite idyllic, and when Rakesh's baby brother, Suresh, came into the world, it seemed we were all set for a long period of domestic bliss; but at such times, tragedy is often lurking just around the corner. Suresh was just over a year old when he contracted tetanus. Doctors and hospitals were of no avail. He suffered—as any child would from this terrible affliction—and left this world before he had a chance of getting to know it. His parents were broken-hearted. And I feared for Rakesh, for he wasn't a very healthy boy, and two of his cousins in the village had already succumbed to tuberculosis.

It was to be a difficult year for me. A criminal charge was brought against me for a slightly risqué story I'd written for a Bombay magazine. I had to face trial in Bombay and this involved three journeys there over a period of a year and a half, before an irate but perceptive judge found the charges baseless and gave me an honourable acquittal.

It's the only time I've been involved with the law and I sincerely hope it is the last. Most cases drag on interminably, and the main beneficiaries are the lawyers. My trial would have been much longer had not the prosecutor died of a heart attack in the middle of the proceedings. His successor did not pursue it with the same vigour. His heart was not in it. The whole issue had started with a complaint by a local politician, and when he lost interest, so did the prosecution. Nevertheless, the trial, once begun, had to be seen through.

The defence (organized by the concerned magazine) marshalled its witnesses (which included Nissim Ezekiel and the Marathi playwright Vijay Tendulkar). I made a short speech which couldn't have been very memorable as I have forgotten it! And everyone, including the judge, was bored with the whole business. After that, I steered clear of controversial publications. I have never set out to shock the world. Telling a meaningful story was all that really mattered. And that is still the case.

I was looking forward to continuing our idyllic existence in Maplewood, but it was not to be. The powers-that-be, in the shape of the Public Works Department (PWD), had decided to build a 'strategic' road just below the cottage and without any warning to us, all the trees in the vicinity were felled (including the friendly old oak) and the hillside was rocked by explosives and bludgeoned by bulldozers. I decided it was time to move. Prem and Chandra (Rakesh's mother) wanted to move too; not because of the road, but because they associated the house with the death of little Suresh, whose presence seemed to haunt every room, every corner of the cottage. His little cries of pain and suffering still echoed through the still hours of the night.

I rented rooms at the top of Landour, a good thousand feet higher up the mountain. Rakesh was now old enough to go to school, and every morning I would walk with him down to the little convent school near the clock tower. Prem would go to fetch him in the afternoon. The walk took us about half an hour, and on the way Rakesh would ask for a story and I would have to rack my brains in order to invent one. I am not the most inventive of writers, and fantastical plots are beyond me. My forte is observation, recollection and reflection. Small boys prefer action. So I invented a leopard who suffered from acute indigestion because he'd eaten one human too many and a belt buckle was causing an obstruction.

This went down quite well until Rakesh asked me how the

leopard got around the problem of the victim's clothes.

'The secret,' I said, 'is to pounce on them when their trousers are off!'

Not the stuff of which great picture books are made, but then, I've never attempted to write stories for beginners. Red Riding Hood's granny-eating wolf always scared me as a small boy, and yet parents have always found it acceptable for toddlers. Possibly they feel grannies are expendable.

Mukesh was born around this time and Savitri (Dolly) a couple of years later. When Dolly grew older, she was annoyed at having been named Savitri (my choice), which is now considered very old fashioned; so we settled for Dolly. I can understand a child's dissatisfaction with given names.

My first name was Owen, which in Welsh means 'brave'. As I am not in the least brave, I have preferred not to use it. One given name and one surname should be enough.

When my granny said, 'But you should try to be brave, otherwise how will you survive in this cruel world?' I replied, 'Don't worry, I can run very fast.'

Not that I've ever had to do much running, except when I was pursued by a lissome Australian lady who thought I'd make a good obedient husband. It wasn't so much the lady I was running from, but the prospect of spending the rest of my life in some remote cattle station in the Australian outback.

Anyone who has tried to drag me away from India has always met with stout resistance.

Up on the heights of Landour lived a motley crowd. My immediate neighbours included a Frenchwoman who played the sitar (very badly) all through the night; a Spanish lady with two husbands, one of whom practised acupuncture—rather ineffectively as far as he was concerned, for he seemed to be dying of some mysterious debilitating disease. The other came and went rather mysteriously, and finally ended up in Tihar Jail, having been apprehended at Delhi airport carrying a large amount of contraband hashish.

Apart from these and a few other colourful characters, the area was inhabitated by some very respectable people—retired brigadiers, air marshals and rear admirals, almost all of whom were busy writing their memoirs. I had to read or listen to extracts from their literary efforts. This was slow torture. A few years before, I had done a stint of editing for a magazine called *Imprint*. It had involved going through hundreds of badly written manuscripts, and in some cases (friends of the owner!) re-writing some of them for publication. One of life's joys had been to throw up that particular job, and now here I was, besieged by all the top brass of the Army, Navy and Air Force, each one determined that I should read, inwardly digest, improve, and if possible find a publisher for their outpourings.

Thank goodness they were all retired. I could not be shot or court-martialled. But at least two of them set their wives upon me, and these intrepid ladies would turn up around noon with my 'homework'—typescripts to read and edit! There was no escape. My own writing was of no consequence to them. I told them that I was taking sitar lessons, but they disapproved, saying I was more suited to the tabla.

When Prem discovered a set of vacant rooms further down the Landour slope, close to school and bazaar, I rented them without hesitation. This was Ivy Cottage. Come up and see me sometimes, but leave your manuscripts behind.

When we came to Ivy Cottage in 1980, we were six, Dolly having just been born. Now, twenty-four years later, we are twelve. I think that's a reasonable expansion. The increase has been brought about by Rakesh's marriage twelve years ago, and Mukesh's marriage two years ago. Both precipitated themselves into marriage when they were barely twenty, and both were lucky. Beena and Binita, who happen to be real sisters, have brightened and enlivened our lives with their happy, positive natures and the wonderful children they have brought into the world. More about them later.

Ivy Cottage has, on the whole, been kind to us, and particularly kind to me. Some houses like their occupants, others don't. Maplewood, set in the shadow of the hill lacked a natural cheerfulness; there was a settled gloom about the place. The house at the top of Landour was too exposed to the elements to have any sort of character. The wind moaning in the deodars may have inspired the sitar player but it did nothing for my writing. I produced very little up there.

On the other hand, Ivy Cottage—especially my little room facing the sunrise—has been conducive to creative work. Novellas, poems, essays, children's stories, anthologies, have all come tumbling on to whatever sheets of paper happen to be nearest me. As I write by hand, I have only to grab for the nearest pad, loose sheet, page proof or envelope whenever the muse takes hold of me; which is surprisingly often.

I came here when I was nearing fifty. Now I'm seventy, and instead of drying up, as some writers do in their later years, I find myself writing with as much ease and assurance as when I was twenty. And I enjoy writing. It's not a burdensome task. I may not have anything of earth-shattering significance to convey to the world, but in conveying my sentiments to you, dear readers, and in telling you something about my relationship with people and the natural world, I hope to bring a little pleasure and sunshine into your life.

Life isn't a bed of roses, not for any of us, and I have never had the comforts or luxuries that wealth can provide. But here I am, doing my own thing, in my own time and my own way. What more can I ask of life? Give me a big cash prize and I'd still be here. I happen to like the view from my window. And I like to have Gautam coming up to me, patting me on the tummy, and telling me that I'll make a good goalkeeper one day.

It's a Sunday morning, as I come to the conclusion of this chapter. There's bedlam in the house. Siddharth's football keeps smashing against the front door. Shrishti is practising her dance routine in the back verandah. Gautam has cut his finger and is trying his best to bandage it with cellotape. He is, of course, the youngest of Rakesh's three musketeers, and probably the most independent-minded. Siddharth, now ten, is restless, never quite able to expend all his energy. 'Does not pay enough attention,' says his teacher. It must be hard for anyone to pay attention in a class of sixty! How does the poor teacher pay attention?

If you, dear reader, have any ambitions to be a writer, you must first rid yourself of any notion that perfect peace and quiet is the first requirement. There is no such thing as perfect peace and quiet, except perhaps in a monastery or a cave in the mountains. And what would you write about, living in a cave? One should be able to write in a train, a bus, a bullock cart, in good weather or bad, on a park bench or in the middle of a noisy classroom.

Of course, the best place is the sun-drenched desk right next to my bed. It isn't always sunny here, but on a good day like this, it's ideal. The children are getting ready for school, dogs are barking in the street, and down near the water tap there's an altercation between two women with empty buckets, the tap having dried up. But these are all background noises and will subside in due course. They are not directed at me.

Hello! Here's Atish, Mukesh's little ten-month-old infant, crawling over the rug, curious to know why I'm sitting on the edge of my bed scribbling away, when I should be playing with him. So I shall play with him for five minutes and then come back to this page. Giving him my time is important. After all, I won't be around when he grows up.

Half an hour later, Atish soon tired of playing with me, but meanwhile Gautam had absconded with my pen. When I asked him to return it, he asked, 'Why don't you get a computer? Then we can play games on it.'

'My pen is faster than any computer,' I tell him. 'I wrote three pages this morning without getting out of bed. And yesterday I wrote two pages sitting under Billoo's chestnut tree.'

'Until a chestnut fell on your head,' says Gautam. 'Did it hurt?'

'Only a little,' I said, putting on a brave front.

He had saved the chestnut and now he showed it to me. The smooth brown horse-chestnut shone in the sunlight.

'Let's stick it in the ground,' I said. 'Then in the spring a chestnut tree will come up.'

So we went outside and planted the chestnut on a plot of wasteland. Hopefully a small tree will burst through the earth at about the time this little book is published.

Adventures in Reading

1

You don't see them so often now, those tiny books and almanacs—genuine pocket books—once so popular with our parents and grandparents; much smaller than the average paperback, often smaller than the palm of the hand. With the advent of coffee-table books, new books keep growing bigger and bigger, rivalling tombstones! And one day, like Alice after drinking from the wrong bottle, they will reach the ceiling and won't have anywhere else to go. The average publisher, who apparently believes that large profits are linked to large books, must look upon these old miniatures with amusement or scorn. They were not meant for a coffee table, true. They were meant for true book lovers and readers, for they took up very little space—you could slip them into your pocket without any discomfort, either to you or to the pocket.

I have a small collection of these little books, treasured over the years. Foremost is my father's prayer book and psalter, with his name, 'Aubrey Bond, Lovedale, 1917', inscribed on the inside back cover. Lovedale is a school in the Nilgiri Hills in South India, where, as a young man, he did his teacher's training. He gave it to me soon after I went to a boarding school in Shimla in 1944, and my own name is inscribed on it in his beautiful handwriting.

Another beautiful little prayer book in my collection is called *The Finger Prayer Book*. Bound in soft leather, it is about the same length and breadth as the average middle finger. Replete with psalms, it is the complete book of common prayer and not an abridgement; a marvel of miniature book production.

Not much larger is a delicate item in calf leather, *The Humour of Charles Lamb*. It fits into my wallet and often stays there. It has a tiny portrait of the great essayist, followed by some thirty to forty extracts from his essays, such as this favourite of mine: 'Every dead man must take upon himself to be lecturing me with his odious truism, that "Such as he is now, I must shortly be". Not so shortly friend, perhaps as thou imaginest. In the meantime, I am alive. I move about. I am worth twenty of thee. Know thy betters!'

No fatalist, Lamb. He made no compromise with Father Time. He affirmed that in age we must be as glowing and tempestuous as in youth! And yet Lamb is thought to be an old-fashioned writer.

Another favourite among my 'little' books is *The Pocket Trivet, An Anthology for Optimists*, published by *The Morning Post* newspaper in 1932. But what is a trivet? the unenlightened may well ask. Well, it's a stand for a small pot or kettle, fixed securely over a grate. To be right as a trivet is to be perfectly right. Just right, like the short sayings in this book, which is further enlivened by a number of charming woodcuts based on the seventeenth century originals; such as the illustration of a moth hovering over a candle flame and below it the legend—'I seeke mine owne hurt.'

But the sayings are mostly of a cheering nature, such as Emerson's 'Hitch your wagon to a star!' or the West Indian proverb: 'Every day no Christmas, an' every day no rainy day.'

My book of trivets is a happy example of much concentrated wisdom being collected in a small space—the beauty separated from the dross. It helps me to forget the dilapidated building in which I live and to look instead at the ever-changing cloud patterns as seen from my bedroom windows. There is no end to the shapes made by the clouds, or to the stories they set off in my head. We don't have to circle the world in order to find beauty and fulfilment. After all, most of living has to happen in the mind. And, to quote one anonymous sage from my trivet, 'The world is only the size of each man's head.'

2

Amongst the current fraternity of writers, I must be that very rare person—an author who actually writes by hand!

Soon after the invention of the typewriter, most editors and publishers understandably refused to look at any mansucript that was handwritten. A decade or two earlier, when Dickens and Balzac had submitted their hefty manuscrips in longhand, no one had raised any objection. Had their handwriting been awful, their manuscripts would still have been read. Fortunately for all concerned, most writers, famous or obscure, took pains over their handwriting. For some, it was an art in itself, and many of those early manuscripts are a pleasure to look at and read.

And it wasn't only authors who wrote with an elegant hand. Parents and grandparents of most of us had distinctive styles of their own. I still have my father's last letter, written to me when I was at boarding school in Shimla some fifty years ago. He used large, beautifully formed letters, and his thoughts seemed to have the same flow and clarity as his handwriting.

In his letter he advises me (then a nine-year-old) about my own handwriting: 'I wanted to write before about your writing. Ruskin... Sometimes I get letters from you in very small writing, as if you wanted to squeeze everything into one sheet of letter paper. It is not good for you or for your eyes, to get into the habit of writing too small... Try and form a larger style of handwriting—use more paper if necessary!'

I did my best to follow his advice, and I'm glad to report that after nearly forty years of the writing life, most people can still read my handwriting!

Word processors are all the rage now, and I have no objection to these mechanical aids any more than I have to my old Olympia typewriter, made in 1956 and still going strong. Although I do all my writing in longhand, I follow the conventions by typing a second draft. But I would not enjoy my writing if I had to do it straight on to a machine. It isn't just the pleasure of writing longhand. I like taking my notebooks and writing pads to odd places. This particular essay is being written on the steps of my small cottage facing Pari Tibba (Fairy Hill). Part of the reason for sitting here is that there is a new postman on this route, and I don't want him to miss me.

For a freelance writer, the postman is almost as important as a publisher. I could, of course, sit here doing nothing, but as I have pencil and paper with me, and feel like using them, I shall write until the postman comes and maybe after he has gone, too! There is really no way in which I could set up a word processor on these steps.

There are a number of favourite places where I do my writing. One is under the chestnut tree on the slope above the cottage. Word processors were not designed keeping mountain slopes in mind. But armed with a pen (or pencil) and paper, I can lie on the grass and write for hours. On one occasion, last month, I did take my typewriter into the garden, and I am still trying to extricate an acorn from under the keys, while the roller seems permanently stained yellow with some fine pollen dust from the deodar trees.

My friends keep telling me about all the wonderful things I can do with a word processor, but they haven't got around to finding me one that I can take to bed, for that is another place where I do much of my writing—especially on cold winter nights, when it is impossible to keep the cottage warm.

While the wind howls outside, and snow piles up on the windowsill, I am warm under my quilt, writing pad on my knees, ballpoint pen at the ready. And if, next day, the weather is warm and sunny, these simple aids will accompany me on a long walk, ready for instant use should I wish to record an incident, a prospect, a conversation, or simply a train of thought.

When I think of the great eighteenth- and nineteenth-century writers, scratching away with their quill pens, filling hundreds of pages every month, I am amazed to find that their handwriting did not deteriorate into the sort of hieroglyphics that often make up the average doctor's prescription today. They knew they had to write legibly, if only for the sake of the typesetters.

Both Dickens and Thackeray had good, clear, flourishing styles. (Thackeray was a clever illustrator, too.) Somerset Maugham had an upright, legible hand. Churchill's neat handwriting never wavered, even when he was under stress. I like the bold, clear, straighforward hand of Abraham Lincoln; it mirrors the man. Mahatma Gandhi, another great soul who fell to the assassin's bullet, had many similarities of both handwriting and outlook.

Not everyone had a beautiful hand. King Henry VIII had an untidy scrawl, but then, he was not a man of much refinement. Guy Fawkes, who tried to blow up the British Parliament, had a very shaky hand. With such a quiver, no wonder he failed in his attempt! Hitler's signature is ugly, as you would expect. And Napoleon's doesn't seem to know where to stop; how much like the man!

I think my father was right when he said handwriting was often the key to a man's character, and that large, well-formed letters went with an uncluttered mind. Florence Nightingale had a lovely handwriting, the hand of a caring person. And there were many like her amongst our forebears.

3

When I was a small boy, no Christmas was really complete unless my Christmas stocking contained several recent issues of my favourite comic paper. If today my friends complain that I am too voracious a reader of books, they have only these comics to blame; for they were the origin, if not of my tastes in reading, then certainly of the reading habit itself.

I like to think that my conversion to comics began at the age of five, with a comic strip on the children's page of *The Statesman*. In the late 1930s, Benji, whose head later appeared only on the Benji League badge, had a strip to himself; I don't remember his adventures very clearly, but every day (or was it once a week?) I would cut out the Benji strip and paste it into a scrapbook. Two years later, this scrapbook, bursting with the adventures of Benji, accompanied me to boarding school, where, of course, it passed through several hands before finally passing into limbo.

Of course, comics did not form the only reading matter that found its way into my Christmas stocking. Before I was eight, I had read *Peter Pan*, *Alice*, and most of *Mr Midshipman Easy*; but I had also consumed thousands of comic papers which were, after all, slim affairs and mostly pictorial, 'certain little penny books radiant with gold and rich with bad pictures', as Leigh Hunt described the children's papers of his own time.

But though they were mostly pictorial, comics in those days did have a fair amount of reading matter, too. *The Hostspur*, *Wizard*, *Magnet* (a victim of the Second World War) and *Champion* contained stories woven round certain popular characters. In *Champion*, which I read regularly right through my prep school years, there was Rockfist Rogan, Royal Air Force (R.A.F.), a pugilist who managed to combine boxing with bombing, and Fireworks Flynn, a footballer who always scored the winning goal in the last two minutes of play.

Billy Bunter has, of course, become one of the immortals—almost a subject for literary and social historians. Quite recently, *The Times Literary Supplement* devoted its first two pages to an analysis of the Bunter stories. Eminent lawyers and doctors still look back nostalgically to the arrival of the weekly *Magnet*; they are now the principal customers for the special souvenir edition of the first issue of the *Magnet*, recently reprinted in facsimile. Bunter, 'forever young', has become a folk hero. He is seen on stage, screen and television, and is even quoted in the House of Commons.

From this, I take courage. My only regret is that I did not preserve my own early comics—not because of any bibliophilic value which they might possess today, but because of my sentimental regard for early influences in art and literature.

The first venture in children's publishing, in 1774, was a comic of sorts. In that year, John Newberry brought out:

According to Act of Parliament (neatly bound and gilt): A Little Pretty Pocket-Book, intended for the Instruction and Amusement of Little Master Tommy and Pretty Miss Polly, with an agreeable Letter to read from Jack the Giant-Killer...

The book contained pictures, rhymes and games. Newberry's characters and imaginary authors included Woglog the Giant, Tommy Trip, Giles Gingerbread, Nurse Truelove, Peregrine Puzzlebrains, Primrose Prettyface, and many others with names similar to those found in the comic papers of our own century.

Newberry was also the originator of the 'Amazing Free Offer', so much a part of American comics. At the beginning of 1755, he had this to offer:

Nurse Truelove's New Year Gift, or the Book of Books for children, adorned with Cuts and designed as a Present for every little boy who would become a great Man and ride upon a fine Horse; and to every little Girl who would become a great Woman and ride in a Lord Mayor's gilt Coach. Printed for the Author, who has ordered these books to be given gratis to all little Boys in St. Paul's churchyard, they paying for the Binding, which is only Two pence each Book.

Many of today's comics are crude and, like many television serials, violent in their appeal. But I did not know American comics until I was twelve, and by then I had become quite discriminating. Superman, Bulletman, Batman and Green Lantern, and other super heroes all left me cold. I had, by then, passed into the world of real books but the weakness for the comic strip remains. I no longer receive comics in my Christmas stocking, but I do place a few in the stockings of Gautam and Siddharth. And, needless to say, I read them right through beforehand.

Be Prepared

I WAS A Boy Scout once, although I couldn't tell a slip knot from a granny knot, nor a reef knot from a thief knot. I did know that a thief knot was to be used to tie up a thief, should you happen to catch one. I have never caught a thief—and wouldn't know what to do with one since I can't tie the right knot. I'd just let him go with a warning, I suppose. And tell him to become a Boy Scout.

'Be prepared!' That's the Boy Scout motto. And it is a good one, too. But I never seem to be well prepared for anything, be it an exam or a journey or the roof blowing off my room. I get halfway through a speech and then forget what I have to say next. Or I make a new suit to attend a friend's wedding, and then turn up in my pyjamas.

So, how did I, the most impractical of boys, survive as a Boy Scout?

Well, it seems a rumour had gone around the junior school (I was still a junior then) that I was a good cook. I had never cooked anything in my life, but of course I had spent a lot of time in the tuck shop making suggestions and advising Chimpu, who ran the tuck shop, and encouraging him to make more and better samosas, jalebies, tikkees and pakoras. For my unwanted advice, he would favour me with an occasional free samosa. So, naturally, I looked upon him as a friend and benefactor. With this qualification, I was given a cookery badge and put in charge of our troop's supply of rations.

There were about twenty of us in our troop. During the summer break our Scoutmaster, Mr Oliver, took us on a camping expedition to Taradevi, a temple-crowned mountain a few miles outside Shimla. That first night we were put to work, peeling potatoes, skinning onions, shelling peas and pounding masalas. These various ingredients being ready, I was asked, as the troop cookery expert, what should be done with them.

'Put everything in that big degchi,' I ordered. 'Pour half a tin of ghee over the lot. Add some nettle leaves, and cook for half an hour.'

When this was done, everyone had a taste, but the general opinion was that the dish lacked something. 'More salt,' I suggested.

More salt was added. It still lacked something. 'Add a cup of sugar,' I ordered.

Sugar was added to the concoction, but it still lacked something.

'We forgot to add tomatoes,' said one of the Scouts. 'Never mind,' I said. 'We have tomato sauce. Add a bottle of tomato sauce!'

'How about some vinegar?' suggested another boy. 'Just the thing,' I said. 'Add a cup of vinegar!'

'Now it's too sour,' said one of the tasters.

'What jam did we bring?' I asked.

'Gooseberry jam.'

'Just the thing. Empty the bottle!'

The dish was a great success. Everyone enjoyed it, including Mr Oliver, who had no idea what had gone into it.

'What's this called?' he asked.

'It's an all-Indian sweet-and-sour jam-potato curry,' I ventured.

'For short, just call it Bond bhujjia,' said one of the boys. I had earned my cookery badge!

Poor Mr Oliver; he wasn't really cut out to be a Scoutmaster, any more than I was meant to be a Scout.

The following day, he told us he would give us a lesson in tracking.

Taking a half-hour start, he walked into the forest, leaving behind him a trail of broken twigs, chicken feathers, pine cones and chestnuts. We were to follow the trail until we found him.

Unfortunately, we were not very good trackers. We did follow Mr Oliver's trail some way into the forest, but then we were distracted by a pool of clear water. It looked very inviting. Abandoning our uniforms, we jumped into the pool and had a great time romping about or just lying on its grassy banks and enjoying the sunshine. Many hours later, feeling hungry, we returned to our campsite and set about preparing the evening meal. It was Bond bhujjia again, but with a few variations.

It was growing dark, and we were beginning to worry about Mr Oliver's whereabouts when he limped into the camp, assisted by a couple of local villagers. Having waited for us at the far end of the forest for a couple of hours, he had decided to return by following his own trail, but in the gathering gloom he was soon lost. Village folk returning home from the temple took charge and escorted him back to the camp. He was very angry and made us return all our good-conduct and other badges, which he stuffed into his haversack. I had to give up my cookery badge.

An hour later, when we were all preparing to get into our sleeping bags for the night, Mr Oliver called out, 'Where's dinner?'

'We've had ours,' said one of the boys. 'Everything is finished, sir.'

'Where's Bond? He's supposed to be the cook. Bond, get up and make me an omelette.'

'I can't, sir.'

'Why not?'

'You have my badge. Not allowed to cook without it. Scout rule, sir.'

'I've never heard of such a rule. But you can take your badges, all of you. We return to school tomorrow.'

Mr Oliver returned to his tent in a huff.

But I relented and made him a grand omelette, garnishing it with dandelion leaves and a chilli.

'Never had such an omelette before,' confessed Mr Oliver.

'Would you like another, sir?'

'Tomorrow, Bond, tomorrow. We'll breakfast early tomorrow.'

But we had to break up our camp before we could do that because in the early hours of the next morning, a bear strayed into our camp, entered the tent where our stores were kept, and created havoc with all our provisions, even rolling our biggest degchi down the hillside.

In the confusion and uproar that followed, the bear entered Mr Oliver's tent (our Scoutmaster was already outside, fortunately) and came out entangled in his dressing gown. It then made off towards the forest, a comical sight in its borrowed clothes.

And though we were a troop of brave little scouts, we thought it better to let the bear keep the gown.

The Four Feathers

OUR SCHOOL dormitory was a very long room with about thirty beds, fifteen on either side of the room. This was good for pillow fights. Class V would take on Class VI (the two senior classes in our Prep school) and there would be plenty of space for leaping, struggling small boys, pillows flying, feathers flying, until there was a cry of 'Here comes Fishy!' or 'Here comes Olly!' and either Mr Fisher, the Headmaster, or Mr Oliver, the Senior Master, would come striding in, cane in hand, to put an end to the general mayhem. Pillow fights were allowed, up to a point; nobody got hurt. But parents sometimes complained if, at the end of the term, a boy came home with a pillow devoid of cotton-wool or feathers.

In that last year at Prep school in Shimla, there were four of us who were close friends—Bimal, whose home was in Bombay; Riaz, who came from Lahore; Bran, who hailed from Vellore; and your narrator, who lived wherever his father (then in the Air Force) was posted.

We called ourselves the 'Four Feathers', the feathers signifying that we were companions in adventure, comrades-in-arms, and knights of the round table. Bimal adopted a peacock's feather as his emblem—he was always a bit showy. Riaz chose a falcon's feather—although we couldn't find one. Bran and I were at first offered crows or murghi feathers, but we protested vigorously and threatened a walkout.

Finally, I settled for a parrot's feather (taken from Mrs Fisher's pet parrot), and Bran found a woodpecker's, which suited him, as he was always knocking things about.

Bimal was all thin legs and arms, so light and frisky that at times he seemed to be walking on air. We called him 'Bambi', after the delicate little deer in the Disney film. Riaz, on the other hand, was a sturdy boy, good at games though not very studious; but always good-natured, always smiling.

Bran was a dark, good-looking boy from the South; he was just a little spoilt—hated being given out in a cricket match and would refuse to leave the crease!—but he was affectionate and a loyal friend. I was the 'scribe'—good at inventing stories in order to get out of scrapes—but hopeless at sums, my highest marks being twenty-two out of one hundred.

On Sunday afternoons, when there were no classes or organized games, we were allowed to roam about on the hillside below the school. The Four Feathers would laze about on the short summer grass, sharing the occasional food parcel from home, reading comics (sometimes a book), and making plans for the long winter holidays. My father, who collected everything from stamps to seashells to butterflies, had given me a butterfly net and urged me to try and catch a rare species which, he said, was found only near Chotta Shimla. He described it as a large purple butterfly with yellow and black borders on its wings. A Purple Emperor, I think it was called. As I wasn't very good at identifying butterflies, I would chase anything that happened to flit across the school grounds, usually ending up with Common Red Admirals, Clouded Yellows, or Cabbage Whites. But that Purple Emperor—that rare specimen being sought by collectors the world over—proved elusive. I would have to seek my fortune in some other line of endeavour.

One day, scrambling about among the rocks, and thorny bushes below the school, I almost fell over a small bundle lying in the shade of a young spruce tree. On taking a closer look, I discovered that the bundle was really a baby, wrapped up in a tattered old blanket.

'Feathers, feathers!' I called, 'come here and look. A baby's been left here!'

The feathers joined me and we all stared down at the infant, who was fast asleep.

'Who would leave a baby on the hillside?' asked Bimal of no one in particular.

'Someone who doesn't want it,' said Bran.

'And hoped some good people would come along and keep it,' said Riaz.'

'A panther might have come along instead,' I said. 'Can't leave it here.'

'Well, we'll just have to adopt it,' said Bimal.

'We can't adopt a baby,' said Bran.

'Why not?'

'We have to be married.'

'We don't.'

'Not us, you dope. The grown-ups who adopt babies.'

Well, we can't just leave it here for grows-ups to come along,' I said.

'We don't even know if it's a boy or a girl,' said Riaz.

'Makes no difference. A baby's a baby. Let's take it back to school.'

'And keep it in the dormitory?'

'Of course not. Who's going to feed it? Babies need milk. We'll hand it over to Mrs Fisher. She doesn't have a baby.'

'Maybe she doesn't want one. Look, it's beginning to cry. Let's hurry!'

Riaz picked up the wide-awake and crying baby and gave it to Bimal who gave it to Bran who gave it to me. The Four Feathers marched up the hill to school with a very noisy baby.

'Now it's done potty in the blanket,' I complained. 'And some, of it's on my shirt.'

'Never mind,' said Bimal. 'It's in a good cause. You're a Boy Scout, remember? You're supposed to help people in distress.'

The headmaster and his wife were in their drawing room, enjoying their afternoon tea and cakes. We trudged in, and Bimal announced, 'We've got something for Mrs Fisher.'

Mrs Fisher took one look at the bundle in my arms and let out a shriek. 'What have you brought here, Bond?'

'A baby, ma'am. I think it's a girl. Do you want to adopt it?'

Mrs Fisher threw up her arms in consternation, and turned to her husband. 'What are we to do, Frank? These boys are impossible. They've picked up someone's child!'

'We'll have to inform the police,' said Mr Fisher, reaching for the telephone. 'We can't have lost babies in the school.'

Just then there was a commotion outside, and a wild-eyed woman, her clothes dishevelled, entered at the front door accompanied by several menfolk from one of the villages. She ran towards us, crying out, 'My baby, my baby! Mera bachcha! You've stolen my baby!'

'We found it on the hillside,' I stammered. 'That's right,' said Bran. 'Finder's keepers!'

'Quiet, Adams,' said Mr Fisher, holding up his hand for order and addressing the villagers in a friendly manner. 'These boys found the baby alone on the hillside and brought it here before...before...'

'Before the hyenas got it,' I put in.

'Quite right, Bond. And why did you leave your child alone?' he asked the woman.

'I put her down for five minutes so that I could climb the plum tree and collect the plums. When I came down, the baby had gone! But I could hear it crying up on the hill. I called the menfolk and we come looking for it.'

'Well, here's your baby,' I said, thrusting it into her arms. By then I was glad to be rid of it! 'Look after it properly in future.'

'Kidnapper!' she screamed at me.

Mr Fisher succeeded in mollifying the villagers. 'These boys are good Scouts,' he told them. 'It's their business to help people.'

'Scout Law Number Three, sir,' I added. 'To be useful and helpful.'

And then the Headmaster turned the tables on the villagers. 'By the way, those plum trees belong to the school. So do the peaches and apricots. Now I know why they've been disappearing so fast!'

The villagers, a little chastened, went their way.

Mr Fisher reached for his cane. From the way he fondled it I knew he was itching to use it on our bottoms.

'No, Frank,' said Mrs Fisher, intervening on our behalf. 'It was really very sweet of them to look after that baby. And look at Bond —he's got baby-goo all over his clothes.'

'So he has. Go and take a bath, all of you. And what are you grinning about, Bond?'

'Scout Law Number Eight, sir. A Scout smiles and whistles under all difficulties.'

And so ended the first adventure of the Four Feathers.

My Best Friend

My best friend
Is the baker's son;
I gave him a book
And he gave me a bun.

I told him a tale
Of a magical lake,
And he was so thrilled
That he baked me a cake.

Yes, he's my best friend;
We go cycling together
On bright sunny days,
And even in rain and bad weather.

And, if we feel hungry,
There's always a pie
Or a pastry to munch on,
As we go riding by!

The Parrot Who Wouldn't Talk

'**Y**ou're no beauty! Can't talk, can't sing, can't dance!'

With these words Aunt Ruby would taunt the unfortunate parakeet who glared morosely at everyone from his ornamental cage at one end of the long veranda of Granny's bungalow in North India.

In those distant days, almost everyone—Indian or European—kept a pet parrot or parakeet, or 'lovebird' as some of the smaller ones were called. Sometimes these birds became great talkers, or rather mimics, and would learn to recite entire mantras (religious chants), or admonitions to the children of the house, such as '*Paro, beta, paro!*' ('Study, child, study!') or, for the benefit of boys like me—'Don't be greedy, don't be greedy.'

These expressions were, of course, picked up by the parrot over a period of time, after many repetitions by whichever member of the household had taken on the task of teaching the bird to talk.

But our parrot refused to talk.

He'd been bought by Aunt Ruby from a birdcatcher who'd visited all the houses on our road, selling caged birds ranging from colourful budgerigars to chirpy little munnias and even common sparrows that had been dabbed with paint and passed off as some exotic species. Neither Granny nor Grandfather were keen on keeping caged birds as pets, but Aunt Ruby threatened to throw a tantrum if she did not get her way—and Aunt Ruby's tantrums were dreadful to behold.

Anyway, she insisted on keeping the parrot and teaching it to talk. But the bird took an instant dislike to my aunt and resisted all her blandishments.

'Kiss, kiss,' Aunt Ruby would coo, putting her face close to the barge of the cage. But the parrot would back away, its beady little eyes getting even smaller with anger at the prospect of being kissed by Aunt Ruby. And, on one occasion, it lunged forward without warning and knocked my aunt's spectacles off her nose.

After that, Aunt Ruby gave up her endearments and became quite hostile towards the poor bird, making faces at it and calling out, 'Can't talk, can't sing, can't dance!' and other nasty comments.

It fell upon me, then ten years old, to feed the parrot, and it seemed quite happy to receive green chillies and ripe tomatoes from my hands, these delicacies being supplemented by slices of mango, for it was then the mango season. It also gave me an opportunity to consume a couple of mangoes while feeding the parrot.

One afternoon, while everyone was indoors enjoying a siesta, I gave the parrot his lunch and then deliberately left the cage door open. Seconds later, the bird was winging its way to the freedom of the mango orchard.

At the same time Grandfather came on to the veranda, and remarked, 'I see your aunt's parrot has escaped.'

'The door was quite loose,' I said with a shrug. 'Well, I don't suppose we'll see it again.'

Aunt Ruby was upset at first, and threatened to buy another bird. We put her off by promising to buy her a bowl of goldfish.

'But goldfish don't talk,' she protested.

'Well, neither did your bird,' said Grandfather. 'So we'll get you a gramophone. You can listen to Clara Cluck all day. They say she sings like a nightingale.'

I thought we'd never see the parrot again, but it probably missed its green chillies, because a few days later, I found the bird sitting on the veranda railing, looking expectantly at me with its head cocked to one side. Unselfishly, I gave the parrot half of my mango.

While the bird was enjoying the mango, Aunt Ruby emerged from her room and, with a cry of surprise, called out, 'Look, my parrot's come back! He must have missed me!'

With a loud squawk, the parrot flew out of her reach and, perching on the nearest rose bush, glared at Aunt Ruby and shrieked at her in my aunt's familiar tones, 'You're no beauty! Can't talk, can't sing, can't dance!'

Aunt Ruby went ruby red and dashed indoors. But that wasn't the end of the affair. The parrot became a frequent visitor to the garden and veranda and whenever it saw Aunt Ruby it would call out, 'You're no beauty, you're no beauty! Can't sing, can't dance!'

The parrot had learnt to talk after all.

Miss Ramola and others

Though their numbers have diminished over the years, there are still a few compulsive daily walkers around: the odd ones, the strange ones, who will walk all day, here, there and everywhere, not in order to get somewhere, but to escape from their homes, their lonely rooms, their mirrors, themselves...

Those of us who must work for a living and would love to be able to walk a little more don't often get the chance. There are offices to attend, deadlines to be met, trains or planes to be caught, deals to be struck, people to deal with. It's the rat race for most people, whether they like it or not. So who are these lucky ones, a small minority it has to be said, who find time to walk all over this hill station from morning to night?

Some are fitness freaks, I suppose, but several are just unhappy souls who find some release, some meaning, in covering miles and miles of highway without so much as a nod in the direction of others on the road. They are not looking at anything as they walk, not even at a violet in a mossy stone.

Here comes Miss Romola. She's been at it for years. A retired schoolmistress who never married. No friends. Lonely as hell. Not even a visit from a former pupil. She could not have been very popular.

She has money in the bank. She owns her own flat. But she

272 2 R U S K I N B O N D

doesn't spend much time in it. I see her from my window, tramping up the road to Lal Tibba. She strides around the mountain like the character in the old song 'She'll be Coming Round the Mountain', only she doesn't wear pink pyjamas; she dresses in slacks and a shirt. She doesn't stop to talk to anyone. It's quick march to the top of the mountain, and then down again, home again, jiggety-jig. When she has to go down to Dehradun (too long a walk even for her), she stops a car and catches a lift. No taxis for her; not even the bus.

Miss Romola's chief pleasure in life comes from conserving her money. There are people like that. They view the rest of the world with suspicion. An overture of friendship will be construed as taking an undue interest in her assets. We are all part of an international conspiracy to relieve her of her material possessions. She has no servants, no friends; even her relatives are kept at a safe distance.

A similar sort of character but even more eccentric is Mr Sen, who used to live in the USA and walks from the Happy Valley to Landour (five miles) and back every day, in all seasons, year in and year out. Once or twice every week, he will stop at the Community Hospital to have his blood pressure checked or undergo a blood or urine test. With all that walking, he should have no health problems, but he is a hypochondriac and is convinced that he is dying of something or the other.

He came to see me once. Unlike Miss Romola, he seemed to want a friend, but his neurotic nature turned people away. He was convinced that he was surrounded by individual and collective hostility. People were always staring at him, he told me. I couldn't help wondering why, because he looked fairly nondescript. He wore conventional western clothes, perfectly acceptable in urban India, and looked respectable enough, except for a constant nervous turning of the head, looking to the left, right, or behind, as though to check on anyone who might be following him. He was convinced that he was being followed at all times.

'By whom?' I asked.

'Agents of the government,' he said.

'But why should they follow you?'

'I look different,' he said. 'They see me as an outsider. They think I work for the CIA.'

'And do you?'

'No, no.' He shied nervously away from me. 'Why did you say that?'

'Only because you. brought the subject up. I haven't noticed anyone following you.'

'They're very clever about it. Perhaps you're following me too.'

'I'm afraid I can't walk as fast or as far as you,' I said with a laugh; but he wasn't amused. He never smiled, never laughed. He did not feel safe in India, he confided. The saffron brigade was after him.

'But why?' I asked. 'They're not after me. And you're a Hindu with a Hindu name.'

'Ah yes, but I don't look like one.'

'Well, I don't look like a Taoist monk, but that's what I am,' I said, adding, in a more jocular manner: 'I know how to become invisible, and you wouldn't know I'm around. That's why no one follows me. I have this wonderful cloak, you see, and when I wear it I become invisible.'

'Can you lend it to me?' he asked eagerly.

'I'd love to,' I said, 'but it's at the cleaners right now. Maybe next week.'

'Crazy,' he muttered. 'Quite mad.' And he hurried on.

A few weeks later, he returned to New York and safety. Then I heard he'd been mugged in Central Park. He's recovering, but doesn't do much walking now.

Neurotics do not walk for pleasure, they walk out of compulsion. They are not looking at the trees or the flowers or the mountains; they are not looking at other people (except in apprehension); they are usually walking away from something—unhappiness or disarray in their lives. They tire themselves out, physically and mentally, and that brings them some relief.

Like the journalist who came to see me last year.

He'd escaped from Delhi, he told me. Had taken a room in Landour Bazaar and was going to spend a year on his own, away from family, friends, colleagues, the entire rat race. He was full of noble resolutions. He was planning to write an epic poem or a great Indian novel or a philosophical treatise. Every fortnight I meet someone who is planning to write one or the other of these things, and I do not like to discourage them, just in case they turn violent.

In effect, he did nothing but walk up and down the mountain, growing shabbier by the day. Sometimes he recognized me. At other times, there was a blank look on his face, as though he was on some drug, and he would walk past me without a sign of recognition. He discarded his slippers and began walking about barefoot, even on the stony paths. He did not change or wash his clothes. Then he disappeared; that is, I no longer saw him around.

I did not really notice his absence until I saw an ad in one of the national papers, asking for information about his whereabouts. His family was anxious to locate him. The ad carried a picture of the gentleman, taken in happier, healthier times, but it was definitely my acquaintance of that summer.

I was sitting in the bank manager's office, up in the cantonment, when a woman came in, making inquiries about her husband. It was the missing journalist's wife. Yes, said Mr Ohri, the friendly bank manager, he'd opened an account with them; not a very large sum, but there were a few hundred rupees lying to his credit. And no, they hadn't seen him in the bank for at least three months.

He couldn't be found. Several months passed, and it was presumed that he had moved on to some other town; or that he'd lost his mind or his memory. Then some milkmen from Kolti Gaon discovered bones and remnants of clothing at the bottom of a cliff. In the pocket of the ragged shirt was the journalist's press card.

How he'd fallen to his death remains a mystery.

It's easy to miss your footing and take a fatal plunge on the steep slopes of this range. He may have been high on something or he may simply have been trying out an unfamiliar path. Walking can be dangerous in the hills if you don't know the way or if you take one chance too many.

And here's a tale to illustrate that old chestnut that truth is often stranger than fiction:

Colonel Parshottam had just retired and was determined to pass the evening of his life doing the things he enjoyed most: taking early morning and late evening walks, afternoon siestas, a drop of whisky before dinner, and a good book on his bedside table.

A few streets away, on the fourth floor of a block of flats, lived Mrs L, a stout, neglected woman of forty, who'd had enough of life and was determined to do away with herself.

Along came the Colonel all the road below, a song on his lips, strolling along with a jaunty air; in love with life and wanting more of it.

Quite unaware of anyone else around, Mrs L chose that moment to throw herself out of her fourth-floor window. Seconds later, she landed with a thud on the Colonel. If this was a Ruskin Bond story, it would have been love at first flight. But the grim reality was that he was crushed beneath her and did not recover from the impact. Mrs L, on the other hand, survived the fall and lived on into a miserable old age.

There is no moral to the story, any more than there is a moral to life. We cannot foresee when a bolt from the blue will put an end to the best-laid plans of mice and men.